BITE THE POWER THAT FEEDS

DIRTY BLOOD
BOOK 3

PENELOPE BARSETTI

HARTWICK PUBLISHING

Hartwick Publishing

Bite The Power That Feeds

Copyright © 2023 by Penelope Barsetti

All rights reserved.

ACKNOWLEDGMENTS

Special thanks to these readers who made this book a reality:

Katy DiPrima

Julia

Shelby Andrews

Alicia Scott

Stacey Gonzalez

Athena Rain

Christal Bolotte

CONTENTS

1. Kingsnake   1
2. Larisa   5
3. Kingsnake   13
4. Clara   33
5. Larisa   57
6. Kingsnake   67
7. Clara   73
8. Larisa   99
9. Kingsnake   119
10. Clara   145
11. Larisa   155
12. Kingsnake   177
13. Larisa   191
14. Kingsnake   201
15. Larisa   211
16. Kingsnake   221
17. Larisa   237
18. Kingsnake   251
19. Larisa   257
20. Kingsnake   277
21. Larisa   281
22. Kingsnake   293
23. Clara   319
24. Larisa   337
25. Cobra   347
26. Clara   351
27. Kingsnake   355
28. Clara   365
29. Kingsnake   375

30. Kingsnake 393

31. Larisa 407

32. Kingsnake 415

33. Larisa 427

1

KINGSNAKE

She lay in our bed, her bandaged body hidden underneath the covers. Her breaths remained short, her skin pale as snow. My duty was to my people, and part of that obligation was recognizing my incapacity. I couldn't lead. I couldn't protect. Not when the person I loved most balanced on the edge of life and death.

My eyes hadn't left her face.

Fang was on the other side of the bed beside her, sitting there like a loyal dog. His broken scales had been bandaged as well, and an ugly gauze was wrapped around his thick body. ***I'm sssorry…***

It's okay, Fang.

You trusted me to protect her. I failed.

Ellasara was fueled by more than her orders.

His eyes shifted to me.

She knew I loved Larisa—and she was furious.

Fang continued to stare.

She didn't want me, but she still didn't want anyone else to have me. The most fucked-up shit ever.

Then it's good ssshe's dead.

Yes. I felt no pain. No remorse. The world was better without her.

Larisa will turn. She's ssstill breathing.

I'm afraid of her reaction when she does.

You had no choice.

No. I had two very different choices. Just as my choice had been taken from me, I took it from her.

He shifted his gaze back to her. **The situations are unequal.**

I still feared her reaction.

It'll be alright, Kingsnake.

I hope so, Fang.

The door opened and Viper entered. "Come with me."

"I can't leave, Viper." I was sunk in the armchair, weighed down by grief and stress. "I gave you the crown for a reason."

Viper entered the bedroom, Cobra behind him. "How is she?"

"She's breathing."

Cobra stared at her for a while before he looked at me again. "She'll be an Original."

"Yes." Because I'd also poured some of the Golden Serpent venom we'd collected into her mouth, we wouldn't share the same venom, which was disappointing.

"We won the war?" I could only assume by the way they'd leisurely walked in here.

"Yes," Viper said. "The Ethereal fled after King Elrohir was killed."

"Who killed him?" My eyes shifted to Cobra.

My brother had an opaque emptiness in his eyes. "Father."

I released a heavy sigh. "Of course he did."

"I tried to stop it," Cobra said. "But I only helped Father..."

"What will you say to Clara?" Viper asked.

"No fucking idea," he said.

"What now?" I asked.

"We lost good people," Viper said. "We'll need to burn the dead. Recover from the battle. Then we'll travel to Evanguard and pursue the truce the new queen has promised. We need to secure it quickly before Father decides to launch an attack instead. Now that Aurelias has been taken from him, he has even more fuel for his rage."

"Sounds like a plan," I said. "Good luck."

Cobra narrowed his eyes. "You're coming."

"I'm not going anywhere while Larisa remains indisposed."

"We'll wait," Viper said. "She's one of us."

I looked at one brother then the other.

"Literally," Cobra said with a slight grin.

2

LARISA

I dreamed of black clouds and dark flames. Smoke and soot. A horrifying grin. My stomach tightened, and I felt sick. I felt pain that was excruciating, but not excruciating enough to stir me from this heavy slumber.

I had no sense of time, only darkness. Sweat was all over my body. I was aware of the way the sheets clung to my skin like sand to wet feet.

My eyes finally opened to the ceiling.

It was dark, and it took several seconds to understand where I was. To my left, Fang slept in a circle, at the very edge of the bed so as not to disturb me. My head tilted the other way—and locked on eyes that were a mix of green and brown. I stilled at the intensity of that stare. Then I felt that intensity, felt the paramount relief of a man who'd nearly lost everything. With my eyes locked on his, everything rushed back.

Ellasara bested me in the battle—and pierced me through my armor and skin. I didn't remember what happened after that, other than collapsing on my back against the stone. My hand immediately went to my wound, feeling the wet gauze that protected it.

Kingsnake moved to the edge of the bed to come closer to me. "Sweetheart." For the first time, I didn't need to feel his emotions to understand every thought that passed through his mind. I could see it written clearly across his face. His eyes were hard with emotion, wet with unspent tears, full of a love he'd previously tried to hide.

I sat up and expected to feel pain in my abdomen, but I felt nothing at all.

His hands cupped my face, and he kissed me on the forehead, his lips lingering as they cherished my cold skin. We stayed that way for a breath before he pulled away to look me straight in the eye. "How do you feel?"

"A lot better than I expected..."

His hands left my face.

"What happened to Ellasara?"

"I killed her." There was no hesitation in his words. They shot right out like a ball from a cannon. There was no emotion to accompany what he said. He felt nothing. Nothing at all. "Sliced her head from her shoulders—like a fucking cockroach."

I remembered the smug look on her face, the horrible things she said to me. She played dirty to get me to drop my guard. I fought her the best I could, but her skills outweighed mine. "Fang, are you okay?" My hand rested on the back of his neck.

I'm sssorry I failed you.

"You didn't fail me. I'm still here."

Fang looked at Kingsnake before he rested his chin on my thigh.

The backs of my fingers stroked his hard scales, feeling like glass. "I'm glad you're alright…"

My wound will heal. My scarsss will shed along with my skin.

"What's happened since?" I looked at Kingsnake again.

"We won the war," he said. "As I'm sure you surmised."

"Your brothers are alright?"

He gave a nod. "Yes."

"What will happen now?"

"We'll travel to Evanguard to broker a truce with Queen Clara."

"That's great news," I said. "Then we can distribute the cure to the kingdoms."

"Yes," he said. "It'll usher in a brand-new era of peace among all races."

It'd be a whole new world.

"When you're well, we'll go."

"You don't have to wait for me," I said. "No one's trying to kill me anymore so..."

His eyes quickly flicked down, and he withdrew his hand from mine. "My brothers and I didn't want to leave without you—because you're one of us."

The smile tugged at the corners of my lips. "You guys are sweet." I'd always been an outsider, always standing on the very edge of every social group, always abandoned in favor of something better. But with Kingsnake, I felt like I was first choice. His priority. "I actually feel pretty good. I think I could leave tomorrow."

He would normally tell me to take my time, to rest for several days before moving a muscle, but he didn't do that now. All he did was stare, his emotions swirling in a cloud.

"Is there something wrong?"

His eyes flicked away, only momentarily.

When he didn't say anything, I felt tension return to my body, felt it pull on my stomach. "Kingsnake?" I distinguished each emotion separately, like a different note on a sheet of music. Guilt. Pain. Dread.

"There's something you should know."

My fingers stilled against Fang's neck. All my relief at being alive disappeared.

"I didn't reach you in time." Now he looked away, turning his head like my stare was too painful. "You were lying in a pool of your own blood when I arrived. Barely breathing. I defeated Ellasara as Fang retrieved Viper and the medic." He still wouldn't look at me. "The medic stitched you up, but he said you wouldn't make it."

Moments like these made my heart race...but that was when I realized I had no heartbeat. No thump against my chest. Just...silence.

Kingsnake turned quiet.

Now I was the one to look away.

He must have known I understood the situation because he didn't speak further.

Shock. Grief. Terror. It hit me all at once. I lifted my hand to look at my skin, to see that it was paler than I remembered. There were no marks from the sun. No more sunshine kisses. I would never be able to stand directly in the sunlight again...without slowly killing myself. My soul had been sacrificed to create this hollow shell of existence.

"Sweetheart..." He must have seen the despair heavy in my face.

I wanted to cry, but I would hide the tears until he was gone.

"It wasn't an easy decision."

I didn't look at Fang either, avoiding both of their gazes.

"I couldn't let you die."

Heat seared my throat. Despair flooded my lungs. My mind, body, and soul had been irrevocably changed—and I couldn't change it back. Now I was a cold-blooded animal, no different from a snake.

His voice was heavy like rainfall. "I can see that I made the wrong decision."

If I spoke, I would cry. I held my silence like my life depended on it...even though I no longer possessed life. Nor could I create life.

Kingsnake left the bed and walked out.

The instant the door clicked back into place, my chest heaved and I cried.

I cried for my soul.

I cried for the children I would never have.

I cried for the decision I wasn't given the opportunity to make for myself.

3

KINGSNAKE

I lay on the couch in my study, my bare feet propped on the armrest. The fire started to burn low in the hearth, but I was out of wood. The coffee table held decanters of gin and scotch that were nearly empty. Booze didn't affect me the way it had when I was human. Now it took so much more just to get a buzz.

Another thing Larisa would discover.

The door to my study opened, and someone walked inside. They didn't see me because the back of the couch obscured me. Viper moved to the front of the desk and searched through my pile of scrolls and maps until he found whatever he was looking for. When he turned back around, he gave a slight jump.

"You're the general of Grayson," I said in a bored voice. "And you had no idea I was here? The fire didn't tip you off?"

Viper returned the map to the desk. "Why do you look like shit?"

"Probably because of the headache."

My brother glanced at all the empty bottles. "You'd be dead right now if you weren't already dead." He moved to the opposite couch and sat down. "I'm guessing Larisa is unhappy with the decision you made?"

I sat up, grabbed one of the bottles, and took a big drink.

"Got it."

I chucked the empty bottle into the fire and made the flames leap a little higher.

"In her defense, she just woke up and received a lot of information."

I slouched sideways and propped my head against my closed knuckles. "What the fuck's wrong with me?"

Viper stared at me.

"I could have any woman I want, but I always choose the ones who don't want me."

"Did Larisa say that?"

"You should have seen her face..."

"Give her some time. Remember how you felt when Father changed you. It took a while, but you came around. You eventually realized that he was right all along. That'll happen with Larisa."

I stared at the fire.

"Just because she's upset doesn't mean her feelings for you have changed."

"But I'm sure they have."

He gave me a hard stare. "This is the woman who traveled to the other side of the world to be at your side. The woman who refused to flee a battle because she'd rather risk her life to be with you. The woman who saved Aurelias—the biggest fucking prick on the planet."

He tried to make me laugh, but it wouldn't work.

"Her feelings won't change, Kingsnake."

I kept my eyes on the fire.

After a long stretch of silence, Viper changed the subject. "We need to leave tomorrow. Father returned to Crescent Falls to regroup. We need to take advantage of his absence. Once we secure world peace, he'll be forced to abandon his revenge."

"Then go."

"We can't go without you, Kingsnake."

"You're the leader of our people now, Viper." I grabbed another bottle by the neck and chucked it at the fire. "I'm just a fucking drunk."

He didn't flinch at the crash and the shatter of glass. "We aren't going without you, Kingsnake. So if we have to tie you up to the back of a horse and have him drag you, so be it."

"Larisa won't come."

"She'll be safe here. She needs space anyway."

I felt uncomfortable leaving her unprotected, but I remembered she no longer needed my protection. She was an Original now, a vampire more powerful than I. And she no longer had enemies.

"I'm not King of Grayson—you are."

My eyes shifted to his.

"You've believed in the greater good since the beginning. You're the one who should secure it."

———

The following morning, I entered our bedchambers to retrieve my things. Putting on my armor so soon after battle was a disappointment, but I wouldn't walk into Evanguard with my head on a platter either.

Larisa sat on the couch in the other room, Fang hanging from the branches of his own tree. She didn't look at me when I entered.

Not that I'd expected her to. But it hurt anyway.

I changed in the closet and grabbed my pack.

That captured her attention. "Where are you going?"

I set the pack on the bed and placed a few things inside. "Evanguard. I need to speak with Queen Clara." I'd told her all of this yesterday. There was no way she could have forgotten. Or maybe she had...in her misery.

She left the couch and walked up to me. While she was still the woman I loved, her appearance had changed subtly. Her skin had grown paler, like she'd never stepped into direct sunshine. Her eyes were darker and also more vibrant, like the eyes of a bird of prey. Her smell was totally different. But she was still the most beautiful damn thing I'd ever seen. Knowing her life-span had increased to eternity pleased me...even if I didn't show it. "How long will you be gone?"

Another slap of disappointment. "A week. Maybe more." Maybe I'd never come back if she didn't want me. I continued packing, masking the raw pain she'd just inflicted. "You'll be safe here. I'll leave Fang with you."

"You're angry. Really angry."

I stilled at her assessment. "How do you expect me to feel?"

"Patient—at the least."

After a breath, I turned to regard her head on. "We have the rest of eternity to be together—and you're disappointed. You have the opportunity to be the strongest kind of vampire—and that's inconsequential to you. Most people would do anything to stand where you stand now."

"But it came at a cost. A cost I'll have to pay later."

"Or maybe never."

She stared at me, her mood distant and cold.

My blood still existed in her veins, making her a part of me forever. I found that beautiful, but she found that despicable.

"It was my dream to have a family. And now I'll never have that."

"If I'd let you die, you wouldn't have had them either," I snapped. "I told you to hide away from Grayson with Fang until the war was over, but you insisted on staying. So don't sit there and act like this is my fault."

Her eyes winced at my cruelty.

"I made the best decision I could at the time, and despite your disappointment, I still don't regret it. Your destiny is greater than dying young. Your destiny is to be the Queen of Vampires, Lady of Darkness." I turned back to my pack and zipped up the top before I threw it over my shoulder. I headed to the door to walk out. "Embrace it."

———

I watched the stable hands prepare the horses for the long journey. The cloud cover had returned to our coastal kingdom, the powerful rays of the sun fractured and minimized. I stared at the sky and remembered the afternoon when Larisa and I rode to the top of the mountain and basked in the sunshine. She'd sat there with her eyes closed, enjoying the warmth on her skin.

She would never have that again.

Cobra came to my side. "Ready?"

It took a second to snap out of the memory. "Yes."

Cobra continued to watch me. "She's not joining us?"

"No." I gave my brother a hard stare, warning him not to press the topic.

Cobra looked away. "Then we should get moving." He approached his large stallion and climbed up into the saddle.

I had just stepped over to my horse when I was interrupted.

Wait.

What is it?

We're coming.

I backed away from the horse and looked to the gate.

A moment later, Larisa appeared in her armor and sword, looking breathtaking with her new strength. Instead of Fang following behind her, he was draped across her shoulders, her newfound power enough to carry his weight.

It was hard not to stare.

She moved to the stable hand. "Fetch me a horse, please." Her eyes eventually found mine, but she didn't stare for long. She avoided my gaze, still resentful of the decision I'd made on her behalf.

But she had come.

They brought her a beautiful white mare, and with Fang on her shoulders, she climbed onto the horse.

The looks on my brother's faces were indescribable. Eyes wide, jaws slack, they looked at Larisa like they'd never truly seen her before. Cobra gave a quiet whistle as he looked her up and down. "Vampire looks good on you, honey." He gave his playful grin.

I was too happy to scold him for the comment, seeing her on her horse next to ours, a part of our pack. "Let's head out."

———

We took the same path Larisa and I had taken together to Grayson. Through the valleys between the mountains, in the dark path below the mountain, and to the forest on the other side. But we weren't even halfway there when we stopped for rest.

We set up camp in the forest once the sun became too high in the sky. Now that we didn't have the cloud cover to protect us, we had to move in the dark, which was feasible since Larisa could see without light.

We secured our horses to the trees and made camp, my two brothers, Fang, and Larisa.

She knew the drill after traveling with me, and she prepared the fire before setting up her own bedroll—which meant she intended to sleep alone. She might have joined me on this journey, but her distance was still enormous.

My brothers grabbed their canteens and drank in front of the fire, choosing to spend their free time drinking.

Larisa stayed away, lying in her bedroll by herself.

Fang moved to the spot beside me in front of the fire, his head resting on top of his coiled body.

Cobra drank from his canteen then glanced at Larisa in the distance.

"She'll come around," Viper said. "She wouldn't be here right now, otherwise."

How is she?

Fang's eyes were closed, like he'd sleep right there until the afternoon passed. **She ssspoke to me in confidence.**

That's not a good sign.

It's hard to reject your lifelong beliefs. She truly believes her soul is lossst—and she's mourning that death. She's grieving, saying goodbye to a life she assssumed she would have, surrounded by hatchlings. You take it persssson-ally, when it has nothing to do with you.

I've given her so much more.

She'll see that eventually—when she's ready.

We packed up and left at sunset. The sun was low in the sky at our backs, blocked by the mountains. The monsters in the forest didn't interfere with our passage, and we eventually made it to the land of the kingdoms.

We passed Raventower, the torches illuminating the darkness, but we continued on our way.

Larisa and I hadn't spoken throughout the entire trip. I wondered what she thought as we passed her old home, if she wished she had married that spineless king and had his brats. The thought made me want to break down their gate and cut his head from his shoulders.

We moved farther west, close to the border where the werewolves resided in the forest. It was unsafe to stop there and drop our guard, so we continued until we reached the barren lands, an arid, dry place that was similar to a desert. The land had been cursed long ago, so nothing grew, except for weeds.

We stopped at the trees just before we crossed, taking cover under the thick canopy instead of exposing ourselves to the blazing sun. We made no fire, not when it was so warm this far out west.

Larisa was on her own again, in her bedroll away from the rest of us.

Cobra leaned against one of the trees, his ankles crossed in front of him. "You want me to talk to her?"

"And say what?" I snapped.

"You know me." He waggled his eyebrows. "Handsome. Charismatic—"

"I don't think hitting on my woman is going to help right now."

Cobra took another drink, still grinning.

"Why don't you hit on Queen Clara?" I said.

The comment wiped the grin clean off his face. "I think I'd have better luck with Larisa."

"Why?" Viper asked, leaning against another tree.

"Well..." Cobra paused as he considered his next words. "I didn't keep my word."

"Father's actions are his actions," I said. "Not yours."

"But I didn't stop it," he said. "Her people must have told her the news once they retreated to their realm. So I doubt she'll be thrilled to see me." He took another drink from his canteen. "Ironic, isn't it? The one woman I'm even remotely interested in...and she's my lifelong enemy, and I killed her father."

"*You* didn't do anything," Viper said. "It's a consequence of battle."

"A battle we only won because of the information she gave us," Cobra said. "Her father would still be alive right now—"

"Her father is evil, remember?" I said. "I'm eager to hear exactly what she discovered."

"I think Father is just as evil." He twisted the cap back onto his canteen.

I couldn't disagree with that.

Viper glanced at Larisa. "You should try talking to her."

That would be pointless.

"Tell her something she doesn't know about you."

I'd shared everything.

"Give her something interesting so she'll listen."

"I'm not that interesting," I said.

"You're fifteen hundred years old," Viper said. "I'm sure you can find something."

"Go," Viper said.

I released an annoyed sigh and rose.

Tell her about usss. She doesssn't know.

I considered the idea for a moment before I moved to where she lay in her bedroll, on the other side of camp with her back to us.

Based on her breathing, I knew she was wide awake, just ignoring me.

I sat beside her, arms on my knees, looking between the trunks to the forest beyond.

She continued to ignore me.

"It was Fang's venom that turned me. My father captured him and forced the venom from his fangs. Now that you know who my father is, you understand how barbaric he can be. And you know Fang well...and know that Fang isn't the obedient type. My father enslaved him, and when Fang refused, my father hurt him..." It was hard to revisit this story, to think of my companion's treatment. It was so long ago, Fang had forgiven me for all of it, but it had still left an invisible scar. "So I released him. Let him go in broad daylight so no one would chase him."

She seemed to be intrigued by the story, because she sat up beside me. Her arms were on her knees like mine. She used to smell like flowers and springtime, but now she smelled like a misty forest.

Before the battle, we were so deeply connected. Even now, I loved her more at our worst than I had ever loved Ellasara at our best. But now, there was this barrier between us—

and I had no idea how to fix it. "He was touched by my gesture...and came back. We've been inseparable ever since."

"Fang called him a snake-killer..."

"Because he is." My father and I had a million miles of distance between us. Every time I disobeyed him, I pushed myself into darker light, but I wouldn't make a different decision to stay in his good graces. My relationship with Fang meant far more to me.

"Has Fang turned anyone else?"

"Yes. But by choice, not servitude. Snakes are very proud creatures. They recognize no crown and no power."

"Why does he stay with you?"

It was starting to feel the way it used to, sharing intimate words in solitude. "His venom granted me immortality. And my blood grants him the same. But I think it's more than that...deeper than that."

"So...Fang is also immortal?"

"As long as he continues to feed from me."

"I've never seen him do that."

"It's not a public affair. He bites my wrist and feeds on my blood." I loosened the vambrace on my wrist and exposed the skin, showing her the snake bite mark in the flesh. It was subtle, unnoticeable if you didn't know to look for it.

She stared at it then ran her finger over the indentations.

Just that single touch made me warm.

I returned the vambrace to my wrist and locked it in place.

"He doesn't have a family of his own?"

"He's had several hatchlings, but once they're born, they're immediately independent."

"Do snakes...fall in love?"

"He's never given me that impression."

"Well, it's nice to know I'll never have to lose him."

It was the first positive reaction she'd had to her newfound immortality. I hoped that attitude would grow—in time.

"Thank you for telling me."

"I want to share everything with you." I hoped to share immortality with her—if she would forgive me.

She was quiet.

It wasn't an outright rejection, but I interpreted it that way in my insecurity.

"I'm sorry for my coldness. I just... I'm having a hard time."

"You can talk to me. Remember, I struggled with the very same things you struggle with now."

"I guess you're right." She kept her eyes on the trees, never looking at me once. "Did you want a family?"

"Yes." I imagined my own home on the farm, a wife in bed beside me every night, the excited screams of children in the house. "I thought I would have five kids. Raise them to look after their mother when I was gone. Raise them to take care of the farm when I was too old and frail to do it myself."

She turned her head slightly and looked at me.

"I do understand your feelings, sweetheart. But I've made my peace with it."

She was quiet.

"It'll get easier."

"If only we'd met at a different time... How different our lives could have been."

I turned to look at her, and for the first time, her green eyes were on mine. "While that would have been nice, I would rather have you forever. A single lifetime just isn't enough."

———

After we crossed the arid desert, we approached the perimeter of Evanguard. Their forests were thicker than others, with trees so close together, it was difficult to navigate on horseback. And the foliage was different from the fresh pines in the mountains or the redwoods outside Grayson. Every different kind of green existed here, trees that were lush with light-green leaves with waxy coats. The sounds of wildlife were audible even on the outskirts, birds chirping, animals screeching.

"Did your girlfriend tell you how to get in?" Viper asked as his horse walked beside Cobra's.

"No." He walked along the perimeter, peering into the trees as the sun set.

"Let's just walk inside and explore," Viper suggested.

"We'll get lost," Cobra said. "No one who's entered their forest has ever come out alive."

"Why?" Larisa asked me.

"Dangerous things live in there," I said.

"Let's set the forest on fire," Viper said. "That will get their attention."

"And you're the general of Grayson?" Cobra asked in surprise. "That's the worst way to be diplomatic."

"You got a better idea?" Viper snapped. "Couldn't you send a missive?"

"None of our birds know the way," Cobra said.

"So, what are we going to do?" Viper asked. "Keep circling? We'll need to find cover before dawn, which means we'll need to cross the desert back the way we came."

I grew tired of their bickering. "They have scouts all throughout this forest. We just need to let them know we're here."

"So, burning it is?" Viper asked.

Cobra rolled his eyes.

"In a way." I dropped off my horse and let him graze. I grabbed an ax from the saddlebag and began to chop at the closest tree. "We'll make a big bonfire—something they won't miss."

"They might shoot us in the dark," Cobra said.

"Queen Clara is expecting us, so I doubt it," I said as I took a break. "Now shut up and help me."

They helped me chop down the tree and branches and set it on fire. It had enough fuel to cast flames high into the sky, to be so distinct that someone would notice and come running. Now we just had to wait.

4

CLARA

It was late.

Normally, I'd be asleep right now. Or at least in bed, wishing I were asleep.

But my scouts noticed the vampires at our border—and I knew exactly who it was.

Now I was in the throne room, low-burning candles placed on every surface to cast enough light indoors. Fires weren't permitted in Evanguard, but I needed to make an exception to take a meeting at this hour.

I sat in my armchair and felt my heart thump in my chest. It was painful and uncomfortable. White flowers had been woven into my hair to signify my status as Queen of Evanguard—because my father had been killed in battle.

No one suspected my treason. No one knew I handed the victory to our enemy.

Now I had to carry that for the rest of my life.

My hands were forever stained with my father's blood.

The vampires did grant mercy to my people by allowing them to flee, but they didn't allow my king to leave with them. Was I stupid for thinking Cobra would honor that request? Or was my father right? That I needed a husband to be a good ruler. Was I a fool?

The door opened, and Toman entered. "Kingsnake, King of Grayson, his general Viper, and King Cobra, King of the Mountain, have ventured to our forest to speak with you. Shall I let them enter? Or shall I kill them instead?" He stood with his hands locked together behind his back, his eyes constantly dead now that he served me rather than ruled with me.

"Let them proceed."

He hesitated, the disagreement all over his face.

"Is that a problem, Toman?"

"They slew our king."

"And they let us flee. If we don't forge peace with our enemies, we'll be slain too."

His disagreement was still potent. "You would betray your people for a vampire good in bed?"

My stare remained stoic, but the blood in my heart boiled. "I'm privy to information you are not, Toman. My father imparted information to me that is so blood-curdling, you would scream. I will pardon your behavior this time, but provoke me again, and I won't be so merciful." I gave a wave of my hand, dismissing him.

He hesitated, his hostile stare still fiery.

I held his look as I sat upon my throne, daring him to oppose me with a single word.

He finally backed down and walked out.

Now my heart started to race again, picturing those dark eyes and shadowed jawline. Cobra stared at me with the kind of ownership no other man could ever emulate. His skill with the blade was stronger than mine, despite my greater experience, and that earned my respect. He earned other things too, like the command of my body...and the beat of my heart. I dreaded this moment and yearned for it simultaneously.

The door opened again, and this time, a group of handsome vampires entered. I recognized Viper from my stay in Grayson. The man beside him was unfamiliar, so I assumed this was Kingsnake, King of Grayson. A woman was beside him, dressed in armor similar to his. I assumed she was his prey, the woman who could grant immortality to the kingdoms, but she was definitely not human.

And then I saw him.

He entered last, wearing the black-and-gold armor of his people, his strong body even stronger in the plates of strength, the cloak that hung behind him. I knew that body so well that I could picture everything that lay underneath. He was tall like his brothers, possessed the same unrivaled confidence embedded in their DNA, and had eyes with so much depth they had no ending.

All I could do was stare.

He stared back. "It's nice to see you again...Your Highness."

Butterflies the size of dragons roared in my belly. Lightning that struck the peaks of mountains burned my veins. "Yes... and not on a battlefield."

The corner of his mouth rose in a smile, but only slightly, so subtly that no one else noticed it.

I could stare at him forever, but I had to shift my attention to Kingsnake. "I've granted entry to you and your brothers only. The woman will have to wait outside with the guards until our conversation has concluded."

"She stays," Cobra said immediately. "You speak to all of us, or you speak to none of us."

I stared at Cobra, surprised by the way he'd snapped so quickly.

"Her name is Larisa," Kingsnake said.

I looked at Kingsnake again.

"My future wife and Queen of Grayson," Kingsnake finished. "She goes where I go. Nonnegotiable."

Larisa looked at Kingsnake beside her, who had his gaze fixed hard on me.

This woman must be one and the same. "You've made her into a nightwalker."

Kingsnake took a moment to answer. "Yes."

"Why?" I asked. "I thought she was the salvation of humankind."

The air had a heft I could feel. A boulder the size of a mountain.

"Ellasara struck her down and nearly claimed her life," Kingsnake said. "I had no other choice."

Larisa dropped her gaze to the floor.

If she had died, her soul would have traveled all the way here...sucked into our Mountain of Souls to fuel our immortality. "I'm sorry that happened to you. But you made the right choice."

Larisa lifted her gaze and looked at me again.

"Toman, you're dismissed."

He remained by the door. "I won't leave you with these fiends—"

"I can handle myself. Now, go."

He lingered a moment longer then looked at Cobra.

Cobra stared back.

Both men seemed to know exactly who the other was without asking questions.

Toman finally dismissed himself and shut the doors behind him.

I left the throne and moved to the grand table covered with my father's old scrolls and notes. "Sit." I sat at the head of the table, arms on the armrests, the candles dripping wax into the silver candlesticks.

They gathered around, Kingsnake and Cobra taking the chairs closest to me.

It was strange to sit exactly where my father had sat during our conversations, to take his place as the ruler of Evanguard.

Now that Cobra was closer to me, I felt the pulse in my neck, the steady beat of blood. I was as aware of his presence as I'd been in the bedroom, his naked body next to mine in the middle of the night. The passage of time had been so brief that it was unlikely he'd already bedded someone else, but his appetite seemed ravenous.

I tried to keep my eyes on Kingsnake because that was easier than looking at his brother. "You received my warning."

"We did," Kingsnake said. "And it won us the war—so, thank you."

A ball of dread dropped into my stomach.

"I'm sorry about your father." It wasn't Kingsnake who spoke, but Cobra, his voice gentle.

I still didn't look at him.

"As am I," Kingsnake said. "It wasn't our intention—"

I couldn't listen to this. "My father was my blood, my kin. To hear of his death is deeply painful. But it's also complicated...because he wasn't a good man. His hatred toward your kind has been fueled by incessant greed."

Kingsnake stared, both elbows on the table, his hands together. "Speak further."

Now I looked at the table, unable to meet the eyes of anyone. "I want to forge an eternal truce with your people.

A binding peace that will hold forevermore. No more death. No more despair."

"Tell us of this incessant greed you speak of," Cobra said.

My eyes lifted, and I looked at Larisa and Viper. "The truce first."

I could feel the change of energy as it moved across the table, the way each one of them tensed in discomfort.

"I told you." Viper looked at his brother beside him. "Whatever secret she's hiding is enough to make us kill her on the spot."

Cobra shifted his gaze to me.

I held the stare.

There was no judgment or anger in his eyes, unlike his brothers.

"Those are my terms," I said. "Agree to this truce between our peoples, and I'll grant you access to this information."

The brothers all looked at one another in silence, as if they could read one another's minds. They all seemed to come to an agreement because Kingsnake turned to me. "We want our immortal races to coexist in harmony, regardless of your crimes, so we'll sign your truce and move forward in a new era of peace."

Viper released an annoyed sigh.

Cobra gave me a stare so heated it made my skin bubble.

I unrolled the scroll with my signature at the bottom and passed it to Kingsnake. With a feather-tip quill, he signed his name in black ink at the bottom. He passed the paper to Cobra, who also added his signature in cursive script.

The scroll was returned to me. "Thank you."

Kingsnake stared at me, more intense than he'd been a moment before. "Speak."

I defeated the dread and moved forward. "Before I share this with you, I want you to understand I was unaware of this until last week. And the great majority of the Ethereal are unaware of this truth—"

"*Speak*," Kingsnake said, his eyes venomous.

My spine was straight, my core was strong, but I still felt weak with shame. "The reason the Ethereal have forged this endless crusade against your people is because we compete for the same resources."

"What resources?" Kingsnake asked.

"The kingdoms of men."

Still confused, he narrowed his eyes.

"You need their blood for immortality...and we need their souls."

No movement. No reaction. But the tension was like the heat from a raging forest fire.

Kingsnake dropped his stare momentarily, his entire face tight with consternation. His eyes eventually made their way back to me. "Explain."

"I can't explain the mechanism. I'm not sure my father could either since it's been operating long before either one of us was born. But when a human passes from this life... their soul is captured here. It travels to the river below the mountain that reaches our city, the river that waters our crops, that fills our canteens. The Ethereal truly believe the gods have blessed us with immortal life, have ordered us to eliminate the nightwalkers, while not realizing that they feed and drink the souls of mortals." I finally got it off my chest, but instead of feeling better, I felt worse. It only made it truer.

Once Kingsnake heard my tale, he turned to look at Larisa beside him.

She looked pale, even for a vampire.

Cobra and Viper did the same, looking at the woman they regarded as a sister.

Larisa didn't look at Kingsnake. Her eyes were on the table, and her fingertips moved over her lips in astonishment.

"I'm sorry..." There was no justification for what my people had done. It was pointless to apologize.

Kingsnake looked at Cobra for a while.

Cobra sank back into the chair, arms flat on the table.

The fact that they weren't drawing their blades and threatening to kill me was a miracle. They seemed too shocked to do anything except sit there.

Kingsnake finally spoke. "My father was right—about everything."

"Fuck," Cobra said.

"The kingdoms believe we're the enemy," Kingsnake said. "But it's the people they worship as gods..."

I used to be proud of my people. Now I was so ashamed.

Viper looked at me, his face tight in hatred. "You disgust me."

Cobra didn't look at me, but he jumped to my defense. "Viper."

"Please don't tell me you still want to fuck this bitch—"

"*Viper.*" Cobra didn't raise his voice, but somehow his voice became more powerful. "She just said she and everyone else in Evanguard had no idea. They're victims of this deceit just like we are."

43

"You do realize our mother isn't in the afterlife?" Viper pressed. "These assholes *ate* and *drank* her fucking soul—"

"*Stop*," Kingsnake said. "Queen Clara could have kept this knowledge to herself, but she didn't. She's not like King Elrohir and the leaders who came before her. We have every right to be angry—but not at her."

"Am I the only one here who's not an idiot?" Viper asked. "You really think Queen Clara or the Ethereal will stop the very practice that keeps them alive? The second they shut this down, their entire race will be gone. Did you think about that?"

Cobra dropped his gaze and said nothing.

Kingsnake had nothing to say either.

Viper looked at me. "You aren't going to stop it, are you?"

"It's—it's not so simple."

With a victorious look on his face, he sat back.

"On the one hand, I'm so disgusted I can't sleep at night. Knowing my beating heart is fueled by the souls of innocents is traumatizing. But on the other hand, if I stop it...I die. So does everyone I know."

"If you were to stop the practice, how long would you have?" Cobra asked.

"I'm not sure," I said. "Maybe we'd age and live the remainder of our lives. Like humans, we'd have our children then die. Or maybe we'd immediately perish..."

"I'd say the souls have halted the aging process," Kingsnake said. "And if you were to stop, you would proceed with a normal mortal life. Yes, your days would be limited. And yes, you would creep closer to death. But you would have your soul—and so would the remaining humans."

I gave a nod in agreement. I'd lived almost two thousand years, plenty of time to enjoy all the fruits of life, but the idea of losing it still terrified me. Children had never crossed my mind because I hadn't found the right person, but knowing my days were limited suddenly affected that urgency. "In truth, the way we practice our immortality is our business, as it is your business how you maintain yours. Whether we decide to destroy the obelisk on the Mountain of Souls and choose a mortal life or we choose to continue harboring the souls of the dead is our decision. There's no reason our races need to be in constant battle."

It was clear Viper hated me from the way he looked at me. "We drink the blood of humans, most of them volunteers. And we don't kill them. And even if we did, we don't take their souls. The two are incomparable."

"And spreading the sickness to their people only benefits you," Kingsnake said. "Because the more deaths they suffer, the stronger you become."

I'd never admitted that was intentional, but the truth was obvious. "I was disturbed when my father admitted that to me."

"Do you have an antidote?" Kingsnake asked.

I shook my head. "We assumed it would have run its course by now, but it seems to be getting worse. The idea was supposed to be temporary, enough time to defeat you at your weakest point."

"We have a cure," Kingsnake said. "So we'll take care of it."

"Because we aren't the monsters," Viper said. "*You are.*"

This time, Cobra didn't interfere on my behalf.

Kingsnake spoke again. "You have to stop the practice."

I looked at him once again.

"You know it's the right thing to do."

I breathed a quiet sigh. "What if this were you? Would you sacrifice your immortality for any reason?"

Kingsnake held my gaze, and when he didn't answer immediately, I knew he possessed the maturity to understand other points of view, even those that opposed his own. "If you stop, we'll grant you immortality—as vampires."

I didn't expect the offer, not after a millennium of war. "But we would lose our souls."

"Which would be fair—if you ask me." Viper chimed in again, looking at me like we were enemies on the battle-field. "You should be grateful that we would make the offer at all."

I looked at Kingsnake again. "Why would you offer this gift?"

"Because the soul is sacred," he said. "Every person deserves to decide how it's used. While I would rather not make your kind our kind because of our bloody history, it's preferable to the abuse of innocent people. We may be vampires and you may be Ethereal, but we were human once."

I could live forever as a vampire—or accept that my time had come.

"What will you decide?" Kingsnake pressed.

"I have yet to tell my people the truth. I suspect that will give me my answer." We were a peaceful race, respecting the gifts of the earth. We chose not to eat meat, respecting the creatures that shared our world. I suspected they would all choose to abolish the disgusting practice and accept their own deaths.

Viper looked livid at that answer. "If you think we'd allow this to continue—"

"Viper." Kingsnake was the one to interrupt him this time.

Viper slammed his hand down on the table then sunk back into the chair, defeated.

Kingsnake continued. "How will you explain this truce without telling your people the truth?"

"I can't," I said simply. "I'll need to tell them everything my father told me in confidence."

"Why did he tell you?" Cobra asked.

I'd deceived him. "I pretended to be intrigued, rather than disgusted. He assumed he was preparing a new monarch, while I was plotting his destruction. I won't pretend I'm not deeply hurt that you didn't spare his life..." I paused, keeping my composure so I wouldn't break down into tears. "But he had an evil heart. I don't think this would have ever been resolved peacefully if he'd continued to live."

"I tried," Cobra said. "I really did."

I wouldn't look at him, not when I expected more loyalty than he'd shown.

Kingsnake spoke. "Would you grant us hospitality in your lands while you inform your people?"

I lifted my chin and looked at him. "I don't appreciate your mistrust after the sacrifice I've made, after everything I've shared with you."

"It's not mistrust," Kingsnake said. "But we'd like to know the outcome of your decision. We'd like to be present as we usher in a new era of peace. Because while you may grant it, it's hard to believe if they can't see it."

I'd known this moment was coming, and the more I tried to postpone it, the more stressful it became. We'd just suffered a terrible defeat against the vampires, and now I would be the one to usher in a new era of camaraderie... and tell my people everything we'd believed had been a lie. Our entire ideology, our entire purpose...gone. I suspected some would take their own lives just to stop the pain. "I will always grant my allies accommodations when they ask for them. However, it does come with one condition."

"We won't feed," Kingsnake said. "Your concern is unnecessary."

I gave a nod. "Then Toman will make the arrangements. I wish you all a good night of sleep." I left the table before anyone could speak and opened the door. "Please make accommodations for our guests. They'll be staying with us briefly."

Toman looked like he wanted to kill me, to stab his sword through my stomach. "This is asinine—"

"You need to trust me."

"Trust someone who continually makes the wrong decisions?"

"Trust me, not marrying you was the right decision," I said. "Now, do as I ask or resign from your position so I can find someone who will."

"I'm a commander. Not a servant—"

"Then you've been dismissed."

He seethed in silent anger.

I looked past him to one of the other guards. "Neo. You've been appointed as the Queen's Guard."

Neo immediately left his post and came to me, issuing a deep bow once he was in my presence. "It is an honor, Queen Clara."

"Make accommodations for my guests. They'll require three rooms."

"Of course, Your Highness."

I stepped aside and watched him enter, ushering the guests down the stairs and to the forest floor.

Except Cobra wasn't with them.

My heart had been steady a moment ago, and now it raced a little faster. I returned to the throne room and found him exactly where I'd left him, sitting in the high-backed chair, the glow of the candles highlighting the contours of his handsome face.

I stared, my face frozen in stoicism. "It's late, King Cobra. You should retire for the evening."

He left the chair, made the walk around the table, and then came up to me. Nearly a foot taller than me, when he was up close, I had to tilt my head back to keep my gaze locked on his.

"I like that dress."

It was white, with a pronounced slit up my right thigh. It had long sleeves but a deep cut down the front that showed my collarbones, the hollow of my throat, and a bit of the top of my chest. Handwoven by our best seamstress, the dress was elegant and beautiful, showing my power as queen but also my humbleness. My heart continued to race, but it raced a little faster at his compliment. It wasn't given with a cheeky smile and his typical smugness. It was simple and genuine.

"And the flowers..." His hand raised and reached for one of my strands, lightly touching a white iris pinned in place. "Beautiful."

I tried to keep my breath even when he touched me. Tried to pretend this intimacy meant nothing to me. But my heart wouldn't slow.

He withdrew his hand and continued his stare.

"Is there something you wanted to say?"

He cocked his head slightly, those intelligent eyes locked on mine. "A lot of things, actually. But are they things you want to hear? Your racing heart tells me yes, but that icy look on your face says no."

I hated that my own body betrayed me. And I couldn't stop it.

"There it goes..." Now that smug grin emerged.

Heat flushed my cheeks. "Are you the only one with this ability?"

"It's specific to Cobra Vampires. We can hear our prey from a distance."

"What special abilities do Kingsnake Vampires have?"

"Night vision."

"I thought all snakes had that ability."

"His is different from mine. He can see heat signatures."

"And Originals?"

"They can feel minds."

"Feel?"

"Yes," he said. "It's very involved."

I didn't ask any more questions, knowing I was purposely filling the silence with words to make it more bearable.

Anytime I was around him, the tension was so tight it could snap my neck from my shoulders. It was worse now, after our time apart.

His eyes watched mine as he rode the wave of silence. "We agreed that your father would be spared. Honoring your request was the least we could do after the information you provided us. But unfortunately, my father felt otherwise. I tried to stop him, even interfered in the battle before they could kill each other...but it wasn't enough."

I didn't ask questions because I didn't want details. Didn't want to know how my father had met his death.

"I'm sorry." His voice rang with truth. And his eyes shone with it.

My eyes flicked away.

"Please don't be angry with me—"

"I'm not."

He studied me a moment longer. "Then why is there this distance between us?"

I'd kept him at arm's length since we'd stepped into the same room. I'd made sure not to stare. Made sure not to show an ounce of emotion. "It's complicated."

"No, it's not." His tone became clipped.

I looked away.

"Tell me."

It took me a moment to muster the courage to look at him again. "You were right about everything...and I'm ashamed."

The hardness in his gaze immediately softened.

"You asked me to stay, and I left."

"I'm not the kind of man to hold a grudge."

"You're not?" I whispered.

Slowly, that handsome smile returned to his lips. "Not with you."

"After everything my people have done, you should despise me the way Viper does."

"I've always been more of a lover than a fighter." The smile stayed, warmer than sunshine on a spring afternoon.

"I'm serious."

"As am I." His eyes smiled too, glowed like moonlight on a clear night. "And by the way, the whole queen thing is a huge turn-on."

I looked away and muffled the chuckle that escaped.

"And as I said...I like that dress." His eyes dropped down and roamed over every inch of my body.

The heat burned my cheeks even more. "Are you hitting on me?" I'd said the same thing to him when I was trapped in that cell. He kept coming on to me, kept soliciting sex from me in exchange for freedom, which was disgusting...but also a turn-on.

His grin vanished as he moved closer me, his hand sliding into my hair as he brought his lips down on mine. His arm hooked around the small of my back, and he squeezed me to him with a masculine pull.

The second his mouth was on mine, it all came rushing back. The emotions. The passion. The fire.

His fingers squeezed the fabric of my dress and made it rise farther as his lips caressed mine, feeling my lips with purpose, giving me his breath and taking mine in return.

My fingers met the hardness of his armor. No matter what I touched, it was cold steel. The only place where I could feel flesh was his face, so I cupped his cheeks as I let his mouth ravish mine.

He slowly backed me up to the table, his hands still grabbing and grasping, his tongue meeting mine with a quiet moan. His hand gripped one of my ass cheeks before he lifted me onto the table and moved between my thighs. With our mouths level, our kisses intensified, growing heated and hard. Sometimes our teeth knocked together, and sometimes we swallowed each other's moans. He yanked down the zipper at my back, so my dress dropped several inches, revealing my tits. He grabbed each one as he continued the kiss, his thumb flicking over my nipple firmly.

My fingers worked his trousers, getting them loose enough underneath his armor so he could pop free. My hands returned to his arms and shoulders, feeling the plates of armor with disappointment, wishing I could feel the powerful muscles that used to bulge at my touch.

He yanked me to the edge and tugged on my panties until they came free and got caught around a single ankle. Our kisses grew louder as we grabbed on to each other, quickly bringing our bodies into place so we could finally be reunited.

He aligned himself at my entrance and then gave a harsh shove.

Once I felt him, everything stopped.

It stopped because it felt so damn good.

My eyes locked on his, with my lips parted for breath.

He looked at me just the way he did before, with sheer possessiveness. Then he started to move, his face burying in my neck, the two of us clinging on for dear life as we fucked like wild animals.

5

LARISA

Our accommodations weren't on the ground but up in the trees. A spiral staircase took us to the very top, a humble abode with a single bed in the same room as the kitchen, with a separate sitting area. Windows were plentiful, and if it weren't nighttime, daylight would flood every corner.

Kingsnake took a quick look around, his red cloak shifting behind him as his shoulders moved. He turned in a circle, and when he faced me again, it was with a hard expression.

"You don't like it."

"No."

"I think it's kinda neat—"

"It's vulnerable and precarious."

"I'm sure Queen Clara would make other arrangements—"

"It's fine." He unfastened his cloak then removed his armor, setting the pieces on the couch because he had nowhere else to put them.

I moved to the small dining table and took a seat. It was dark, but I could make out the details of the room and the outside perfectly. There were more color variations than I'd realized, different ways of seeing the world.

Kingsnake entered the room, dressed in his trousers and nothing else. He took the seat across from me, his large body sinking into the chair, his jawline covered in a thick shadow because he hadn't shaved on the journey. For a man spoiled by luxury, he could take the rough road and adapt to it perfectly.

He crossed his arms over his chest and stared. His mood was heavy like storm clouds, his dark eyes bright like strikes of lightning. His anger was palpable, even if I couldn't feel it pressed right up against me.

I didn't speak.

He continued to stare.

I suffered his anger in silence, too uncomfortable to speak.

"I'm waiting for an apology."

I couldn't do that either.

"And an acknowledgment that I was right—about everything."

My eyes shifted away.

"Look at me."

I refused, focusing out the window over the kitchen sink.

"Larisa—"

"Yes, I heard you." I kept my gaze averted.

He turned quiet, his stare hot on my face.

"It's so fucked up." I thought of my mother. My father. Friends who'd died because of a disease our gods had released. "Every person for the last...thousands of years. And I could have been one of them."

His anger slowed from a boil to a simmer. The emotion in my voice could tame him on his worst day.

When the hostility vanished, I looked at him again. "That's the only thing we have—our soul. And some arrogant bastards decided it was theirs. It's so disturbing. If you'd made a different decision...imagine hearing that news."

He looked away abruptly, the mere suggestion too much.

"You'd never recover from something like that." I knew Kingsnake would have struggled to carry on after that. Would have been forever scarred by the decision he could have made. There would be no peace with the Ethereal. He would probably burn this forest to the ground.

"No," he said. "I wouldn't." His voice was quiet, contemplative.

My eyes shifted out the window again, seeing fireflies hovering near the canopies. The forest was quiet, with the exception of a bird that cawed into the night. The breeze moved the branches as it passed through. It was the most peaceful place I'd ever visited—besides Kingsnake's bed. "Wanting to be with you was never the issue...and I hope you know that." He'd told me he loved me, and that should have been the most romantic moment of my life. But it turned into a precursor to the most difficult conversation ever. "I've given up everything for a man before, and we know how that turned out."

"Don't compare me to him ever again."

"I'm not. I'm just saying—"

"I understand that asshole fucked you over, but I've proven many times over that I'm dedicated to you and only you. You knew I loved you long before I said it because you felt it every time we were in the same room together. Don't pretend to be insecure in a relationship that I've made ironclad."

"I didn't mean to offend you—"

"Ellasara fucked me over too, but never once did I compare you to her."

I stopped talking, knowing he had a rebuttal to everything I said.

We turned quiet again.

Silence.

I was tired after our travels, but my mind was too fried for sleep. "Where does this leave us?"

He turned to regard me, one eyebrow slightly cocked.

"I know that I hurt you."

He stared for several seconds, his mind empty. "I told you we're ironclad."

How could a man toss me aside for someone else, but another man love me so unconditionally? I was unremark-able to the first man, but irresistible to the second. But I also didn't understand how Ellasara could have used Kingsnake so cruelly without falling for him. He was the most handsome man I'd ever seen, strong and noble, was kind without being weak. But she didn't see that. "How long did it take you to accept your new way of life?"

"Months. But I probably never would have truly accepted it without knowing the truth."

I knew the god-awful truth, and I still grieved for the soul I'd lost.

"I owe my father an apology...but I'm still unsure if I can give it."

"Why?"

He didn't speak for a long time. "I fear it'll make no difference. His resentment is permanent."

"I find that hard to believe."

"When you live so long, those ill feelings grow and fester to epic proportions. His relationship with Aurelias has deepened into a brotherhood, and he knows where he stands with Cobra and Viper. But with me...there's been nothing but silent contempt and heavy grudges."

"I'm surprised you care when you dislike him so much."

"A relationship between father and son is always complicated." His eyes moved out the window again.

"What if the Ethereal refuse to stop what they're doing?"

"They better."

"Would you give up your immortality?"

His eyes came back to me. "If it were under the same circumstances, yes."

"You're a lot more empathetic than your brothers."

"Probably because I was closest to our mother. She lived for love and peace, not cruelty."

"I'm sorry you lost her..."

"As am I." His emotions were quiet, as if he didn't feel anything at all. Time had buried his heartache.

"But what if they refuse?"

"Then we'll have another battle," he said. "Their affairs are their own business, but their practices are so inhumane we'll need to intervene. My mother's soul is already gone, but she would want us to stop this for the rest of humankind."

"Yeah...you're right."

"I've been a vampire far longer than I was ever human, but a part of me will always retain my humanity."

———

A hot shower had washed away all the sweat and grime from our travel. I stepped out in a towel, feeling refreshed with clean skin and hair. My fingers ran through the strands as I moved into the room with the bed.

His thoughts assaulted me the moment I entered the room. Heat from the summer sun burned my flesh as if I stood in the middle of a desert at high noon. Invisible hands grabbed me everywhere, tugged on the towel to make it come free. His need was so potent, it was borderline angry.

My eyes found his as he lay on the bed, his back against the headboard, sheets bunched at his waist. His muscles were chiseled and strong, big bulges all over his arms. His hair was slightly damp from his shower. He didn't bother to fully dry off before he got into bed.

His eyes dropped to the cotton towel that covered my body. They stayed there a moment before they returned to my gaze.

My nipples were hard against the cotton, and my skin prickled like the temperature had just dropped. The last time I'd slept with him was before the battle, before I became a nightwalker. My body felt different now. Paler. Stronger. Now that my blood was unusable, I'd wondered if he would want me less, but it felt like nothing had changed.

He grabbed the towel and tugged it gently, the material coming out of my hands and dropping to the floor. The cool air hit my skin, made the bumps pebble more. He pushed down the sheets to show his big dick, ready before my body was even exposed. His fingers clasped around my wrist, and he pulled me to him, wanting me on his lap.

My thighs parted over his hips, and he guided his length inside me as I came down, our bodies sliding together in perfect harmony.

He inhaled a deep breath as his fingers kneaded my ass.

My senses were stronger, so it felt even better than it had before. My hands palmed his chest as I rolled my hips and treasured the feel of him inside me, right where he belonged. My eyes closed as I savored it, the feeling of his powerful hardness.

He grew impatient and lifted my ass, wanting me to rise up and slide back down and sit on his balls.

I started to move, my tits gliding past his face, my back arching before it straightened again.

His fingers continued to knead my ass as he moaned, as his cock throbbed inside me.

I kept it slow and steady, treasuring the way his body felt with mine, getting used to it all over again. I basked in the glow of his desire, feeling how much he wanted me every moment. No matter how quickly or slowly I moved, he loved it. When I looked at him, I saw a ripple of pleasure. When my fingers moved over his heart, I felt another throb of pleasure. He loved everything I did, no matter how insignificant.

And when I came...his body rumbled like an earthquake.

His arm hooked around my back as he guided me to the bed and moved on top of me, our bodies positioned at the foot of the bed rather than the head. He folded me the way he liked, getting the angle deep like he wanted, and then fucked me as he gripped me by the throat.

6

KINGSNAKE

It was afternoon when we woke up.

The last time I'd fed was before the battle—and I had started to feel it. I'd be lying if I said I didn't miss the taste of her blood, but I'd rather live without it than live without her. Never again would I be that strong unless I found prey that possessed something similar.

But just the thought made me feel guilty.

She would have to feed too. I knew she must be hungry, even though she never mentioned it. The idea of feeding on someone's blood probably revolted her, but at some point, her hunger would outweigh her disturbance.

Someone knocked on the door before they walked in.

Larisa was already dressed in the clothes they'd supplied us, a deep green dress with one sleeve. A prominent slit was up one thigh, so high that her undergarments were nearly exposed.

I might not be a fan of the elves, but I appreciated their design style.

It was Cobra, wearing a big-ass grin on his face like he was in paradise. "Morning."

"It's past noon," I said.

"Didn't notice." He helped himself to the dining table, wearing his armor and cape. He looked at Larisa, who sat beside him. "The elves have great fashion sense, don't they?"

"Cobra." I pulled out the chair across from her and sat down. "Hit on my fiancée, and I'll have to slide my dagger between your ribs."

"Can she be your fiancée if you haven't asked her to be your fiancée?" he asked, an eyebrow cocked.

When I looked at Larisa, her eyes were on Cobra, as if to purposely avoid my gaze.

If her answer would have been yes, I would have asked her before the war. I would ask her now, but everything still felt tense. "Now that you've made a pass at my fiancée and provoked us both, can you tell us why you're here?"

"Do you always smile like that?" Larisa asked.

Cobra waggled his eyebrows. "Queen Clara and I had words..."

"Sounds like a lot more than words," I said.

"You know me. Always a gentleman." He waggled his eyebrows again.

"What does this mean?" Larisa asked. "Are you two together?"

"That would never work, Cobra," I said.

"Why not?" he snapped. "If they destroy their obelisk, she'll become a vampire. We would be the same."

"But we'll always be different—and you know that."

Cobra's good mood evaporated, and he gave me his hard stare. "You shouldn't hold a grudge against someone who didn't commit a crime. The person who did is gone now. Let's move on."

"It's not that simple, Cobra. They've pledged war against us for thousands of years. You can't just erase that."

"Kingsnake." Larisa caught my attention with her serious voice.

My eyes shifted back to hers.

"If the elves agree to disband this practice entirely on their own, we should focus on a new horizon. We should focus on peace. You and Cobra are both kings, and there's no reason you can't make this happen."

Cobra kept his eyes on me. "Maybe Larisa should rule in your stead while you take a vacation or something."

I ignored the insult. "Viper won't be happy."

"Is he ever happy?" Cobra countered.

I stayed quiet when I didn't receive the answer I wanted. "So you came here to tell us you got laid last night?"

"No. I came here to tell you Clara has been speaking to the elves since early this morning."

"She didn't waste any time," Larisa said.

"No," Cobra said as he looked at me. "Because she's a good person. She told me how horrible she feels about everything, that she draws breath because someone lost their eternal soul. It eats her alive."

I didn't have much pity. Not after all the battles that had been fought needlessly. "You expect me to feel bad for her? You know who I pity? Our mother. Our other relatives. Larisa's family. All humankind. That's who I feel bad for."

"She didn't know—"

"I understand that," I snapped. "But she's still benefited for all these centuries. Until she says they'll abolish the practice and accept a mortal life or an immortal one as a night-walker, I'll continue my resentment."

"You sound like Father." It was meant as an insult—and it definitely landed as one.

"What will you do if she says no?"

"She won't—"

"What if she does? What if her people refuse to cooperate? Then what?"

"She has faith in her people."

My eyes burned into his. "We always do the right thing until it becomes hard to do the right thing. They claim to be spiritual creatures who worship their trees and abstain from meat. But once their perfect lives are in peril, they'll become feral."

Cobra stared at me.

"I hope I'm wrong. I hope she embraces immortality as one of us. I hope you get everything that you want. But be prepared for a very different outcome."

7

CLARA

"The obelisk absorbed the souls of those who've passed. Those are then transferred to the water under the mountain, the water that leads to our rivers, that irrigates our crops, that quenches our bodies with every drink. I don't know how long it's been there. I don't know who built it. But the power that keeps us alive...is the souls of others."

The Ethereal stared back at me, the generals in the front, the others behind. We sat in the wooden amphitheater where we held our plays and played our music. It was rarely used for announcements like this. "My father shared this with me before he passed. The information was passed to him by his father before he perished in battle. I could have kept it to myself as my father wanted, but I was too disturbed by what I learned. I couldn't carry on, knowing someone lost their immortal soul so I could continue to live...and I know you must all feel the same way." In truth,

I didn't know how they felt. I'd just shared the news with them, and most of them were so shocked they were stunned into silence. "I know this is a lot to take in..."

"What are we supposed to do?" one of the generals asked. "If we destroy the obelisk, we'll all perish."

"I've shared this information with the vampires—"

"You did what?" the general snapped. "You shared our secret with our enemy?"

"They aren't our enemy. I've just told you that they've never been our enemy. They simply competed for the same resource. We've committed genocide against them needlessly. And they've offered us a gift."

"What gift?" he asked.

"They've offered us immortality if we abolish the act."

Heavy silence spread across the amphitheater. They all stared at me, disturbed.

"Yes, that means we'll be vampires, but I think that's better than what we are now. It's better than what we've been doing. It was generous to offer, considering the destruction we've caused their people."

Now all their eyes were down on the ground.

"As Queen of Ethereal, I've decided to destroy the obelisk. That means you have a decision to make. You can live the remainder of your lives as humans and pass on when your time comes. And those who prefer immortality...can choose to be nightwalkers. I know this is hard to digest, so take your time."

———

I sat in my study, my eyes on the wall across the room. A flower had fallen out of place in my hair, but I didn't bother to fix it. I'd assumed the weight would be lifted from my chest once I confessed the truth to my people.

But now it was heavier.

Seeing their horrified faces looking back at me was the worst thing I'd ever experienced. I could see they were paralyzed by the news, shocked by their own upcoming demise. Giving them a secondary option of being a vampire didn't seem to go over well. They wanted to live forever—and keep their souls.

I'd been queen for such a brief time, but I already felt like the worst ruler who ever lived. Perhaps I should have just destroyed the obelisk without their knowledge and explained their aging as a curse from the gods.

There was no good answer.

The door opened, and the Queen's Guard entered. "King Cobra, King of the Mountain, requests a word."

I wasn't in the mood for company, not even from him, but I refused to shoo him off. He was all I had right now. "Send him in."

A moment later, Cobra entered, regal in his king's uniform. He took the seat to my left and pivoted the chair so he faced me. One ankle crossed and rested on the opposite knee, and with his elbows on the armrests, he brought his hands together in his lap. He stared, his charming smile absent, his eyes deep and serious. "Are you alright, sweetheart?" The tenderness in his voice was a direct contradiction to his usual hardness.

My eyes hadn't been on him that entire time, just taking him in through my peripheral. But now I shifted my gaze to his directly, seeing dark eyes that reminded me of lonely midnights. "No...not really."

"What happened?"

"They took it pretty hard."

"What did they say?"

"Nothing..."

His eyes, full of pity, were still glued to mine.

"I told them I would destroy the obelisk. So they need to decide whether they want to live the remainder of their lives as human...or embrace immortality as a nightwalker. I'm not sure what they will decide."

"I thought you were going to put it to a vote."

"But then I realized how cruel it is to make people choose. It's a bit easier when someone else makes the hard choice for you."

He gave a subtle nod. "This makes me a bit uneasy."

"Why?"

"What if they stage a coup?"

"We're peaceful—"

"You're taking away their way of life. Not everyone will agree with your decision. Since you're the only one who knows where it is, if they kill you, their immortality perseveres."

I found it hard to believe my own kind would do something so barbaric, but it wasn't out of the realm of possibility.

"I will stay with you until it's done."

"I have guards—"

"I don't trust them."

"Cobra, you have your own obligations—"

"None of those obligations is more important than you."

I kept a straight face, but my heart clenched like a closing fist.

"What will you decide?"

Not understanding the question, I stared.

"Will you live the remainder of your life as human...or join me?"

I hadn't made any choice, not when I had so many other things to think about. I could live a short life and keep my soul...or I could live forever as a hollow vessel. It was obvious what Cobra wanted me to choose. "I don't know."

He did his best to hide his disappointment, but it flashed across his eyes like a meteor in the sky. "If you become a vampire and live forever, your life would be exactly as it is now. You planned on living forever—and now you can."

"But if I die—"

"Now that a truce has been granted between our people, there would be no reason to die."

"I'm not arrogant enough to assume I'm invincible."

"You're invincible with me." His confident eyes stared into mine. "You think I'd ever let anything happen to my queen?"

It happened again, my heart clenching painfully. "We hardly know each other—"

"I know you better than anyone else. And you know better than anyone else." He said it so confidently, with eyes that were bright with power. "I've lived a long time and bedded a lot of women. None of them has ever meant a damn thing to me—except you."

I could feel the pulse in my neck, feel it race in both excitement and fear, and that meant he could hear it. The last time someone professed their love to me, it was a lie. But I knew it wasn't a lie with Cobra. The only thing he wanted was me. "Why me?"

There was a long pause, like he didn't have an answer. "I don't know."

"You don't know...?"

"I know that's not the romantic answer. But whatever we have between us is deeper than logic. It's chemistry, the way our bodies hum to life when we're in the same room together. It's the way I love talking to you as much as I love fucking you. After I bedded you once or twice, I should have been bored and ready for the next thing, but I wanted more. I still want more." His eyes looked so beautiful when he spoke with such sincerity. "It's more than physical. It's emotional too, because when you left, I was an utter mess. Ask my brothers, and they'll tell you."

"I was a mess too."

A ghost of a smile moved across his lips. "If you choose to remain mortal, we'll have our time together, but it'll be brief, and then I'll be inconsolable once it's over. Or you can join me, and we can take our sweet-ass time. I know there's an issue of children...because that's important to most women—"

"I'm not sure if I want them. I always assumed when I found the right person, I would have them, but that's just because of my duty to reproduce and continue the family line. Now that my father is gone and my sister isn't speaking to me and the Ethereal are essentially no more...it doesn't matter."

"Then it makes even more sense."

I felt his presence push into me, asking for the answer he wanted to hear. "I pledged myself to someone before, and it ended up being the biggest mistake of my life. Now you're asking me to sacrifice my soul when we haven't had much time together—"

"First of all, don't compare me to that asshole who used you. Don't pretend you don't realize you've got me wrapped around your finger and pinned under your thumb. I'm so fucking hard for you—all the time. And secondly, I'm not asking you to decide this very moment. We have time. I just want to know you're open to it."

"I am open to it." I said it without thinking. Before Cobra, I never would have even considered it, considered sacrificing my soul for a guy after the last man in my life had stabbed me in the back. But I considered it because something about him felt right—even when I was locked in that cell and he was bringing me food, it felt right.

He stared at me with a hard expression, his eyes slowly shifting back and forth between mine. I'd give anything to know his thoughts the way he could hear my heartbeat, but I suspected he felt a dip of pleasure when he heard me say that. "Let's go to bed."

———

He rested his blade against the nightstand and placed his dagger on top. Piece by piece, his armor and clothing were removed, revealing the chiseled muscle underneath tight skin with corded veins. He was the one nearly naked, but he looked at me like I was wearing nothing. He dropped everything until he was fully naked, his hard cock anxious.

I swallowed, having never seen a man so gorgeous. I still wore my dress with the flowers in my hair, but I felt paralyzed by that hungry stare. Today had been the worst of my life, but he somehow made it seem like a distant memory.

He came around the bed toward me, eyes locked on mine, and once he reached me, his hand gripped my back and tugged me close. The zipper came down, and the dress came loose, exposing my tits to the cool air. It slipped to my ankles, and then his big thumbs hooked into my panties and pulled them down. Once I was buck naked, he lifted me to his body then adjusted me onto his length. He pulled me down over his cock like he slid his hand into a glove.

I breathed out as my arms circled his neck. I expected him to lay me down on the bed and dominate me, but he held me with his strong arms and started to guide me up and down, strong enough to hold my weight like it was nothing.

Fuck, that was hot.

With minimal effort, he continued to move me, sliding me down his length over and over, his eyes locked on mine with our lips close together. Our breaths started to deepen, started to grow louder. Soon, we panted for each other, our wet bodies moving together perfectly.

I squeezed him as I came, turned on by his strength, the way he made me feel lighter than a feather, when I had muscles in both my arms and legs. I clung to him and sliced his skin with my nails, my tits dragging against his chest as I moved. "Cobra..." My hand cupped his face, and I kissed him as I finished, feeling more pleasure between my legs than I ever had before.

He carried me to the bed and dropped me on the sheets before he moved over me. He folded me into a ball and planted one of my feet against his chest before he ravished me, banging the headboard against the wall, making my toes curl because the pleasure continued. "Be my baby."

My eyes found his, the possessive need in his stare.

"You're my baby," he said against my ear. "Let me call you that."

My arm hooked over his shoulder, and I gripped his wrist as he pinned one of my legs back. The last man who called me that made a fool out of me, didn't deserve to call me that in the first place. But this man did. "Okay."

————

"Baby, get up."

My eyes stayed closed, still dead asleep.

"Clara. Now."

The danger in his voice made my eyes snap open. That was when I smelled it—the unmistakable aroma of smoke. I sat up and saw Cobra was already fully dressed in his armor with his sword at his hip. "What's happening?"

"I hear twelve heartbeats nearby. They're frantic, like they're running or fighting."

I rolled out of bed and hurried into my closet, throwing on clothes. My armor was there, pristine white like pearls, and I pulled it on before I grabbed my sword. When I returned to the room, Cobra had his blade in his hand with his eyes on the ceiling.

"We need to leave."

"That's exactly what they want us to do."

I started to cough, the potency of the smoke too much for my lungs. "If we stay here, we'll die."

Cobra moved forward and stepped into the hallway, but instead of going to the main entrance, he moved to one of the windows. He slammed his elbow into it and shattered it into pieces. "Come on." He gave me his hand and helped me over the edge. It was a ten-foot fall to the balcony below, and I made it without losing my balance. Cobra dropped down a moment later. "Follow me." He moved around the balcony toward the front, but the fire had burned it through, creating a massive gap between the two different parts. The drop below us was twenty feet, and while he might survive that as a vampire, I wouldn't as a human.

He turned back to me. "I'm going to throw you."

"I can make the jump—"

"It's twenty feet." He got on his hands and knees. "Run and push off my back. You aren't going to hurt me, so give it your best."

I thought I could make it without the help, but it would suck to be wrong. "Alright." I scooted back then sprinted, running and stepping up onto his back before I pushed hard, flying across the divide and barely making it to the other side. I grabbed on to the edge, dangling over the chasm below.

"Pull yourself up!" he shouted from behind me. "You can do it."

I ground my teeth as I pulled myself up and over the edge.

"Attagirl."

I pushed to my feet and backed up so he could make the jump, but then I spotted the enemy behind him. "Cobra!"

He turned at the right time, seeing the Ethereal soldiers coming at him. There were three, all wielding their blades with deadly precision.

Cobra unsheathed his blade with record speed and deflected the first sword. He kicked the other Ethereal back and then dodged the attack aimed at his neck. It all happened in the blink of an eye, and then he wielded his blade against all three opponents.

Before I could jump back across to help, I had my own assassins to deal with. Five of them came at once, all intent on putting me in the ground for the decision I had made. It hurt that Cobra had been right, that my own people could be so barbaric.

I pulled out a dagger and threw it into the neck of the first assassin, then caught the blade of the next. I couldn't handle four men at once, but I did my best to block and evade their weapons. Otherwise, I'd lose an arm or my neck. The flames cast light in the darkness for me to see their movements, and while I kept up my defense, my energy was draining quickly. One of them got their blade on my armor, and my vambrace popped right off. The other one caved in, pressing hard into my forearm and making me wince. With my guard down, their blades sliced across my stomach. My armor took the brunt of it, but it still knocked the wind out of me.

"*Clara!*" Cobra's horrified yell came across the chasm.

I hoped he was more worried about himself than me. I rolled out of the way of a deadly blow to my neck and got to my feet, but someone tugged me back and I fell down once again. Then I saw their black-and-red armor, looking like glowing embers against the backdrop of the flames. Kingsnake took on two by himself, slicing down the middle of one and then decapitating the other, as if it took no effort at all. Viper destroyed the other two, pushing one down into the chasm and then snapping the neck of the other.

Kingsnake yelled across the gap. "We got her!"

Cobra kicked his opponent into the chasm then looked at me. "Baby, are you alright?"

"I'm fine," I said, still out of breath.

Viper came over and tore the vambrace off my arm when he realized the damage it had caused my forearm. The bruising was immediately noticeable.

Cobra took off at a run and jumped across the opening, making it all the way across without faltering. He looked me over himself to make sure I was alright before he glanced at Kingsnake. "Are there others?"

"Viper and I killed them at the entrance," Kingsnake said. "Larisa felt their intentions, and we came immediately."

"Where is she?" Cobra asked.

"I asked her to hide," Kingsnake said. "That didn't go over well, and I'll pay for it later."

Cobra came straight to me and grabbed both of my shoulders. He gave me a once-over before he let me go. "I feared this would happen."

"Why?" Kingsnake asked.

"Clara told her people she would destroy the obelisk," Cobra said. "They clearly weren't happy with that decision."

"It seems to have been isolated to a few rebels," Viper said. "Anyone else who has the same idea will be wary."

"You need to destroy the obelisk," Cobra said to me. "Be done with it so this doesn't happen again."

I still couldn't believe my own people had tried to kill me and the vampires were the ones who'd saved me.

"We'll escort you there," Kingsnake said.

Cobra waited for my agreement. "Clara?"

"I'm sorry... I just need a second." I walked away from their group and left the flames behind, trying to access cool air to cleanse my lungs. My life had fallen apart piece by piece, and now that my own people had tried to murder me, I hit rock bottom. I looked into the tree houses, knowing that the Ethereal stood on their balconies and stared at the flames that would have claimed my life. When I looked at the stairs, I saw the dead guards who had fought to protect me. I saw the other Ethereal who had come out to witness the horrific sight. Some of them grabbed buckets and formed a line, moving the pails from the river to the palace to douse the flames.

All I could do was stand there.

My eyes were on the forest, but I could feel him beside me. Feel him standing there and staring at me, accompanying me in my misery. My arms were crossed over my chest and I was on the verge of tears, but I was too proud to let them fall. "I feel like I'm living a nightmare...and it just gets worse."

He came closer at the silent invitation.

"My life wasn't great before I knew the truth, but it wasn't horrible either. Now everything I've ever believed in is a complete lie. My own people whom I've served tried to burn me to death. My father was killed by my treason. I'm destroying my own immortality. I have to decide whether I want to live an unremarkable life as a human or forever as an undead. It's all happened in such a short amount of time... It's hard to process."

"Heavy is the head that wears the crown."

I slowly turned to him.

"You're ushering in a new era for the Ethereal. You're making the right choice, albeit the hard choice. There will be defiance. There will be disappointment. That's your burden to bear for as long as you wear that crown."

"Is that supposed to make me feel better?"

"It's supposed to harden your spine. It's supposed to invigorate you with courage. You inherited a kingdom of lies and deceit. Now it's your responsibility to make the Ethereal as glorious as they should have been. If you thought that would be easy, then you're a fool."

I'd expected the man I was sleeping with to console me, to tell me I was doing a great job, to say all the things I wanted to hear. Instead, he told me the things I *needed* to hear. Spoke the truth instead of cushioning me with lies.

And I liked that. "It sounds like you speak from experience."

"It wasn't easy to start our kingdoms. And it hasn't been easy to make the tough calls. If the job is ever easy, then you aren't doing it right." He stared at me with that hardness in his gaze, a king in a different kingdom. "You know I'm here for you—always. My blade is yours. My brothers serve you. But it's your job to lead."

"I'm surprised one of you doesn't just take over..."

His eyes took in mine. "The Ethereal don't need us when they already have a mighty queen."

When his stare became too much, I looked away.

"Who happens to be the sexiest little thing I've ever seen." His smile was in his voice, charming and flirtatious.

My sadness was too potent to feel joy.

"Some of your people tried to kill you, not all. Others still follow you. Others respect you for speaking the truth. You've killed your enemies, and now you stand tall. Show them that Queen Clara can't be stopped by blades and fire. This is your chance to show your strength and remind people why you're the one on the throne."

After a couple breaths, I let the sadness disappear. There was no time for self-pity. No time for doubt. "We'll leave for the obelisk at first light. But truthfully, I have no idea how to destroy it. It's made of solid stone."

"Viper has explosives."

I turned to him. "And why has Viper brought explosives into our forest?"

"He always has them on hand, just in case we come across an obstacle we can't cross or we need to block the path of an oncoming enemy. Nothing personal."

After they'd defended me against my own people, they were nothing but trustworthy, so I let it go.

"How long is this trek?"

"My father and I made it there and back in a single day. But it will take us longer because I don't know the path as well as he did. I know the general route, know what markers to search for, but there will definitely be some mishaps along the way."

He gave a nod. "Then we may need to put this trek on hold."

"Why?"

His eyes avoided mine for a moment. "We didn't anticipate our stay lasting so long, and it's been a while since we've eaten."

My heart dropped into my stomach. I'd never seen him feed, so it was easy to forget that he was a vampire who feasted on the life-force of others. His fangs were never visible, and other than the paleness of his skin, it was hard to tell that he was undead.

"We'll honor your rules and fulfill our needs outside the forest."

"How long will this take?"

"A couple days, probably."

"And...you'll just grab someone and take what you want?"

"That's not really how it works."

"Then how does it work?" I asked.

His eyes faded, like the question was unwelcome. "It's offered freely."

"And why would someone just do that?"

He looked away for a moment. "You're asking questions when you don't want the answers. So let's just leave this conversation unsaid."

Enthusiasts lived everywhere, obsessed with vampires, the beautiful, immortal beings. Most humans worshipped us, but many worshipped them too. "So you find a pretty girl who wants you and lets you go to town?"

He shifted his weight but held my eyes all the while. "Your heart is racing so damn fast..."

In embarrassment, I looked away.

"Not because you're excited. Not because you're nervous. But because you're angry. So damn angry. So drop the conversation."

"Why don't you feed from a man—"

"Because I'm not going to." His voice was clipped and hard. It held no room for negotiation. "I feed, and then I leave. There will be nothing else, Clara. I've been faithful to you since the moment I laid eyes on you. You're mine now, and I'm not going to fuck that up with a lesser woman—"

"Why haven't you asked to feed on me?"

He stilled at the question.

All the jealousy and anger made my tone change, made it deepen.

"Because I respect you too much to ask."

"Isn't that what you do with your other lovers? Feed and then fuck them—"

"You aren't one of them. You're so much more. I would never ask you to do something you so vehemently oppose.

And you don't need to offer now just because I'm hungry. I will feed, and that's it."

My heart still pounded in my chest. Like an army of hooves against the earth. "I don't want you to."

He came closer, our exchange so charged that anyone who saw us together would know there was something between us. His chin was dipped to meet my look, and the intensity in his eyes became so much more. "Are you sure, baby? Because the others will have to leave anyway."

"I could ask for volunteers."

"That's a bold move."

"You and your brothers are very...attractive. I wouldn't be surprised if there are women here who would be interested, especially after you let us retreat at the end of the war. And more so now that you've offered to make us your kind after what we've done to you. Some disagree, I know this, but others have been touched. Feeding you is the least we can do."

He continued to stare at me. "If that's what you want."

"Is it not what you want?"

His eyes flicked back and forth between mine. "I want your blood with the same intensity that I want your body. It's something I think about every time we're together. When your body is folded under mine and you're shedding tears of pleasure, I want to sink my teeth into your flesh and have you. Yes, it's what I want. But I only want it if you want it too. Only if you want me to own you. So make sure it's what you really want...because I'm going to want it all the time."

———

The flames were doused, and the rest of the forest was spared from the inferno. My accommodations were destroyed. My father's possessions were torched to ash. I was forced to retreat to my previous home, the tree house high in the canopy. I didn't have the same privacy I had with the throne room, so the Ethereal knew I'd taken one of the vampires with me.

Cobra took a quick look around, checking every door and closet to ensure we were alone before he put down his sword. "Will the guards at the base be enough? Someone could come with an ax and chop it down."

"Not these trees. When they're in their prime, they're practically stone. It would take months to chop it down with a hundred men." I shed my armor and felt pounds lighter. Last time I was here, I'd mourned the loss of Cobra, the passionate affair that made me realize I deserved more than Toman. Cobra was the best thing that had ever happened to me...in a lot of ways.

"You're sad." Cobra came to me, most of his armor gone and on the couch.

"How do you know?"

"I've become well acquainted with your heart." His hand slid into my hair and cupped my face, taking me with the kind of ownership that turned me on. He grabbed me when he felt like it. Tugged me when he felt like it. "Tell me."

My fingers slid over his wrist. "Last time I was here, I'd just left you."

A subtle smile moved on to his lips.

"I missed you..."

"I missed you too, baby." His thumb moved underneath my chin and forced my stare up to his. "Your letter made me smile, listening to you demand more and refuse to settle for less. To wait for a man worthy of your heart."

I found myself in the same position I'd been in before, much sooner than I anticipated. He was wrong for me in every way, but I yearned for him the way I yearned for the sun. The way I yearned for flowers in spring. Heat in summer.

"A man like me."

My heart quickened. If I felt it, so did he. Felt it flutter like the wings of a hummingbird.

His arm tugged me into his body as his lips caught mine. He gave me a squeeze as he kissed me, a kiss that quickly morphed into something deeper. Breaths and tongues were exchanged as we moved closer to the bed, articles of clothing falling along the way. The beginning of our night had been full of passionate fucking, and now the early morning would be filled with lovemaking.

He got me onto the bed and moved over me, his heavy body carved with bulging muscles. He kissed me as he grabbed my knee and propped it back, pinning my thigh against my hip. With his lips directly above mine, he spoke. "Last chance, baby." His throbbing dick was right against my clit, and the flesh of my thigh was exposed.

My heart continued to race, both in fear and excitement. "Yes..."

He didn't give me a chance to change my mind. He was already at my exposed thigh, his fangs now visible as he brought his face to my flesh and bit me.

I inhaled a deep breath when I felt my skin break against his teeth. It hurt like a knife that cut the surface. Blood dripped down my thigh to the sheets. The pain was quickly overridden by the most exquisite pleasure. Instead of a cry, I gave a moan. My fingers dug into his hair as he fed on me. I was suddenly flooded with arousal as if I hadn't been turned on in the first place. I wanted this man every time I saw him. Every time I saw that charming smile, those intense eyes, those broad shoulders. But now it was so much more. "Cobra..."

He withdrew his fangs and licked his lips before he moved back up my body. He lifted my hips as he tilted his own and slid inside until he was deep within, so deep it hurt. His thrusts were hard and forceful, his breaths stifled with quick moans.

I rocked with him then flung my hair out of the way, exposing my flesh for him.

"Fuck, baby." His hand dug into my hair, and he closed his lips over my neck, piercing me with the same pain and pleasure again. He continued to move inside me, tilting my hips farther so he could fuck me and feed from me at the same time.

There was nothing else like it. My arms hooked over his shoulders, and I held on as he brought me to heaven with his touch. A rumble started in my stomach then spread to my extremities. Pleasure no other man had ever given me rocked through my body like waves in a violent storm. Tears burned down my cheeks as I was racked with ecstasy. "Cobra..."

8

LARISA

I saw Kingsnake approach the place where he'd ordered me to hide. I knew he was coming because I felt his emotions as he drew closer. My abilities had expanded since I'd become a vampire, and I could feel him the entire time he was gone, feel him locked in the throes of battle.

It was a horrible thing to experience, his potent anger and focus as he cut down his enemies. But it was also welcome, because I always knew that he was alive. I emerged from the tree when he drew near, seeing a powerful king approach me, his armor scuffed from the blades that had tried to reach his flesh.

The second he saw me, I felt it. Searing heat from unbridled flames. A longing that stretched across the seas. A relief like rainfall on a forest fire. His love wasn't a particular sensation that I could detect, but it was the foundation for all those other emotions he felt. He cupped my cheeks with both palms and kissed me, a gentle kiss full of love instead of lust. He was the one in battle, but he feared for my life instead of his.

Before he pulled away, he kissed my forehead. The first time he'd ever done such a thing. The first time anyone had done such a thing. Engulfing me in the glow of unconditional love. I could feel Elias's arousal the second his wife entered the room. Knew he wanted to fuck her. But Kingsnake had never felt that way in anyone else's presence. Even when he spoke with Ellasara, he only emanated rage.

His eyes, his heart, his body...it was all just for me. "I love you."

His arms were at his sides now, but his eyes hardened more than they ever had. He didn't take a breath. Still as a statue, he looked as if he felt nothing at all, but underneath that mountain were rivers with infinite depths. Warmth flooded his body like sunlight in his veins, and the depth of that feeling was unlike anything I'd ever felt.

"I'm sorry about before—"

"It's forgotten."

"I want to be with you forever—soul or no soul."

He absorbed that declaration for seconds before he stepped close to me again. His arm hooked around the arch in my back, and he drew me into him, his forehead coming back to mine. "Marry me."

With my eyes on his lips, I gave a slight nod. "Yes."

"It wasn't a question, sweetheart."

―――――――

We sat across the table from each other, sunshine coming through the canopy and the windows. Kingsnake had pushed the table away from the walls so we could be in the shade as much as possible. Now that I was a vampire, I understood the discomfort he mentioned before, the way the rays felt so hot, it was as if they were melting your flesh.

Since the palace had burned to the ground, we didn't know where to find Cobra. He was shacked up with Clara somewhere, so we'd have to wait for him to come to us. In the meantime, we sat together, enjoying the silent companionship that was born over a lifetime. But for us, it had happened in just a few months.

The door opened, and Viper entered. "Have you heard from him?"

"No." Kingsnake kept his gaze out the window.

Viper took the chair at the head of the table. "Then I guess we'll just sit on our hands and wait until his dick is thoroughly satisfied."

My first breath as a vampire had been full of strength and enhanced abilities. But with every passing day, I started to grow weaker. My stomach began to cramp, and now it gnawed at my insides. I didn't bother with the food I used to eat, because that wouldn't satisfy me whatsoever.

I knew I needed blood.

Repulsive. Disgusting. But if I didn't eat at some point, I would die.

Kingsnake must be hungry too, but he didn't mention it. His eyes were the dark color of earth now, not the brilliant green they once were.

Minutes later, the door opened again, and Cobra entered. "Morning."

"Take your morning and fuck right off," Viper snapped.

With a ridiculous grin on his face, he took a seat. "You need to get laid, man."

"And you need to get laid less," Viper said. "Get that stupid smile off your face—"

"I'm far too hungry and tired to tolerate this." Kingsnake spoke in a quiet voice, like he, indeed, was exhausted. "How far is the journey to the obelisk?"

"A couple days, maybe," Cobra said. "I know you guys are hungry, so once you've eaten, we'll begin the trek."

"We're hungry?" Viper asked. "Why are you excluded from that statement?"

Cobra shrugged as the grin remained on his face.

"You fed on Clara?" Kingsnake asked.

His grin only grew. "Turns out, she's the jealous type. Which is fine by me because I think that's pretty hot." He waggled his eyebrows. "She's asked for volunteers for the rest of you, and a few men and women have stepped forward."

"Why?" Viper asked. "Why would they agree to that?"

"For a lot of reasons," Cobra said. "But mainly gratitude. We agreed to a truce, when we could have slaughtered them instead. And after centuries of war, it's the least they can do. Plus, we have admirers everywhere." He winked.

I felt sick to my stomach, not just because of what I had to do, but because Kingsnake would feed on someone besides me. I'd been his only prey since the moment we'd met, and knowing he would sink his teeth into another beautiful woman immediately made me insecure. My blood was what made him desire me in the first place. And now...I didn't have that to offer anymore.

Kingsnake felt the same dread. It slowly spread through his body like a poison.

"After you've eaten, we'll go," Cobra said. "Viper, we'll probably need your explosives to destroy this thing. Apparently, it's made out of solid stone."

"I just want to eat," Viper said as he stood up. "Let's go."

Cobra got to his feet too but halted when we remained in our seats. His eyes flicked back and forth between us before he headed to the door. "We'll wait for you at the bottom." He walked out with Viper and shut the door behind them both.

Kingsnake didn't look at me. His eyes were out the window again.

The only reason I stared at him was because he didn't stare at me. If his look met mine, my eyes would dart away.

Silence passed, accompanied by the hundreds of birds that chirped in the trees.

Kingsnake drew a slow breath before he looked at me once again. "This is hard for both of us. But it's something that needs to be done. The weaker we are, the more vulnerable we are to our enemies."

"What enemies?" We'd made peace with the Ethereal. The humans would welcome us with open arms once we healed the sickness.

"You and I will always have enemies, even in the times of greatest peace. I'm King of Vampires, Lord of Darkness, and soon you will be my queen. A queen more powerful than her king as she possesses the blood of the Originals. People will always want to kill us, sweetheart. But I'll watch your back—and you'll watch mine."

My eyes glazed over as I pictured this new life, wearing the armor of the Kingsnake Vampires, at his side during times of war and times of peace. Years would feel like days. Days like minutes. While I would be married to a powerful man, I would be a powerful woman myself. As long as no one cut us down, we would be together forever. Literally forever. But if I wanted that to happen, I had to feed.

I had to stick my fangs in another person...and drink their blood.

And Kingsnake had to do the same, with a woman, someone other than me. That part of our relationship was officially over.

His eyes shifted back to me. "It gets easier, in time."

"It feels wrong."

"You aren't taking anything that's not freely given."

"Still."

"I won't pretend I'm totally comfortable with this. I've never been on the opposite end of this situation."

"Ellasara was a vampire." I was told not to mention her, but I had to.

A burst of quiet anger erupted through him, but he didn't scold me. "I didn't love her the way I love you. Didn't feel the jealousy that I feel right now. The idea of you feeding on a man...I don't like it."

"I can feed on a woman." The whole thing was despicable to me. Whether they were male or female, I wouldn't enjoy it.

He watched me. "Trust me...you'll want a man."

"Why?"

"Because it's intimate. Once their blood hits your tongue, it's more than just a feed. It's...a moment. It's like kissing. You wouldn't want to kiss a woman, but a man."

"I'd kiss a woman."

"Once the elements of their blood hit you—" He stopped once he realized what I'd said, and a distinct rush of arousal scorched his veins. "What did you just say?"

"I'm not attracted to women, but I'm not repulsed by the idea like you are with a man."

He gave a subtle nod as he continued to stare. "Can I watch?"

"Watch me feed?" I asked in surprise.

"Yes." The tense conversation suddenly became far less strained. His despair had faded like mist over the ocean once the sun popped out of the clouds. He straightened in the chair, secured his arms over his chest.

"Didn't realize you were into that."

"Every man is into that, sweetheart."

"Then will you feed from a man—"

"No."

"So, I'll make the sacrifice, but you won't—"

"You offered. I didn't ask. And you don't have to do it if you don't want to."

All this talk made me hungrier, made me hungry for something that repulsed me. But the natural urges of my body took over. "A woman is fine."

"Then let's go." He rose from the chair, far more invigorated than he'd been moments ago. When I didn't rise, he stared down at me. "It took me a long time to accept my new life. A long time to accept this eternal darkness and everything that comes with it. But it'll get easier...and easier."

———

One of the elves led Viper and Kingsnake away, taking them to their respective tree houses to feed on the women who'd volunteered themselves. I was relieved I didn't have to see what she looked like. Didn't have to see the desire flash across her eyes when she looked at my fiancé. She must have seen him when he first came to Evanguard and jumped at the chance to be alone with him. As much as I despised the darkness they possessed, vampires were sexy.

"Larisa?"

I turned to Cobra beside me, who'd offered to wait with me while Kingsnake was away.

"Don't let it bother you."

"Easier said than done..." I looked away again, watching the light come through the canopy at the top of the trees.

"It's just a meal. Nothing more."

I knew Kingsnake hadn't fed yet. His mind was devoid of emotions at the moment. With my heightened abilities, I could feel him over greater distances, and while that was a blessing in battle, it was a curse now. "Now that he can't feed from me, I'm afraid he'll want me less...and less. That someone else will come along with exquisite blood, and that'll be the end." I told Cobra the outright truth when I couldn't share a sliver of it with Kingsnake.

"As long as you have those same tits and ass, he'll never want you less."

My eyebrows cocked.

"Don't tell him I said that." He grinned. "He'll break my arm."

"I'm serious, Cobra."

He gave a quiet sigh. "I've known Kingsnake a long time. He's never been attached to his prey before. Their blood became stale, and then they were replaced. I'm talking weeks, at the most. And with Ellasara, that was a different kind of love. None of us ever really liked her."

"Why?"

"She was arrogant."

"And you aren't?" I asked incredulously.

He grinned again. "That's why I like you. You say how it is. Ellasara would have turned up her nose and walked away like she was too good to speak to us. That bitch was stiff. So stiff that I bet he couldn't even tell when she climaxed—if she even could have an orgasm. That woman was made of stone." He crossed his arms over his chest. "But with you, it feels right. You already feel like family. So don't worry if that woman up there is the hottest bitch he's ever seen, it's not going to make a difference."

At that moment, Kingsnake emerged in the clearing, regal in his uniform, with his eyes clear and focused. There was no sign that a feeding had taken place, no spots of blood on his clothing or at the corner of his mouth.

"He's already done?"

Cobra turned to look at him. "See? All over."

"But I..." I'd felt his presence as he'd made his way up the stairs. Felt his presence once he'd entered the tree house. It was a dull presence, the type of energy I felt when he was trying to fall asleep. There was no rush of excitement. No desire. Nothing at all.

Kingsnake walked up to us, his eyes on me.

"Did you feed...?"

"Yes."

The second Elias had stepped into the room with the woman who would become his wife, searing heat flushed through his body. I'd dismissed it the first time because attraction couldn't be overcome, but it happened every time he was around her...and around some of the maids. But with Kingsnake, I never felt those feelings, even when a woman asked for his bite alone in a bedroom up in the trees. He had no idea I could feel him across distances like that, and even if he did, he couldn't block off his mind that well.

"Ready?" he asked.

I'd been so concerned with his feeding that I forgot about my own.

"Word of advice," Cobra said as he placed his hand on my shoulder. "Just enjoy it."

"You still want a woman?" Kingsnake asked.

I nodded, not wanting to put him through what I'd just gone through.

"Whoa...what?" Cobra asked. "Daaaammmn. Are you going to watch?"

"Yes," Kingsnake said.

"Lucky son of a bitch." Cobra dragged his hand down his face and across his jawline. "Maybe I can talk Clara into it someday."

"You asked her to turn?" Kingsnake asked.

Cobra shrugged. "That's the only way we can be together, and I know she's crazy about me." He smirked and clapped Kingsnake across the back. "Enjoy, asshole."

The woman the Ethereal presented to me was beautiful, with glowing skin, long blond hair in loose curls around her shoulders. She'd volunteered for Kingsnake or Viper, but she agreed to feed me when Queen Clara asked. I saw the man who had volunteered for me. He served in the army, so he was strong and well-built like Kingsnake, and he was handsome too.

That made me want the woman more.

We were escorted into a private building on the forest floor, the sunshine suddenly absent inside the enclosure. I hadn't said a word to the woman. What was I supposed to say? Thank you? Did the wolf speak to the lamb before he fed?

Kingsnake accompanied us and closed the door behind us.

Her eyes immediately went to him and stayed there, the vampire she originally wanted. My novice fangs were about to pierce her glowing flesh, but she seemed unperturbed by that. She was either a farm animal too stupid to see her imminent end, or she was brave enough to accept the inevitable.

Kingsnake came to my side. "The process is simple. Draw close, release your fangs, and then bite. The blood will flow into your mouth instantly. Only take until the hunger subsides, then withdraw. Since it's your first time, you'll want more, but you'll need to cut yourself off. Otherwise, you risk killing the source."

I remembered when he'd first bitten me. He was an experienced vampire, but even he struggled to control himself when he had a taste of my blood. I feared my response would be even worse.

"I'll be here the entire time." He couldn't feel my unease the way I could feel his, but he could see it written across my face like text on a scroll. "It's your first time, so don't burden yourself with unrealistic expectations. I will interfere once you go too long."

I suddenly felt the hunger in a painful wave. It tightened my stomach. Made me weak and anxious at the same time. Now I didn't care that I was about to bite a woman instead of a man. I just wanted to eat.

He seemed to see it in my eyes, the hunger of a vampire. "Go for it." There was an armchair in the room, so he took a seat, his knees planted far apart, one elbow on the armrest, his fingertips rubbing together like there was a grain of sand between them.

I looked at her, the blond woman who continued to stand there, her eyes shifting from Kingsnake once she had my attention. We were the same height, our eyes level, so my teeth should reach her throat with ease.

It was an out-of-body experience, an unease that crept down my spine. I was so unsure of myself, incapable of walking up to her and taking what I wanted. But I was hungry, and that fueled my first few steps.

I drew near, so close together like we were lovers. My eyes watched hers. Hers watched mine.

Then I reached up and grasped her golden curls before I brushed them back from her neck.

Kingsnake's arousal was instant, like the moment a kettle on the hot stove started to whistle. From the shadows of the armchair, he watched us with his closed fist covering his hard mouth.

My fingers sank deeper into her hair and pushed it back to leave her neck exposed to me, the flesh so smooth and unblemished. My hunger increased tenfold, and I felt my fangs protrude entirely on their own, as if on instinct. Now the momentum was in place, and as if swept up in the speed of the stream, I was moved forward. My fangs were so sharp that I pierced her flesh instantly, and I listened to the quiet gasp she released at the pain.

The pain I would never feel again—because I was undead.

The blood hit my tongue...and it was indescribable. Like a drink of water in the hot desert, a hot meal after a long fast, it was pure bliss. My arm automatically tightened around her back, and I pulled her to me, sinking my fangs deeper as more blood flooded my mouth. My hunger was unsatiated. In fact, it was deeper than before.

Kingsnake's arousal had deepened the moment I'd gripped her around the waist. His heat was an inferno in that room, watching me take my first prey with conviction. Instead of feeling the despair I felt when he satisfied his hunger, he got a show that jolted his desire.

It made the feeding better, feeling his hotness surround me as I fed from the woman who offered her body openly. My hand stayed in her hair and kept it back as I feasted on her flesh. My hunger was eventually satisfied, but I kept going, overeating just the way I did when I was alive. The food tasted so good that I continued to shovel it into my mouth and force it into my stomach. My fingers deepened on her body as I drained her, taking more than I needed, without regard to her well-being.

Kingsnake's strong voice came to me. "Sweetheart."

I kept my grip on her, refusing to let her go.

"Enough."

I couldn't do it. I couldn't stop.

Now he said my name, something he hadn't done in a very long time. "Larisa." He raised his voice, scolding me like a parent scolded a child. I only had seconds to behave before the punishment came. "You don't want to kill this woman."

That severed the trance. My fangs left her flesh, and I withdrew, still feeling the rush of euphoria in my veins. I saw the blood drip down her neck. Felt the fullness I hadn't felt since I was last alive.

She drifted away, moving to a chair nearby.

Kingsnake stepped in front of me, his hand landing on my arm to balance me. His eyes burned into mine, his heat still searing because his arousal hadn't died with his admonishment. He watched me, watched me work through the experience.

My eyes dropped, ashamed by what I'd done and how much I'd enjoyed it. I was officially a nightwalker, taking the blood of others for my own pleasure. The only consolation I had was the fact that I'd experienced it myself, knew how good it could feel.

As the seconds trickled by, I felt the rejuvenation, the strength that came from nowhere. I felt better than I ever had, even the moment I'd first opened my eyes. The strength in my arms and legs was undeniable. My focus was suddenly sharp as a blade. I always knew I had the power of the Originals, but now I actually felt it.

His hand moved into my hair and wiped the drop of blood in the corner of my mouth. "How do you feel?"

My answer emerged as a whisper. "Better…"

He tilted my head, making my eyes meet his.

"A lot better."

Subtly, a smile entered his hard mouth.

"Stronger and more powerful than I ever have."

9

KINGSNAKE

I threw her onto the bed before I removed everything in a rush. Harder than the steel of my sword, I had tunnel vision for this woman, blocked out the world and all my responsibilities. As if I hadn't fed, I was starving, starving for the woman who would be my wife.

My knees hit the bed, and I bent her to my will, planting one foot to my chest and pinning back her other leg with my arm. She was stronger than I was, but unaware of her strength, she let me dominate her exactly as I pleased.

I entered her with a hard thrust then gripped her by the throat.

Her hand clutched my wrist, and she released a moan at my entry.

I fucked her viciously, fucked her like she was a whore rather than making love to her like a fiancée. Watching her feed on another woman was one of the sexiest things I'd ever seen, made me so tense that my breaths became hard and labored. I'd wanted her right there on the spot, but I had to spare that woman's life first.

Now I finally had her, seeing the way her eyes glowed in a different way because she was full. Mine turned green when I had her power in my veins, but hers turned golden like the most expensive jewelry money could buy.

Her hand held on to my wrist as she shook with my thrusts, my fingers so tight she struggled to breathe, not that she needed to. I hadn't removed my pants, just dropped them down to my thighs because I wanted to burrow myself in that channel immediately. I wanted to claim the woman I'd already claimed a long time ago.

She was more than mine. She was mine forever. Soulless, in eternal darkness.

I squeezed her throat like I hated her rather than loved her, but it was the possessiveness that turned violent. She was no longer a fragile human who would crumple at my strength. Now she was a powerful nightwalker who shared my affinity for blood. Now she was my equal, the woman who was as entitled to my kingdom as I was.

Fucking hot.

She liked my violence because she came, panting as I choked her, tears watering her eyes. Her pussy was so tight, like it had the strength of my iron fist. She clenched around my dick like she wanted to bruise it.

"Fuck." I hit a threshold I didn't see, and then my dormant seed filled her, claiming her once more. When I fed, the blood satisfied my hunger, but it was a disappointment from beginning to end. It was like stale bread with wine that had been uncorked too long. It filled my stomach, but it didn't fill it with delight. The Ethereal who had offered herself wanted to satisfy more than my hunger, my body as well, but I'd pinned her down and took what I needed before I left her there.

Larisa's hand gripped my ass as she tugged me into her, claiming me as her man the way I'd just claimed her. All her hesitations and regrets had evaporated, and now she was as committed to me as she had been before the battle.

I was a man of many grudges, but I held none against her.

Not after I got what I wanted.

———

You sssaid this would only take a few daysss.

Every plan has a hiccup.

What kind of hiccup?

I can ask Queen Clara to grant you entry. She'll allow it.

I don't need anyone's permission. I'll be there ssshortly.

"Fang will be joining us." I reached the bottom of the stairs then extended my hand to Larisa, not that she needed it.

"Good." She took it and let me help her to the ground. "I miss him."

We walked to the clearing where Cobra and Viper stood, dressed in their full gear for our adventure.

Cobra turned first, his eyes scanning Larisa's face for the differences in her appearance. "You look like a whole new woman."

"I feel like a whole new woman," Larisa said, joining my brothers like she was one of us. She had a different relationship with each one of them, even Aurelias, a vampire made of stone. Her assimilation into my family had been effortless. Ellasara had made no effort at all, and it had felt like shoving a square peg in a round hole.

"So…" Cobra looked at me. "How was it?"

I ignored the question.

"You really aren't going to tell me?" he asked in disbelief. "I'm your brother."

"No."

"No, you aren't going to tell me? Or no, I'm not your brother?"

"Both."

Viper released a quiet chuckle.

Cobra brushed off the insult. "We'll talk later, then." He gave a wink. "Got it."

My eyes shifted to Viper. "Where's Queen Clara?"

"She's my woman," Cobra said. "So ask me."

"I'm tired of hearing you talk," I said.

Larisa's eyes shifted back and forth between us as the conversation unfolded.

Cobra leaned toward Larisa. "He's just jealous he's not the only one with a girlfriend."

"*Fiancée*," I corrected.

Cobra nudged her before he rolled his eyes.

She chuckled.

My eyes immediately shifted to hers at the betrayal.

Her eyes shifted away.

Queen Clara joined us, dressed in earth-colored trousers and a white linen top. She carried a backpack, and her hair was pulled back in a thick bun. The rest of us were armored with our blades, but she carried nothing. "That's a lot of unnecessary weight to carry."

"We prefer to be prepared," Viper said.

"It's nothing but wilderness out there," Clara said. "A bear is your worst foe."

"We're used to it, baby," Cobra said. "Lead the way." He gestured with his arm.

She dropped her argument and took the lead.

Cobra took the moment to admire her ass with a nod of approval. "She's got one hell of an ass, doesn't she?"

It made Larisa chuckle again.

Viper and I would never look.

We headed off, leaving the main city of Fallonworth and entering the wilds. As we withdrew from the city center, it grew quieter, the rivers our only company. Sometimes the breeze moved through the trees and shook the branches. A bird would caw before flying overhead. But it was silent the rest of the time.

I kept Larisa in front of me, just in case she slipped along the trail or needed my help. Even though she was a more powerful vampire, my impulse to care for her would never die. I would always treat her like the delicate human she used to be.

Cobra and Queen Clara took the lead, the two of them talking quietly as they navigated the forest. There were times when we came to a stop, as if she couldn't remember the way her father had shown her. Minutes passed as she tried to think, as she tried to search her memory for the path to take.

Larisa looked up to the canopy far above, the branches that shaded our venture. "It's beautiful here."

I watched her tilt her head back and admire the ceiling of the forest, the gold in her eyes bright. She wore her armor and sword, carrying the extra weight without issue. It'd weighed her down on the journey to Evanguard, but now that she'd fed, she was infinitely stronger. I'd expected more resistance at her first feeding, but the hunger must have been so powerful that she couldn't question it.

"I never left Raventower my whole life." She continued to look up. "It's nice to see new places...near and far."

I admired the side of her face, seeing a woman so thoroughly enthralling I couldn't get enough of her. When I first saw her, I'd felt literally nothing, but now...damn.

She must have felt my stare because she looked at me.

"I'll take you anywhere you want to go, sweetheart."

"What else is there to see?"

"So much more," I said. "And we have all the time in the world."

For the first time, throbbing pain didn't flash across her eyes. A subtle smile softened her already rose-petal features. "I look forward to it."

———

It was a journey that should have only taken a day, but it took much longer than that.

"Good thing we ate before we left," Viper said as he came to my side.

"Yes."

He looked at Cobra and Queen Clara up ahead, the two of them on the top of the hill to admire the surroundings. "You think she'd have some idea..."

"She's only been here once," I said in her defense.

"For something so important, she should have remembered every little detail," Viper said coldly. "Unless this is all a ruse. Just for us to think she wants to destroy it, but in actuality, she has no intention—"

"Viper."

"What?" he snapped. "They can't hear."

"Clara is here to stay, so you should make an effort to like her."

His entire face tightened in annoyance. "You're telling me you trust her?"

"She told her people she would destroy it."

"That's what she says...but who knows."

"Her people wouldn't have tried to kill her otherwise." The moment rebels turned against her and tried to burn her to death, I knew Clara had spoken the truth, had been fully transparent with us since the beginning. "Yes, I trust her."

Viper looked away, releasing a heavy breath.

"And our brother is clearly smitten, so we need to make every effort possible."

"Don't pretend your request isn't tremendous."

"You gave Larisa a chance."

"Larisa?" he asked incredulously. "There is no comparison between the two. You insult your own woman by using both of their names in the same sentence."

"You inherited Father's stubbornness."

"And Cobra has inherited Mother's naïveté."

"Viper." I deepened my tone. "I believe she's truly lost. I also believe she'll find her way."

He continued to stare up the hill at the two of them, watching them converse about their surroundings.

"Your hate will never be powerful enough to save Mother's soul."

He continued to stare.

"It pains me too, but we have to drop our prejudice against the innocent. Clara's doing everything she can to make this right. That takes character. Without knowing her, I would say Cobra is lucky to have found a woman so courageous."

Viper eventually turned back to me. "Kingsnake, I've always admired your intellect and empathy. It's made you a great king. But you haven't thought this through. You haven't realized just how complicated this will be."

Larisa sat on a rock in the distance, entertained by the lush landscape that surrounded us. Fang was wrapped around her body, perched on her lap like a loyal companion. Her fingers absent-mindedly stroked the scales upon his head, something I'd never done. I watched her before my eyes shifted back to his. "Speak your mind."

"You know how much Father loved Mother." He turned his head to regard me head on, his eyes burning with a quiet fire. "Her death haunts him, even all these centuries later. The very reason we became nightwalkers was to kill those assholes who desecrated her dignity as well as her body. We both know his hate has no boundary. We both know that hatred will only grow once he knows the truth—that the Ethereal destroyed his wife's soul."

A flush of coldness moved down my spine.

Viper continued to peer into my gaze. "Even if we destroy this obelisk, it'll make no difference. Not to him. He'll never stop until they're massacred."

My eyes dropped, feeling the dread that his assessment provoked. "We'll speak to him."

"Which will do nothing."

"We can't keep living this way. We need to move on—"

"If you hadn't turned Larisa and she was dead right now, would you move on?"

My eyes stayed down.

"If she had to suffer an eternity of nothingness because the Ethereal—"

"*Stop.*" The thought was intolerable. Fucking intolerable.

"Then you know Father will never move on."

———

Finally, the Mountain of Souls was in sight. We had been on the wrong mountain, so we'd waited until sunset to make the trek back down the hill and onto another path.

We slept in our bedrolls every night, the mild temperatures making it comfortable to slumber under the starlight.

"Everything alright?" Larisa's voice brought me out of the vault of my thoughts.

I turned to her beside me, her concerned eyes combing over my face. "Yes."

Her stare continued, unable to believe my lie when she felt my truth. "I can feel your...I'm not sure how to describe it."

"Dread. That's what you feel."

"And what are you dreading?"

Everything Viper had said was spot-on. Even with the obelisk destroyed, my father would be furious that we'd offered a truce, that we'd offered to impart our immortality to the people who had stolen my mother's afterlife. "We'll discuss it later." In private. Where Cobra and Queen Clara couldn't overhear my concerns.

Larisa didn't let her curiosity get the best of her. She accepted my refusal without argument. "I wish we could communicate the way we speak with Fang. How nice would that be..."

"Yes, it would be nice."

We stopped halfway up the mountain when it was fully dark, Queen Clara unable to see anything in the pure blackness. "We'll continue at dusk." She unslung her pack and carried it close to a tree where she would retire for the night. Cobra always joined her, the two of them sharing a single bedroll and a pillow. On occasion, they snuck off into the darkness to fulfill their desires in private.

I would have done the same with Larisa, except I'd been in a foul mood since my last conversation with Viper.

Larisa got her bedroll ready, Fang immediately helping himself and snaking inside to where her feet rested. He was a large snake, taking up most of the space, but she never seemed to mind.

She loved my best friend as much as I did. Bonded with my brothers, too. I had been blinded by Ellasara's beauty, infatuated with her poise and intelligence, and became oblivious to all the shit she lacked. I'd loved her when I didn't know what love really was. Now I did.

I got into my bedroll beside Larisa and looked up at the cloudy sky. Tomorrow would be overcast, so we would have a great opportunity to destroy the obelisk and make ground on the return journey. That trek should be much shorter than the one here.

"How do you think Aurelias is doing?"

He crossed my mind every day, wondering if he was dead or alive. "I'm sure he's fine." He was the only person who had enough clout to sway Father's opinion, and it was a shame he wasn't here to do that.

"Yeah, me too."

"If he doesn't return by the time this is over, we'll go after him."

"I think that's a good idea."

She worried about my brother like he was her brother—and that made me love her more.

At dusk, we packed our things and left.

We continued up the path to the mountain, the steep hill a strain on our bodies. The temperature was cool, so at least we didn't have to conquer the elements as well as the terrain. Hours passed before we reached the top, the black stones erect and enigmatic in the dull light. I thought I heard a quiet hum against my ear, but it was so faint I wasn't sure if I was imagining it. Every single one of us was absorbed in the sight of them, the pillars that towered over us with an unquestionable solidarity.

If it weren't a graveyard of souls, it would look like art.

Queen Clara suddenly released a scream.

We all turned at the sound, and as I unsheathed my blade, I moved in front of Larisa, even though she was covered with armor.

Queen Clara was on the ground, an arrow just beneath her shoulder.

"It's an ambush!"

Cobra sprinted faster than I'd ever seen him move, getting to her just as the next arrow fired. It bounced off his armor right below his neckline, an arrow meant for her lung. "Come on." He grabbed her by the arm and dragged her behind one of the pillars of stone, protecting her from the arrows that continued to fire.

I dragged Larisa behind the closest pillar. Viper appeared on the other side.

"What the fuck did I tell you?" Viper snarled, pulling his bow from his back.

"Rebels," I said. "The same from Evanguard."

"Clara said she was the only one who knew about this place," he snapped. "So she's a damn liar."

"If she staged this, why would they shoot her?" Larisa said. "She wouldn't have left her armor behind."

"To make us think—"

"Viper, we can argue about this later." I peeked around the corner, seeing a group of five soldiers approaching the stone that protected Cobra and Queen Clara. I recognized the first one on the left. "Toman. She dismissed him from her service when we first came here."

Viper took a peek too, but then quickly moved back for cover when an arrow fired off. "You're right."

"Her father must have told him when he assumed they would be married."

Viper poked his head out, dodged the arrow that came at him, and then fired off an arrow himself. "Got him in the shoulder."

"Stay here with Fang," I said to Larisa.

"Why?" she snapped. "You're outnumbered."

"We can handle it. Now, do as I say."

"I'm an Original, remember?" she spat.

"We don't have time for this—"

"I'm not going to hide every time you risk your life. Am I your queen or not?"

I breathed hard, furious that this conversation was taking place now. "You're my woman first."

"We've got to move," Viper said. "They're closing in, and Clara will die without armor." He stuck his head out again, his bow at the ready. "I'll cover you. Go."

If I continued this argument, then Queen Clara would die, so I didn't say a word to Larisa as I left the protection of the rock and ran ahead.

One of the archers aimed his bow at me, but before he could fire, Viper fired first. Hit him right in the neckline between his armor and helmet.

I kicked him back, so the bow flew from his hands as he collapsed on the ground.

Toman was wounded but not dead, so he came after me with vengeance in his eyes.

Cobra fought two men alone, keeping Clara behind him as he protected her body with his.

More men came, and then we really were outnumbered. I sliced down one then grabbed him by the arm, protecting my body from the volley of arrows that fired down.

Cobra pushed Clara back farther in the stone, protecting her from the arrows that would have pierced her everywhere without her armor.

I dropped the corpse I held and reached for a dagger in my pocket. I threw it at the neck of the first, getting blood to squirt from his mouth before he hit the dirt. It turned into chaos after that, men everywhere, coming for the four of us with rage on their side. They fought for their immortality—so this fight would be their best. Overrun, I didn't even have time to think about Larisa. I just hoped she'd listened to me.

I struck down my opponent then saw Fang break the neck of another foe. The crunch of bones was audible over the screams of the dying.

"Kingsnake!"

I turned to Cobra, who had taken on three fighters alone.

He couldn't even make eye contact with me, his blade spinning in a flurry of blows. "Larisa!"

I turned to look, and that was enough for me to nearly lose my neck.

But Fang got there first. His body tripped their feet, and then he opened a nasty gash on the man's neck. *Go*.

I saw Queen Clara run with Larisa. In the short glimpse I got, it was clear that Larisa was trying to get her to safety while we fought off the battalion of rebels. Two rebels chased after them.

Go!

I left Fang's side and sprinted as hard as my body could go, rushing to Larisa before the rebels could get to her first.

They entered the maze of stone pillars, the men hot on their tails.

"Larisa!" I shouted, giving away my position so she would know I was there.

A man jumped out at me when he heard me, swinging his blade for my neck. I barely ducked in time. My sword burrowed in the opening between his arm and his torso, bringing a swift death before I kept going.

I made it around the pillars, seeing Larisa and a soldier locked in a battle of swords.

Clara was defenseless without her weapons, so she grabbed a rock and threw it at the soldier's head.

They both moved so quickly that it missed.

The soldier challenged Larisa with his flurry of blows, moving so fast that she could barely keep up. Her blood wasn't enough to best him, not when he had far more experience. But then she ducked his blade, elbowed him in the face, and swiped her blade at his neck. It went clean through, severing his head from his shoulders.

She stepped back and inhaled a deep breath when she saw the massacre.

My impulse was to run to her and cup her face in my palms, but now that they were both okay, my priority was my brothers and Fang. I sprinted back, seeing the pile of bodies that Fang alone had caused. He had the last soldier pinned to the ground with his body, and he bared his fangs and squirted venom into the sky.

"Noooo!"

I love it when they ssscream. Fang struck, ripping a hole in his flesh with his powerful bite. Blood poured to the dirt. The man was dead instantly.

Cobra kicked his assailant off him then Viper came behind and finished, slicing his blade through his neck.

The last foe fell—and then it was quiet.

Cobra had a nasty gash on his temple, but he was unharmed otherwise. Viper was untouched. And Fang looked like he wanted more bloodshed. I sheathed my blade and returned to Larisa. I went straight for her, gripping her in my arms to make sure she was okay. I looked over her wordlessly, seeing the absence of a single scratch.

"Baby." Cobra ran to Clara and cupped her face in his hands, his fingers trapping her hair against her face. He looked her over, visibly distressed and terrified. He sprang into action and ripped the arrow out of her shoulder before he applied pressure with the gauze he pulled out of his pack. He lifted her shirt, her back to us, and wrapped the material securely over her skin. "Just a flesh wound. You'll be alright."

She gave a wince but didn't complain about the pain. "Thank you for covering me, Larisa."

"Of course," Larisa said, Fang snaking up her body at the same time.

"Everyone okay?" Queen Clara looked around at us all.

"We're fine," I said. "Take a moment to rest."

She sat on the ground, her hand still over her shoulder. "Fucking asshole..."

Cobra stood over her, watching her with a level of concern I'd never seen him express before. He kneeled down and came to her side, his hand gently moving to her uninjured shoulder. "It's over now."

Larisa avoided my gaze, as if she knew how angry I was. This attack could have easily ended with a much different outcome. The stakes were higher now, because her body didn't possess a soul. I could forfeit mine, but never hers.

"You sure you're alright?" Viper asked Clara.

She gave a nod. "I just need a minute."

"Then let's get to work." He turned to walk off, exchanging a look with me as he went.

I looked at Larisa again.

Her eyes were purposely on Clara.

I decided we could have this conversation at another time and joined my brother.

———

"I don't know what to make of this." Viper had struck his sword against the stone, and all he did was scuff his own blade in the process. "These slabs are twelve feet thick. I'm not sure if my explosives will do anything."

"We don't know if the stones are responsible," Cobra said. "And Clara doesn't know either."

I glanced at the women. They sat together, leaning against one of the pillars, Queen Clara's arm in a sling Cobra had made out of bandages. "The pillars must be responsible. They absorb the souls and transfer them to the soil underneath, and then the water."

"How did they even make this?" Viper asked.

Cobra shook his head. "It might be something to do with the crystals. People say they have different kinds of energy. Maybe they have different kinds of powers too."

"What if the Ethereal replace them after we destroy them?" Viper asked.

"I think everyone who knew about them is now dead," I said.

Cobra nodded in agreement. "Hope those explosives are enough."

"We only have so many," I said. "We should dig around the base of the stones to make their foundation weaker."

Viper looked around. "There are at least twelve."

"Yes," I said. "It'll take a while."

"More than a while," Cobra said. "But I agree."

I placed my palm against the stone and felt its smoothness, free of dust and elemental stains. "Let's grab the shovels and get to work."

———

We worked all night and parts of the day when the sun was minimal. Days passed, and once Clara's wound had healed enough, she joined us. Larisa helped as well, while Fang napped on and off the entire time.

After a week, we'd successfully dug around the stones and toppled a few of them. The others were buried too deep into the bedrock, and we would need explosives for those. When darkness returned, we would finish the project and walk back.

I waited for Queen Clara to get cold feet, but she never did.

Larisa and I sat in the shade in a clump of trees, both of us leaning against trunks as we drank from our water canteens. The work was exhausting, so we were both tired. We hadn't spoken about what had happened, but it was coming.

"I appreciate your valor, but you need to understand—"

"A king can serve his people, but a queen can't?" Her response fired off quickly, so she'd clearly practiced this in her head.

"You didn't choose to be a queen. You became one by default. The responsibilities aren't equal."

"But I've chosen to marry you—and accept all the responsibilities that come with it."

"Larisa, I don't need to remind you what's at risk here. Before, you had a soul, but now you have nothing."

"The same is true for you."

"But I chose that." I stared at her, seeing the pushback in her eyes. "You didn't."

She stared back. "I'm an Original. When I sliced that blade through his neck, it was like a hot knife through butter. I feel the difference in strength now, feel the change in my body from a single feeding. Those powers should be put to use."

"Power will never triumph over experience."

"But you give me no experience, Kingsnake. You tell me to run and hide. You've known me long enough to know I don't like to turn my back on a fight. If we're to be king and queen, then we fight together. I should fight for our people as much as you do."

Her dedication to our kingdom brought a warmth to my body. She no longer identified with humankind, with her old village of Raventower. She'd fully embraced this new life, even before she was turned into a vampire. "I could train you every day myself, but your skills would never compare to mine, to another vampire, to the Ethereal. Your life is too important to risk. That's final."

"That's final?" Her voice was quiet, but her eyebrows narrowed sharply.

"In times of war, you'll lead our people while I'm on the battlefield. You have a lot to offer beyond your blade."

"I'm tired of you ordering me to run like I'm some helpless animal. You don't order Fang to run—"

"Did you see what he did to his enemies?" I snapped. "He killed more of them than the rest of us—combined. You're not a two-hundred-and-fifty-pound snake, Larisa. You're barely a hundred pounds."

She looked away, her mood palpable.

"I need to keep you safe. I need you alive for a very long time."

"I understand that, but I'm not helpless."

"I never said you were. But you'll never possess my abilities. Or Viper's. Or Cobra's. Or Clara's."

"If we start now, in fifteen hundred years, I will." She looked at me again.

"I've already trained you—"

"But not as a vampire. Not as an Original."

Looking into the ferocity in her eyes, I knew nothing would sway her decision. "When things settle down, we'll work on it."

"Thank you."

"And I'm sure my brothers will help too."

"Even better."

10

CLARA

I was up at sunrise and dead asleep shortly after sunset. That was how the Ethereal were, living for the sunshine that pierced our canopy. We tilled the earth in our farms, nurtured our plants, thrived in the sunshine like all living things.

But now that I was in the company of vampires, we slept during the day and worked in the night.

It was an hour before sunset, and I sat with Cobra under the tree. We were scattered from the others, Larisa and Kingsnake far away in their own grouping of trees. Viper was the only one alone, usually with the snake Kingsnake was bound to.

Cobra leaned against the tree, his water canteen in his fingertips as his arm rested on his knee. With every passing day, he grew weak, tired. His charming smile was absent. His jokes were gone.

"Feed from me."

His eyes remained on the landscape, on the next mountain. "No."

"You're weak—"

"And so are the others. I won't feed while they starve."

"They can feed from me as well—"

"Never." He gave me his hard stare, and that ended the conversation.

I looked forward again, seeing the three stones that were still embedded deep in the hard rock of the mountain. The others had been toppled by our shovels, but the rest were indestructible.

"Having second thoughts?"

"No." I pulled my knees to my chest and circled them with my arms. "I think enough damage has been done anyway." Most of the stones were gone, so it probably didn't work anymore, or worked at a minimal capacity. The canteen I brought had water from the streams, had liquid souls that were fueling my immortality this very moment. It made me sick.

"I admire you. Most people wouldn't be so brave."

"I'm not brave. I just feel sick." Cobra had told me how he'd lost his mother, and knowing that my people had destroyed her entry into the afterlife made me hate myself, hate my father beyond the grave.

"You feel sick because you have a conscience. Most people don't."

"I used to think all people did, but I was wrong." It made me wonder about my own mother. When she died, did we ingest her soul too? My father knew that but didn't care? "Will you guys be able to make it back?"

"If these explosives work," he said. "And if there are no more rebels waiting for us to return."

"I think that was the last of them."

"Hope so."

Sunset finally arrived, the sun disappearing behind the branches in the trees. The sky turned pink and orange. A chill instantly crept over the land. "It's time." I got to my feet, as did the others.

We walked to the pillars, and Viper began his work. "Stand back." He placed an explosive on each side of the first stone then moved back behind the next slab of stone for cover.

We all did the same.

Viper grabbed a rock and threw it at the explosive, and the second he hit the mark, an eruption of fire and dirt appeared. Rocks were chucked into the air and sprinkled down on us. A moment later, we heard the slab topple over and thud hard on the ground.

Our ears had been covered, but we'd heard it all.

Viper dropped his hands from his head. "One down."

———

We finished the last stone—and then the obelisk was no more. The slabs were on the ground. The earth was dug up in various places. Some of the stones had snapped at the base, their edges razor-sharp.

The place used to be an enigmatic monolith—and now it was a graveyard of stone.

It was done. No going back.

I inhaled a breath and released it, choosing to accept my mortality. When I didn't perish on the spot, I knew I would begin to age naturally from that moment on. But instead of getting old with crow's-feet and wrinkles, I would creep closer to death.

Cobra's hand went to my back. "Are you alright?"

"I'm fine." I'd betrayed my father before he died and beyond the grave. But I had to do the right thing.

"Doing the right thing is usually the hard thing." Kingsnake regarded me, tall like his brothers with the hardness of a king, but the softness of a man. "And you did it courageously—and with grace."

———

We made the return journey to Fallonworth, and it still took several days, despite knowing the way. The vampires were all fatigued, including Cobra since he refused to eat when his brothers had to starve.

When I returned to the forest, it felt entirely different. The peaceful serenity had been replaced by a heavy burden. My kin weren't enjoying the sunlight on the forest floor, picking flowers and bringing crops to the market. Most people sat in despair, their eyes empty, thinking about the choice that lay before them.

A decision I'd forced them to contemplate.

We returned to the city center, the rubble of my former palace still on the ground. The Ethereal would have normally cleared the debris and exposed the earth and grass beneath, but there was no longer a motivation to do anything anymore. "I'll ask for volunteers for you. I know you're hungry."

"Thank you, Queen Clara," Kingsnake said with a nod.

I asked my men, the ones I had left, to gather up those who wished to feed our saviors. It was the same volunteers as before, and the vampires immediately excused themselves to nourish their bodies. Cobra and I retreated to my tree house so he could feed, and instead of removing my clothes and taking me roughly, he only fed. He was that hungry and weak. He fell asleep shortly afterward, collapsed on the bed beside me.

I moved to the dining table and made myself a cup of tea and a fruit bowl. I tried to eat after he ate to keep up my strength. I sat there alone and looked out the window, knowing this place would never be what it had been. This life was based on lies and deceit, and now that the truth had been revealed, it was nothing.

Hours drifted away as I remained lost in thought, contemplating my new life and the path I needed to choose. My tea had grown cold, and so much time had passed that my stomach tightened with hunger again.

Cobra left the bed and joined me at the table, in nothing but his boxers. "How long did I sleep?" he asked in a gruff voice.

"I don't know...a couple hours." Now I had a bite mark on my neck, a mark that was visible because it was so raw.

He sank back in the chair as he stared at me, his eyes still tired.

"Now what?"

He cleared his throat like it was still asleep. "We'll return to Grayson. Kingsnake and Larisa need to distribute the cure to the kingdoms, we need to speak with my father... and I suspect there will be a wedding." He watched me for a moment. "I suggest you take that time to confer with your people and decide what's best for them. I know the decision won't be unanimous, so you'll have to decide how that dichotomy will work. Those who choose to be nightwalkers will need to join us in Grayson and the other vampire kingdoms. Those who choose to remain mortal... will remain behind."

"Why can't the new nightwalkers stay here?"

"You think humans would want to live among vampires?" He tilted his head slightly. "They want their next-door neighbor to be a nightwalker who wants to feed on their blood? The living and the dead have very different ways of life, different cultures, different rules. You can be allies, but not neighbors."

That was probably all true.

"Those nightwalkers will submit to Kingsnake's rule. And those who choose mortality will either follow you as their queen...or will have to appoint a new ruler."

If I became a vampire, I would lose all my power. Being queen had never been my ambition, but now that I wore the crown, it was hard to give away.

"I know it's a lot to think about."

"Yes...it is."

"When I return, I'll accept whatever answer you give. You should have the opportunity to consider your options without my distraction." A subtle smile moved on to his lips. "And we both know how distracting I can be."

The same smile tugged at me.

"But I'll say this." His eyes wandered for a moment before they came back to me. "If you do choose immortality...I would ask you to marry me."

Those dragon-size butterflies were back, breathing fire and scorching everything. "Why?"

"So you wouldn't be giving up your mortality for only a man, but a husband. And not just any husband...but a husband who's a king. You would give up the crown you wear but don another. You would leave the only life you've known but be secure in the new one."

"We don't know each other that well."

"And we'll have forever to become well acquainted."

I looked away and swallowed, excited by the prospect but also terrified. I could remain a mortal, hope to fall in love with my equal, start a family. Or I could forsake my soul and marry this sexy vampire king.

"Your heart is racing." He grinned.

"It's a heavy decision."

"That's why I'm giving you plenty of time, baby."

11

LARISA

We said goodbye before we embarked on the return journey.

Cobra took the longest, like he didn't want to leave her. His hands cupped her face, and he gave her a slow kiss, a kiss reserved for private bedrooms. The intimacy was scorching and made me turn away, thinking about the way his brother kissed me.

Cobra eventually joined us, his shoulders slumped, his head slightly bowed. "What if leaving her is a mistake?" I expected him to address Kingsnake or Viper, but he addressed me instead.

"Why would it be a mistake?"

"Two packs of rebels tried to kill her."

"I think we've killed them all, Cobra. And I'm sure she'll be on her guard, regardless."

He gave a slight nod. "Yeah, you're probably right." He moved forward and joined Viper, determined to leave the border without looking back.

I turned to look at Clara, her eyes heavy and glued to a spot between his shoulder blades. She watched him walk away, didn't let herself blink, as if it was the last time she would ever see him.

"Ready, sweetheart?" Kingsnake's voice brought me back to reality.

"Yes." I felt Fang slide up my leg, wrap around my torso, and then perch himself across my shoulders.

A gentle smile tugged at his lips. "He prefers your shoulders to mine now."

"Fang doesn't have a favorite."

The smile lingered. "He does. And that's okay."

———

We crossed the desert at sunset and rode hard into the darkness. It was scorching and arid during daylight, but the temperatures immediately plunged without sunshine. The armor and clothing kept me warm, and I preferred the cold to the unbearable heat anyway.

At sunrise, we were past the domain of the werewolves and near the kingdoms, and we settled for the afternoon.

I forced myself to accept my new condition because there was no other choice. I had to appreciate everything that it offered rather than grieve what I lost. But being confined to the shade instead of the sunshine would forever cause me misery. Sunshine used to be my friend. When I'd first arrived in Grayson, I would sit on the balcony and absorb the rays. Now I would have to hide from them, like they were an old friend who had become a stranger.

Whenever we traveled, the guys always pulled out their liquor canteens and drank in the shade, swapping stories or talking shit to one another. There was an invisible camaraderie between them, despite the insults they launched back and forth.

And I felt like part of it.

"Larisa's turn," Cobra said. "Have I or have I not?"

Kingsnake turned to me. "You don't have to play."

"Fuck yeah, she does," Cobra said. "She's practically our sister."

Kingsnake continued to look at me. "Ignore him."

Cobra moved forward. "Have you or have you not slept with two people in one day?"

Kingsnake turned to Cobra, his eyes flashing in rage. "What the fuck is wrong with you—"

"Yes."

Cobra's eyebrows jumped up.

Kingsnake snapped his head back in my direction.

Viper gave a subtle nod in appreciation. "Damn."

"Yes?" Cobra asked. "*You?*"

"It's not a sexy story," I said. "I was with this guy, and he left me for someone else. He fucked me and then told me afterward, because he's an asshole like that. Well, I went to the bar and picked up this guy to get back at him. Not that it made any difference."

Kingsnake was angry, figuring out the identity of the guy right away.

Cobra raised his canteen to me. "I respect that. And if my brother ever pisses you off and you want to get back at him—"

"Do you want to die?" Kingsnake stared at him across the circle.

Cobra grinned and took a drink. "Fuck, you make it so easy."

"You have a woman."

"And I'm sure she would think it's hilarious."

Kingsnake tossed his open canteen at Cobra, spraying him with the liquor.

"Are you insane?" He wiped his hand across his face to clear out his eyes. "That shit's like gold. And I'm not giving you mine."

Kingsnake chucked the canteen at his temple next.

"Okay, now you're just being an asshole," Cobra said.

"My turn," I said. "Cobra, have you or have you not?"

He gave a nod. "I'll play."

"Better be something good," Viper said. "Because I already know all his transgressions."

"That's what you think." Cobra took another drink. "Go ahead, sweetheart."

"Call her that again," Kingsnake said. "And see what happens."

"Fine," Cobra said. "Go ahead, *sis*."

I liked that endearment a lot more. "Have you or have you not been in love?"

Tension immediately settled over the campsite, and all the gloating in Cobra's features evaporated. Now he was pale, even for a vampire. He shook his canteen just so he would have something to do with his hand. "That's a fucked-up question..."

"And yours wasn't?" Kingsnake asked. "Now answer it."

Cobra looked away as he massaged the back of his neck. "You guys are assholes—"

"The answer must be yes," Viper said. "Otherwise, he would have said no by now."

Cobra kept his eyes averted, like he had no intention of giving an answer.

I waited and waited, but he never said anything.

I moved on to Viper. "Have you or have you not—"

"Yes." Cobra's answer was quiet, so quiet it was almost inaudible. "Yes...I have."

———

We hoped to make it back to Grayson before the sun was too high in the sky, but we weren't close enough. We were forced to camp in the shade, on the other side of the mountain but still several leagues from the city.

We dropped our bags, gave the horses oats and water, and got comfortable in the darkness under the trees.

Cobra had been in a somber mood since we'd played our game, and I felt guilty for causing his misery. "I shouldn't have asked him that."

"He shouldn't have asked you his question first."

"I didn't have to answer."

"Then he didn't have to either." Kingsnake placed our bed rolls side by side. We didn't share a single cot around his brothers, not when we also had an enormous snake to accommodate in the warm temperatures.

Cobra leaned against a tree, drinking from his water canteen, choosing to relax away from the rest of us.

"I'm going to apologize."

"You don't have to do that, sweetheart," he said. "You did nothing wrong."

"I still feel bad." I left Kingsnake's side and took a seat beside Cobra, leaning my back against the same tree trunk.

He acted as if I weren't there. Didn't start the conversation by mocking his brother or commenting on my one-night stand. He was the only one who always had something to say, but now he was a dried-up well.

"I shouldn't have asked you that. I'm sorry."

He continued to stare at the canteen in his hand. "I'm not upset with you."

"But you're definitely upset."

"It's complicated."

"Well...you can talk to me."

He said nothing, and it seemed like he wasn't going to.

I stayed quiet and watched Kingsnake sit with Fang beside him. Even though nothing was audible, I knew they were speaking to each other. Fang had wrapped around one of Kingsnake's legs and rested his chin on his thigh.

"Life used to be a lot easier."

I slowly turned at his statement.

"Now I worry. Now I'm scared. Emotions I've never felt in my life."

"What are you scared of?"

"Something happening to her. I want to protect her always, but I can't do that when we're in different places. I can't do that if she chooses to remain mortal and within her own lands. I asked her to be a vampire, but I'm afraid she'll say no."

"You seemed confident before."

"It's just a front," he said, arms on his knees. "I don't know what I'll do if she says no."

"You can still be together."

"For like a decade...and then she'll age, and everything will change."

"You wouldn't love her anyway?"

"I'll always love her. But the relationship will change and become a relationship I no longer want. I'd rather end it if she chooses to be mortal than subject myself to that torture. You wouldn't expect a woman to be with a man if there was an expiration date, so why should I?"

I gave a nod in understanding.

"If she says no, I'll go back to my old life. Meaningless flings with women who want my bite as well as my dick. But it'll never be quite the same, not when I know there could have been more."

"Tell her how you feel."

"It's too late for that."

"How so?"

"I should have told her before I left, but I chickened out. I offered to marry her instead. She's smart, so hopefully, she realizes it's pretty much the same thing. She's supposed to give me her answer when I return. And in the meantime, I can't influence her decision. It's too soon to say that shit anyway."

"It's never too soon if that's how you really feel."

"I've never told a woman that before, and I'd rather not say it straight out of the gate. I'd rather take my time, make sure she feels the same way first. In all honesty, I'm not sure if she's there yet."

"I think she could be," she said. "She let you bite her."

"True."

"Maybe I could talk to her."

He looked at me. "And say what?"

"Tell her about my reservations about immortality...and how I've changed my mind about it."

"You have?"

I nodded. "I want to be with Kingsnake, no matter the cost."

"Is that how you really feel? Or is it because that's how you have to feel?"

I stilled at the perverse question.

"I won't tell him what you say."

"He's your brother."

"And you're my sister."

Truth be told, Kingsnake's brothers had made this transition far easier. I wouldn't have my own family, but I would always have them. "I would have chosen this, in time, but it would have always been hard. I wish there were another way."

"Would you prefer the both of you to be mortal?"

"In a perfect world."

"Why?"

"That's how it's supposed to be. How we can have children."

"Imagine if we could. Then literally everybody would want to be a vampire."

"I don't know about everybody, but it would be desirable."

His arms remained on his knees. "I think children are overrated, personally."

"You do?"

"I mean, look at us. We're just a bunch of assholes."

"None of you guys are assholes."

"Come on." He nudged me in the side. "Don't pretend Aurelias isn't the biggest prick you've ever met."

"I actually really like him."

He gave me an incredulous stare.

"I mean, not right at first..."

He chuckled then took another drink from his canteen.

"Does Clara have reservations about that?"

"No. She's not one of those women who's obsessed with having kids. She says she's indifferent."

"Then she'll probably join you."

"Maybe," he said with a shrug. "Hope she does. Because this is the first time I've felt this way, and I doubt it'll ever happen again."

———

We finally returned to Grayson, and it felt like an eternity since we'd been here. The place was exactly as it had been, completely restored to its glory before the battles. The ash from the pyres had washed away in the rain, as well as the blood from the dead. It was overcast and cool, the clouds a thick blanket in the sky. It didn't rain, but random drops of precipitation struck our skin from time to time.

"I need a shower," Cobra said. "And a drink."

"I need a real bed," Viper said.

"Old man," Cobra said under his breath.

Viper punched him hard in the shoulder, making Cobra jerk sideways.

They were kings and generals, but brothers all the same.

"I'll travel to Crescent Falls in the morning and speak to Father," Kingsnake said.

"That sounds like a job for all three of us," Cobra said. "Four, if Aurelias were available."

"I wish to speak to him in private." Kingsnake's tone was clipped, like it wasn't up for negotiation. "Larisa will stay here. Please keep an eye on her in my stead."

"Whoa...hold up." I watched them all turn to look at me. "First, I don't need someone to *keep an eye on me*, and secondly, why am I not coming with you?"

Kingsnake constrained his rage around his brothers, but he couldn't keep it from me. "I wasn't suggesting they supervise you. Just to be here if you need anything because I'll be unavailable."

"And the second question?" I asked.

He held my gaze for a long moment. "I need to speak to him in private."

That didn't explain why I couldn't wait in the bedchambers until he was finished. He must expect this conversation to be an incendiary one.

"It's another long journey in addition to the one we've already taken," he said. "Rest."

I wanted to press deeper, but I knew I had to respect his privacy in this. His relationship with his father was even more complicated than the one he'd had with Ellasara. "Alright."

"Don't worry." Cobra clapped me on the back. "We'll supervise you real good." He walked off, joining Viper as they headed to their chambers in the palace.

Kingsnake hadn't withdrawn his stare from my face. "Don't take offense. This is something I need to do alone."

I gave a nod in agreement. "I wish you the best."

His eyes remained a moment longer before they dropped. "Thank you."

———

Once we were showered and in the comfort of our bedchambers, he joined me under the covers, his arms immediately gripping my body and drawing it close. He tugged me to him, pressed a warm kiss to my forehead. Instead of ravishing my body, he wanted to hold me close, one hand in the back of my hair, his other big hand on my ass.

"How long will you be gone?" I smelled the scent of pine, the soap from the shower that cleansed his body of travel.

"A couple days. Maybe longer, depending on how it goes."

I wanted to press for information, but I chose to stay quiet. "You should take Fang."

"I will. And you should prepare for our wedding."

"Wedding?" I asked.

"I asked you to marry me, didn't I?"

"Well, technically, you told me, not asked. And I didn't know it would happen so fast."

"It would happen faster if I didn't need to speak to him first."

"Do you think he'll come?"

He didn't answer.

Now I understood why a conversation with his father was so paramount.

"The seamstress will help you with your dress. Make sure it shows lots of skin."

I chuckled, assuming it was a joke.

But he was dead quiet—like it wasn't.

"The ceremony will be private, just us and my family. And then we'll have a public coronation."

"Is that really necessary—"

"Yes. In the event of my death, you will lead our people."

"The crown wouldn't pass to Viper?"

"Viper is the general of Grayson—and he'll serve you as he served me."

I'd been excited about the wedding, becoming something more than just his prey, his woman. But now, I was about to inherit an abundance of responsibilities. "You really think I'm the right person for this—"

"Absolutely. I trust you with my life. And I trust you with the lives of my people."

I was touched by it all. The fact that he wanted to marry me after his last marriage was an utter sham...and he trusted me with the well-being of his people, the people he put above himself, always. "Thank you."

He turned his head slightly and pressed his lips to my forehead. His fingers moved into my hair deeper as he squeezed me to him. Warmth emitted from his body, a temperature I couldn't feel, but a depth I could sense. It was still and quiet like a spring morning, golden like daylight. It wasn't passionate like crackling flames in an inferno, but gentle like red embers in a fire snuffed out. Like the last piece of a puzzle falling into place, he felt complete.

It was far more powerful than the words he didn't say.

"I wish you could feel what I feel..." I wished he could feel the way I loved him, the way I felt him love me.

"It's okay, sweetheart," he whispered. "I can see it."

———

He packed his bag again and prepared to depart, fully dressed in his armor as if he anticipated trouble along the way. Fang was hooked around his shoulders since he'd join him for the journey.

I was disappointed, but I knew I couldn't hog Fang all the time.

I walked with Kingsnake to the front of the palace, one of his men taking his pack and carrying it down to the stables to secure it to his horse.

The look Kingsnake gave me...it was like he was saying goodbye forever.

I wanted him to stay, but I didn't dare ask. I wanted to join him, but I didn't ask that either.

That searing heat emanated from him, like he wanted to lock his arms around my body and never let go. He possessed me with just his stare, bound me to him forever without a ring. He moved into me, one hand sliding into my hair as his arm tightened across my back. He tugged me close and kissed me, suffocating my mouth with his desperate desire. It was scorching, his mouth kindling my lips until a fire consumed us both.

Then he abruptly pulled away, and it felt like a winter wind had struck my face. He took the stairs to the bottom without looking back, his cape blowing in the breeze behind him, his massive shoulders supporting the plates of his armor, Fang's scales iridescent despite the cloud cover. He made it to the bottom and disappeared.

I continued to stare, even though I knew he wouldn't return.

The seamstress showed me the different fabrics that I could choose from. Ivory, eggshell, lace, everything elegant and delicate. Any of them would be suitable, but I didn't care for a single one. "Do you have anything in black?"

"For a wedding dress?" the seamstress asked in surprise. "The bride always wears white."

"Because she's a virgin, and I'm definitely not," I said. "Most brides aren't, actually." It was an archaic tradition, especially considering I wasn't even alive anymore and wouldn't be welcomed by the gods once I was killed.

She blinked several times before she gathered the fabrics and left. "Let me see what I can find."

As I sat there alone, I wanted to talk to Fang, the companion I'd always had at my side when Kingsnake was gone. But I didn't have him, not this time. It was a lonely experience, and even though Kingsnake had only been gone for a day, it felt like forever.

The seamstress returned with different fabrics for me to choose from.

I held the first in my hand. "This is perfect." It was silky and shiny, without lace, something simple and elegant. "Let's use this."

She still looked at me like I was tasteless, but she did as I asked. "What kind of style were you thinking?"

"Simple. Just two straps. Tight on the waist. A gown that trails to the floor."

"Let me take your measurements."

I stood in my underwear while she placed the tape measure over my body, getting the inches of my bust, hips, and waistline. When she was finished, she jotted down her notes in her notebook. "I'll have it for you in a couple days."

"Thank you."

She dismissed herself, and I was back to my loneliness.

Then a knock sounded on the door.

"Come in."

Cobra poked his head inside, dressed casually in trousers and a black shirt. Even without his armor, he was still a big guy, his muscles stretching the fabric of his clothing. "Want to play a round?" He held out the deck of cards.

I'd probably be playing with Fang right now if he were here. "You don't have to keep me company—"

He turned behind him. "She said yes." He pushed the door open and made himself comfortable on the couch.

Viper came in too, holding several bottles of liquor.

I joined them and watched Cobra deal the cards. "You guys play for money?"

"Yep." Cobra opened a box and took out a couple cigars. He handed one to me.

"No thanks," I said. "I don't have any money."

"But Kingsnake does." Cobra waggled his eyebrows. "And what's his is yours, right?" He nodded to the dresser. "Third drawer down."

"How do you know that?" I walked over and opened it, finding a wad of currency just sitting there. I took a couple bills and returned.

"That's where he kept his money as a kid." Cobra finished dealing the cards and grabbed his hand, his cigar hanging out the side of his mouth.

We played a couple rounds, both of them smoking and drinking, treating me like I was one of the guys, when I was a woman who barely knew how to play. Fang and I played a very different game, but these guys liked poker. However, I caught on quickly and earned back the money I lost and then some.

We had a silent camaraderie, like I was one of them rather than a pity invite. They embraced me as their own, took me in as the sister they never had. I feared a life without children would be lonely, but it was nothing of the sort. I'd lost my family to nightwalkers and sickness, but now I had a new one.

Cobra put down a card.

"Thank you."

He looked up at my words. "For what?"

Viper stared at me.

"For..." I couldn't find the words. "Being my brothers."

12

KINGSNAKE

My horse was taken to the stables, and I was guided to my bedchambers. It was the same one I always used when I visited, and the last time I was here, Larisa shared the space with me. I dropped my bag, showered, and then told the servant I wished to speak to my father when he was ready to receive me.

Fang was on the bed, his head and neck angled up to regard me. **You're anxiousss.**

Yes.

You're never anxiousss.

Because I'm about to have a conversation I should have had fifteen hundred years ago.

You ask for his forgivenessss.

Yes.

And you fear he won't grant it.

It's very unlikely that he will.

Fang stared at me, his tongue slipping in and out of his closed mouth. **A father who refuses to forgive his son is no father at all.**

He hasn't been my father in a long time.

Another travesty.

He refused to come when I married Ellasara. I said I didn't care...but I did. And now that I know Larisa is truly the one, I don't want to regret his absence.

You can't regret someone else's decision, Kingsnake.

The servant opened the door. "He'll see you in his study now."

I moved to the door when Fang slithered to the floor and up my leg, positioning himself around my body and then across my shoulder. **I'll accompany you.**

It's okay. I know you don't like him.

But I like you.

I walked down the hallway and stepped into his study, a fire in the black hearth, his large body taking up most of the armchair. A glass was in his hand, probably scotch, his favorite. He didn't rise to greet me like he would Aurelias, but he didn't seem as hostile as usual either.

I took a seat, Fang still across my shoulders.

The servant poured me a drink then disappeared.

"Must you bring him?" He looked into his glass before he took a drink.

I said nothing.

Sssnake killer.

"I hate the way he smells."

I ignored that too.

Fang released a quiet growl.

My father set down the glass. "The Ethereal have lost their king, and a novice queen wears his crown. Victory is as certain as the rising sun. We'll ride to their forest, and if they refuse to face us in battle, we'll burn their forest and all those inside." He was back to war and bloodshed, the only things he cared for.

"Or we can move forward and find peace."

His eyes shifted to me, black coals. "My commanders informed me of your visit. You were there a long time." Disapproval was in his tone, as well as a veiled threat. "A very long time."

"I've come to discuss other matters. The Ethereal can wait."

He took another drink, purposeful and slow. "Their extinction is unavoidable. I suppose it can be postponed." He set down the glass again and regarded me head on for the first time. "Speak your mind, Kingsnake."

If I had a heart, I would feel it pound in my chest. Aurelias's words came back to me, a conversation we had in the ice-cold snow. "You were right about everything. And I'm sorry." I thought I would have more to say, but once I was put on the spot, that was all I could muster. So many years of resentment. So many years of coldness. It was hard to face the winter storm in his eyes and hope it would thaw to spring.

He said nothing.

Neither did I.

It stayed that way for minutes.

But he never took his eyes off my face. Never dismissed me. Just absorbed the apology.

"My anger was unjustified. You wanted to spare your son—and I was too naïve to see that. This life was the only option for us, and I should have appreciated it for the gift that it was."

"Where does this come from?"

I looked away.

"Over a thousand years have passed in silence. And now you speak. Why?"

"Larisa." I met his gaze once again. "I wanted us to be together in eternity, but she wanted to keep her soul. I loved her long before I said it, but I knew my declaration would end the relationship rather than deepen it. Then in the battle, Ellasara nearly killed her...and a very difficult choice was placed in front of me. I could let her die with her soul...or we could be together forever. You know what I chose."

He stared, his gaze so hard it didn't possess a drop of emotion.

"She was disappointed...and it killed me."

For the first time since I could remember, his hardness waned.

"She's come around since. Understands that I made the right choice. But it wasn't that way for a while, and now I understand your predicament. Eternal darkness is the only choice. I wished I'd seen it sooner before I said all those horrible things to you."

This was the moment where he should speak, but all he delivered was silence.

I looked away, severing eye contact. "You don't forgive me."

"You'll never understand how it feels to be hated by your own son. Forgiveness is not the issue."

"I don't hate you—"

"But you did. For a very long time. Until you realized that the Ethereal were the monsters I said they were."

I kept my eyes on the fire. "I apologized. I admitted you were right. What more—"

"There's nothing more you can do, Kingsnake."

It was like a slap to the face.

"I'm ready to put this in the past."

I lifted my chin and looked at him again.

"I granted forgiveness long before you asked for it. I've just been stubborn...as stubborn as you."

I stared at my father, seeing him look back at me in a new way. It was so cathartic I didn't know what to say. "What about Aurelias?" My father had been beside himself with sorrow when my brother left—and he blamed me for his departure.

"Aurelias made his own decision. His power and strength will return him to us."

I nodded, hoping that was the truth. "I believe that too."

Silence ensued, but instead of being filled with unbearable tension, it was filled with calm.

"Larisa had a change of heart far quicker than you did." There was no question in his words, but definitely one in his gaze. He knew I had been inside the borders of Evanguard for several weeks, and of course, he suspected exactly what I'd learned.

But once I confirmed his suspicions, he would fly off the handle. "When I return to Grayson, we'll be wed. I'd like you to be there."

His eyes remained hard for a moment, refusing to release his grasp on the earlier topic. But he eventually let it go. "I regret missing your first wedding."

"You didn't miss anything."

"Your brother said she died by your hand. That must have been difficult."

"It wasn't difficult at all." The love of my life had lain in a pool of her own blood, barely alive. Swiping Ellasara's head from her shoulders was the easiest thing I'd ever done. I could have incapacitated her with a wound and spared her life, but I wanted her dead in the ground.

"You could say she did you a favor."

My eyes found his, immediately flushed in anger.

"If she hadn't, do you think Larisa would have turned willingly?"

That was an answer I would never have. "She's always wanted children." If we could have them as vampires, there probably would have been far less resistance.

"Like most women. They are a blessing. There's nothing more satisfying than seeing your boy become a man, become your equal. The pride is worth the long nights and the tantrums and the discipline."

Now I felt guilty for taking it away.

"Do you have any regrets?"

I held his stare, my throat empty of words.

"Would you do it differently if you could?"

My eyebrows narrowed as he pressed the conversation.

"I know how to change it—if that's what you wish."

If I'd had a heart, it would have dropped into my stomach. I felt a jolt of terror that rushed to every extremity of my body, a tightness that seized all my muscles. I swallowed even though my mouth was dry. "I don't understand..."

"Many years ago, I captured a witch in my lands. After months of torture, I discovered it was her magic that created the werewolves. And I also discovered it's possible to undo the permanent, to restore the soul to the body."

Ssscorcery.

My father's face disappeared from view. Now all I saw was Larisa, her skin golden as she stood in the sun, her eyes like emeralds in the light. Her neck twitched with the small pulse that no one else noticed but me. The taste of her blood suddenly flooded my mouth, exquisite.

My father read the expression written across my face. "Then we'll keep this between us."

———

Fang lay in a bundle on the floor in front of the fire, his eyes open and on me as I sat in the armchair.

Hours passed, and I remained still, not even reaching for my drink, my eyes focused on the flames.

Fang hadn't spoken, but his eyes were on me as if he expected me to address what we'd just heard at some point.

I intended to leave in the morning and return to Grayson. Larisa's dress should be ready, and the wedding would take place shortly after my arrival. While there was no rush, I'd felt an urgency since the moment I asked her to marry me.

You mussst tell her.

My eyes moved to his.

You can't keep this sssecret.

I looked at the fire again.

Kingsssnake.

When I ignored him for the third time, he pressed on.

She hasss the right to know—and you know it.

I left the chair and walked away, slowly pacing my bedchambers as every ounce of joy left my body. My father and I had finally put the past behind us, after a thousand years of discontent, and now I was hit with this misery. "You want her to be human? Is that what you want? For her to die in sixty years?"

No. But that'sss her decisssion to make.

I continued to pace.

I know ssshe'll choossse you.

I faced the other wall, shirtless in my sweatpants, staring at a random painting a servant put on the wall. "Then why tell her?"

Becaussse you love her, and you would never betray her.

I turned back to Fang, seeing him perched up now that the argument had escalated. "Omission isn't a betrayal."

Omisssssion is as treasonous asss a lie.

She'd finally gotten to a place of acceptance. Finally looked at me the way she did before. Wanted me the way she did before. Not having to choose made the transition easier for her, and once I gave her the option again, it would only complicate everything. "I'm not going to tell her—and you aren't either."

Kingsssnake—

"Can I trust you?"

He stared at me with those piercing yellow eyes, his disapproval as hot as the fire behind him.

"Fang."

You want me to lie to her?

"It'll just fuck with her head. You know that."

Fang continued his ruthless stare.

"That conversation was between me and my father. It's my business—not yours. Are you loyal to me or not?"

Always.

A burst of relief hit me. "Then we're finished with this conversation."

Fang looked at me like prey, like he would strike and leave a bloody gash on my face. ***You need to trussst her, Kingsnake. Ssshe wouldn't leave you.***

I stopped in the middle of the room, my hands on my hips. "That's not what worries me."

Then what doesss?

I kept my gaze on the fire.

Ssspeak.

"She'll ask me for something I can't give..."

I don't understand.

At one point, I thought that was the life I wanted. Thought I wanted it more than anything. Thought it was how life was meant to be lived. But I quickly discovered the truth—that I wanted to live forever. And now that I had Larisa, I wanted immortality even more. "She'll ask me to give up my immortality—and live a mortal life with her."

———

I headed back to Grayson in the middle of the night, taking advantage of the darkness to cover as much ground as possible. My father had affairs that required his attention and would leave the following day to attend the wedding.

We only had to stop once, and that was because it was an unusually sunny day.

It was different with Fang now. He gave me the cold shoulder—and it was as cold as ice. He didn't speak to me on the ride. Instead of being wrapped around my shoulders, he chose to sit in his bag like he wasn't there at all. When we made camp, he did the same, like my company was unbearable.

I refused to address his anger. If he had something to say, he could say it to me.

After a couple hours had passed, he slithered out and propped himself up, his eyes level with mine. **You can't marry her.**

I ignored him.

Not unless you tell her.

I stared into the tree line, the sunlight casting short shadows because it was midday.

Marriage is sssacred.

"Fang." I regarded him head on. "Do you want me to be mortal?"

He stared.

"Because that's what will happen. My life will be over in the blink of an eye, and you'll go on for lifetimes without me. Yes, I'll have children, but their lives will be over just as quick as mine. You'll know my future descendants, all of them, but you'll never be able to see me again. Is that what you want?"

Fang broke eye contact and turned his head slightly.

"That's what I thought."

But you could sssay no.

"Then she would leave me. I'd rather die than lose her, so I would have no other choice than to live the life I don't want."

You don't know that.

"Yes...I do."

13

LARISA

I looked at myself in the mirror, seeing the satin gown fit me like a second skin. It was simple, with no texture at all, but that was exactly what I wanted. The material was high-quality, so it had a shine when I turned toward the light. It bunched in the front, the material loose like rose petals about to fall.

Cobra gave a low whistle as he looked me up and down. "Damn, that is one hell of a dress."

"A black wedding dress," Viper said with his arms crossed over his chest. "He'll like it."

"Shit, he'll love it." Cobra moved to check me out from a different angle. "Wear your hair down. You know, with those big spiral things. He'll like that."

"Curls?" I asked.

"Yes." He snapped his fingers. "Clara does that with her hair sometimes. Very sexy."

I looked at myself in the mirror once more before I turned to both of them. "I need a favor—from both of you."

"Anything, sweetheart," Cobra said.

Viper drew close. "You know we're here for you."

They teased Kingsnake and each other viciously, but their loyalty was transparent when they tended to me. I knew they liked me, but their commitment to my needs was for a stronger reason than that. "Traditionally, the dad walks the bride down the aisle, and my dad died when I was little. So...I was wondering if you guys would do it?"

Cobra's eyebrows jumped high up his face in surprise.

Viper's expression hardened into stone, not in a cold way, but that seemed to be how he expressed his shock.

"Us?" Cobra planted his hand against his chest and looked at his brother. "You want us to do it?"

"You don't have to. I just thought—"

"We would be honored," Viper said immediately. "We're just surprised you'd want us."

"We're idiots," Cobra said.

"You are not idiots," I said. "You're the closest thing I've ever had to brothers...and your kindness and companionship have meant the world to me. I know you do it for Kingsnake, but it's touched my heart, nonetheless."

Cobra stared at the floor for a while, like he wasn't comfortable with all the touchy-feely stuff. "When he was married to Ellasara, none of us made an effort with her. Aurelias hated her the most. So we aren't kind to you just for Kingsnake. We're kind to you because we like you." He raised his eyes and looked at me. "You're the hottest sister a guy could ask for." He smiled, telling me it was just a joke. "But don't tell him I said that."

I smiled. "I won't."

"Should we do the hug thing?" Cobra asked. "Have we ever hugged?"

"I—I'm not sure if we have," I said.

Both men hugged me, and it turned into an awkward group hug.

Then the door opened, and Kingsnake entered.

"Shit, get out!" Cobra turned and blocked my body with his. "Don't you knock?"

"Don't look." Viper tried to cover his brother's face with his hand.

Kingsnake smacked it down. "What the fuck are you doing with my fiancée?"

"I'm in my wedding dress," I explained. "And it's bad luck if you see it."

Kingsnake stopped fighting his brother and closed his eyes. "Good. I thought I was about to kill both of you."

Viper got him out the door before he shut it.

"Damn, that was close." Cobra stopped blocking me and faced me again. "Change before he sees you. Otherwise, he's going to marry you right here, right now, and we'll all miss it." He winked before he walked into the hallway.

"Why are you guys looking at my wife in her wedding dress?" Kingsnake said from outside the door.

"She wanted us to see it," Cobra said. "Asked for our opinion."

"You guys don't have opinions," he said coldly.

"I don't know..." Cobra said. "I had a pretty strong opinion about that dress—"

"I just got home, and you want to start shit?" Kingsnake said.

"Only because it's so much fun."

By the time Kingsnake entered the bedroom with Fang, I had changed out of my dress. Now it hung in the closet in a protective covering so he couldn't see it. I was in just my bra and underwear and didn't bother to put on something else, because after a couple days apart, I suspected he would rip everything off anyway.

His sour mood that his brothers caused was immediately gone when he looked at me. He stepped into me, his big arms circling me and giving me an embrace that was so strong it was practically crushing. He was still in his armor, so it was my skin against steel, but that was still better than the softness of the empty bed. His mouth met mine and took it aggressively, and then the blazing heat followed. All those emotions wrapped around me like the safest cocoon, and I felt just how much he'd missed me.

Then his hands were in my hair, on my body, yanking off my panties and snapping my bra open. He kissed me as he removed his own clothing, as he dropped every piece of armor and backed me up to the bed. His sword was placed at the edge, and he kicked off his boots before he removed his pants.

Once he was totally free, he was on top of me, my body folded underneath his. Even if I couldn't see his face or feel his touch, he would still turn me on. How he felt about me...was the biggest turn-on in my life. It was so heavy, so pressing, so desperate. It made me wet without a single touch, without even hearing his voice.

His hand took its usual place around my throat, and he squeezed it as he entered me. "Did you miss me, sweetheart?"

"Yes."

He sank deep inside, surrounded by my wetness. "You did." His thumb rested in the corner of my mouth as he anchored me to the sheets. Then he started to thrust, slow and steady at first, working up to a pace that made the headboard tap against the wall.

"I missed you so much..."

———

A passionate night passed into morning, and when I woke up, he was still beside me, his arms my blanket. His smell smothered me and made me think of mighty pines after an afternoon rain. My sleep had been irregular and disrupted while he was gone, but once he was back, I slept like a log.

I woke up before he did, so I watched him sleep. I knew the moment he was awake because his emotions stirred from their slumber and grew in intensity. His arms suddenly squeezed me, and his lips brushed my forehead as he planted a quick kiss.

"Morning, sweetheart." He said it against my ear, his deep voice a quiet rumble.

"Morning..."

He pulled me close and planted a kiss on my shoulder.

I didn't want to disrupt the peaceful morning with serious talk, but I wondered how the conversation with his father had gone. "How'd it go?"

He sat up against the headboard, a sleepy look still in his eyes, and he stared off at nothing in particular. "He's coming to the wedding."

"Oh, that's great."

"I think the past is behind us now." There was a lightness to his body as he said it, like his emotions had molded into soft clouds that drifted across the sky. The last time I'd witnessed a conversation between him and his father, he had been bursting with jagged shards and rage.

"I'm so happy to hear that." I didn't ask for more details, because however the conversation happened, it didn't matter. All that mattered was my future husband had repaired the irreparable relationship with his father. "Perhaps he and I can get to know each other...on better terms."

A small grin moved over his lips. "He's still an asshole, so I don't expect you to like him."

"I'd still like to try."

"Fang will never like him, but that's understandable."

"Yes," I said. "So...tomorrow?"

"I'm ready if you are."

The man I'd once hated would be my husband. Life was a strange journey, but this was a path I'd never expected to take. "I'm ready. I asked your brothers to give me away."

Several seconds passed as he looked at me, taking a moment to absorb the heartfelt words I'd just said. "They said yes?"

I nodded.

"They've embraced you as their own—and I didn't have to ask."

"They're sweet guys."

"Let's not get carried away."

"While you were gone, they played cards with me, had dinner with me, made sure I never felt lonely. And it didn't feel awkward either, like they weren't just there to please you. I told you I wanted a family...and I got one."

A warmth should have filled his body at that moment, but I felt a twinge of sadness. It happened in an instant, a shooting star across the sky, disappearing so quickly it was unclear if it ever happened in the first place. "My brothers are your brothers, sweetheart."

14

KINGSNAKE

The night before the wedding, we chose to sleep apart.

I wasn't a man of tradition, but I'd rather save all my eagerness for the following evening, when I could rip her dress to tatters and leave them on the bedroom floor. I never wore a crown, my scratched armor my symbol of leadership, but I pictured her in a gold crown with red rubies, and that made the wait that much more unbearable.

I sat on the couch in my study, the fire burning in the hearth behind me, the bottles scattered across the table. Whenever I retreated into this room, it was usually with a heavy heart, a mind bowed by war or social obligation. But tonight, I was only there to wait until tomorrow, to the moment I would marry the woman I should have married in the first place.

Cobra sat across from me, in casual pants and a shirt, lounging on the couch with a glass in his hand. His head was tilted back on the circular armrest. The soft padding cushioned the back of his head as he continued to drink. "The eve of a wedding should be spent in great debauchery…"

"You want to walk to the tavern and feast on all the naked girls there?"

A subtle grin moved on to his lips. "I've got a woman now—and she's the jealous type."

"You'll need to feed at some point," Viper said, sitting in the armchair, stiff and straight like he was still on the clock.

"Animal blood will do until we're reunited." Cobra took another drink.

"She requested that?" I asked in surprise, knowing Larisa would never ask for such a sacrifice.

"No," Cobra said. "But I know it bothers her."

"How would she ever know?" Viper asked. "Feed. You need your strength."

"She wouldn't know—*but I would know*." Cobra sat upright and sank into the back of the couch. "It's not like we have any upcoming wars, so I don't need to be at my best anyway. It's fine."

Viper stared at him a moment longer. "Never imagined you for the pussy-whipped type."

His smug grin returned. "For a pussy like that...absolutely." He swirled his glass as he looked at me. "Second thoughts? Cold feet?"

My answer chimed like a bell. "No."

"You're pussy-whipped too, huh?" Cobra asked.

I ignored the question by taking a drink.

"Larisa, Queen of Vampires and Lady of Darkness..." Cobra savored the words on his tongue. "Sounds great. When you see her in her dress, you're going to lose it, man."

"It's nice," Viper said. "She made it her own."

I hoped it showed her beautiful skin, the sexy hollow of her throat, maybe a shoulder. She had the sexiest legs, so I hoped there was a slit that put one on display. In a white gown, she would have a glow that rivaled a diamond.

One of the commanders knocked on the door before he opened it. "King Serpentine has arrived. Wishes to speak with you in private. Shall I fetch him?"

I gave a nod.

The commander disappeared.

"I can't believe he came," Cobra said. "And wants to give you a little pep talk before the big day."

"He wants to talk about the Ethereal." It was his top priority, at all times, and he didn't even know of the horrible tragedies that the Ethereal had inflicted. "I sidestepped it in Crescent Falls, and I know he wants to pursue it now."

"So, he knows nothing?" Viper asked.

"His spies know about our visit to their border," I said. "I know he suspects what I've tried to hide. He'll drill me for that confirmation, and I can't lie to him. Larisa was resistant to her new identity but had a change of heart, and I know he's suspicious of that as well."

Cobra set his empty glass on the table. "What are you going to do?"

"I don't know." Once my father knew the truth, vengeance would be his only thought. "Stall."

"You'll only be able to stall until the coronation is complete," Cobra said. "That buys you almost no time."

"And he'll declare war against the Ethereal," Viper said. "The final war."

"More like a massacre." Cobra sat with his forearms on his thighs. "We can't let that happen."

"I'm not sure how to stop him," I said. "Unless I lie." My relationship with my father had finally been repaired, and if he discovered that I'd denied him the truth, that relationship would be forever broken. An apology wouldn't fix it. But refusing to kill the people who harvested Mother's soul would also be seen as an epic betrayal. "I'll tell him that we'll have this discussion when the coronation is complete...and we'll have to do our best to convince him to let it go."

"That won't work," Viper said. "Nothing will work."

"We have to try." For once, Cobra was fully on my side, because the woman he loved possessed the blood of the enemy. "We must get him to listen to reason. Every Ethereal who knew the truth of the practice has died by our hand. Everyone else who remains is a naïve victim. Surely, he must understand that. He's the smartest man I know."

"But he's also the bloodiest—as we all know," Viper said. "Mother's death is how we ended up here, fifteen hundred years later, because some assholes took her from us. Once he knows that the Ethereal took her soul, which is infinitely worse, he'll never stop."

"Then what will we do?" Cobra asked. "What will we do if he decides to burn Evanguard to the ground?"

I stared at my empty glass.

Viper's eyes had dropped to the coffee table between us.

Cobra started to massage his knuckles in unease.

I didn't want to think about the extremes we'd have to go to. "We'll worry about that when we have to."

———————

The empty bottles and glasses were cleared away before he walked inside. My brothers had vacated and retired to their bedrooms. Larisa was probably fast asleep by now. Or my absence had left a chill in the sheets that she couldn't ignore.

He entered my study, a room he'd never been in, and then took the seat directly across from me. The energy was instantly different. Even if his forgiveness was sincere, he always possessed a quiet veil of hostility. Now I knew it wasn't personal, just who he was.

His posture was stiff, his back straight. The venom had preserved his age, so he was still a handsome man. He wasn't in the same shape as my brothers and me since he spent most of his time being waited on by hundreds of servants. Most battles were fought in his name, but not with his sword.

Silence stretched. The fire crackled and popped.

I grabbed one of the bottles and filled his glass.

He stared at it before he took a drink, downing the entire thing like it was a single shot.

I refilled it.

"I remember the night before my wedding. I've never slept so hard."

"You always knew she was the one—"

"The moment I saw her." His words cut right through me, probably his intention. "In the market square, three zucchinis in her arms. I knew she would give me my sons. And when she looked at me, I knew she felt the same way. Love at first sight, some might say."

"That's beautiful."

"Is that how you feel about Larisa?"

"Well, it wasn't love at first sight. More like hate at first sight. I guess you could say it was a slow burn, but now our fire burns hotter than the forges at the smithing station. I wish she could give me children, but she's more than enough."

He gave a slight nod. "Then I'm happy for you."

"Thank you."

"She's infinitely better than—"

"I don't want to hear her name ever again, especially if my fiancée's name is in the same sentence."

He wore an empty gaze before he gave a nod. "Fair enough."

The heaviness in the air between us was exactly as I remembered. It started to feel the way it did before, a real conversation in which we could fully be ourselves.

"I'm assuming Larisa chose to remain immortal with you."

All I could do was stare.

"She resisted the temptation—which means her dedication to you is irrefutable. Your marriage will be long and prosperous and, hopefully, eternal."

My gaze shifted elsewhere. "I never told her." I used to keep my cards close to my chest when I spoke to him, but now, I put them on the table like with my brothers. Even though there were four of us, he somehow managed to maintain a relationship with each one of us individually. He seemed to be more present after Mother died, even though we were all adults at the time, becoming two parents in one. He wasn't always the cold and empty man he presented himself as.

He watched me for a while, judgment and anger absent from his gaze. "Why?"

"It would complicate my life."

"So you think she'd make the wrong choice."

"She might." Everything Fang had said was right. It was wrong to keep this from her, to deny her an option because it was her life and her soul.

But I didn't care.

I'd finally gotten everything I wanted, and I wasn't going to risk that for anything.

Anything.

"Some people are incapable of making the right decision. Which is why men like us must make the right decision for them."

I should have assumed my father would understand.

"We have other matters to discuss. Just because it's the eve of your wedding doesn't mean you're dismissed from your obligations as king."

The moment was upon us.

"You will tell me exactly why you and your brothers were in Evanguard for so long—and what transpired there—"

"Father." If I dealt with this now, there wouldn't be a wedding. "We've been at war with the Ethereal since the beginning. It can wait until I've had my wedding and coronated my queen. Then we can decide how to proceed."

A flash of anger moved across his eyes, quick like a lightning strike.

"We vanquished the Ethereal in the battle and struck down their king. Can we treasure this moment of peace?"

The tightness remained in his face, his eyes still and locked on mine.

"The Ethereal are too weak to come for us. It can wait."

A fire burned in his belly, and smoke rose from his nostrils.

"It can wait."

15

LARISA

I stood in front of the mirror, in the midnight-black wedding dress. One of Kingsnake's servants had opened the vault and presented me with jewels to wear with my gown, and I selected a necklace of black stones mixed with diamonds. I took Cobra's suggestion and curled my hair, soft and bouncy down either side of my chest. My hair had grown longer and longer since I'd been captured, and now it nearly touched my belly button.

Fang was perched on the bed behind me, his image visible in the reflection of the mirror. *Niiiiiccccceeee.*

"Thank you."

I won't be ssseeing either of you for daysss.

I gave a quiet chuckle. "Probably not."

A knock sounded before Cobra stepped inside. "Ready to do this?" Instead of wearing his gold-and-black uniform that represented the Cobra Vampires, he wore the garb of the Kingsnakes, black and red, in a uniform similar to the one Kingsnake wore. "Damn." He looked me up and down appreciatively. "You are ready."

"How's he doing?"

"You know Kingsnake. Doesn't say much. But I know he's eager to see you walk down that aisle."

A soft smile moved on to my lips, picturing him at the end, handsome in his uniform. There was one moment I particularly looked forward to, but I didn't want to hype it up in my head and be disappointed by reality.

Cobra extended his arm to me.

My arm hooked through his, and I let him guide me away. When we stepped through the door, Fang slithered past us and turned the corner, to join Kingsnake before I arrived. Viper stood there, and it was the only time I'd seen him without his sword and bow. My arm hooked through his, and we walked together.

The grounds were lit up with torches because it was fully dark. The night was clear, so the stars overhead were bright like mini suns. It was a cool evening, but there was no temperature cool enough to make me don a jacket.

They guided me down the stone-laid path around the cliff, following the line of torches until we reached the stone gazebo overlooking the ocean below, an ocean that was black with the exception of the waves that broke against the shoreline. Under the full moon, the waves were packed with momentum, and every time they crashed against the shore, it was audible.

Kingsnake hadn't noticed me yet. He stood with Fang wrapped around his shoulders, his eyes slightly down like he was locked in a conversation with his snake. His father was there, sitting in one of the few chairs provided.

Cobra and Viper escorted me forward, and that was when Kingsnake turned.

His eyes captured me, my body illuminated by the roaring flames of all the torches in the clearing. It took only a second for his own fire to burn—and burn hotter than the sun. So hot the sun melted in inferiority. His eyes remained locked on my face like he was too entranced to look away, to examine the dress that fit my body like a glove.

As I drew closer, his flames subsided to a quiet burn, and then the most exquisite warmth emitted from him. Instead of roaring flames and melting suns, it was the light that blanketed a bed of flowers in spring, a gentleness that rivaled the wings of a butterfly. Passion morphed into love, a love so deep it was the bottom of a quiet ocean.

I felt him touch me when he was still far away. Felt him squeeze me like we were in bed, his arms around me through the coldest part of the night. My heart had been empty for a long time without a family of my own, after a man had promised all those things then replaced me with someone else. But Kingsnake gave me all of that—and kept his word.

I drew close, wishing he could feel everything I felt.

He hadn't blinked once, looking at me like he'd never truly seen me before. Like this was the moment we were meeting for the first time—and it was love at first sight.

When I was directly in front of him, just inches away, his emotions quieted. His mind cleared, as if he felt nothing at all.

But I knew what it really was.

Peace.

Cobra and Viper released me and stepped away, joining their father in the seats.

Kingsnake took my hand, holding me with the same gentleness he would handle a butterfly. He drew me close, grasping my other hand as he held me in front of the robed vampire who would marry us. Vampires weren't religious, as far as I knew, but the man was dressed like a priest.

In the darkness, surrounded by torchlight and a crashing ocean, the priest brought us into a binding union. He presented the rings, and when Kingsnake grabbed my left hand to place my ring, I realized it was a carving of a snake, its eyes made of small diamonds. The ring fit on my finger perfectly, snug but loose enough to be removed if I wished.

The second it was on my finger, it felt right.

Like I'd always worn it.

He presented his ring to me, a simple black band with a snakeskin pattern across the surface.

I examined it in a glance then placed it on his left hand, sliding it to the knuckle.

"As the undead, your souls can't be bound to each other, but your blood can." The priest presented the small dagger.

Kingsnake took it.

I kept a straight face, but a small jolt of fear gripped me.

He made a small cut in the center of his palm then held it up for me to drink.

I hesitated before I dragged my tongue across, getting his black blood on my tongue. It burned at first, dark and acidic with floral tones.

He took my hand and made the tiniest cut along my finger. It felt like a small scratch. Then he brought my finger into his mouth and sucked the drop away.

My moment of hesitation turned into one of desire. The pain was brief and insignificant, and the meaning behind it was paramount. In a single moment, I felt more bound to him than I ever had.

He returned the dagger and grasped my hand again.

"The king has claimed his bride. I declare you husband and wife."

The instant it was official, his body released a tension that'd wound him so tight. He smothered me with love no one could see, only I could feel. Like a snake had wrapped its massive body and squeezed, I knew there was no escape from his clutches. If I tried to get away, he would only squeeze me tighter.

His hand slid into my hair, and he pulled me flush against his body, kissing me like there was no one there to witness it. With crushing force from his lips and his hands, he gripped me tight and seared my lips with his insatiable desire. His emotion was so great, his hands shook with tiny tremors.

My hands cupped his face, and I let him claim me, handed myself over completely and utterly to this eternal night. I'd married a vampire—but I was a vampire myself. It wasn't the life I'd wanted initially, but it was one I embraced fully.

He pulled away slightly, his lips almost on mine. "I love you." He'd only said those words to me once, the very first time he declared the way he felt for me. Words were unnecessary when I could feel his love the way I could feel the warmth of his skin, feel the way he gripped me in those strong arms.

I'd also only said those words to him once, when I should say them every day. He wasn't privy to my emotions the way I was to his, the way my heart rose from the dead and beat for him and only him. If only he could feel the depth of my emotion the way I felt his, the way I would lay down my life for his without blinking twice. But he couldn't, so I told him. "I love you too."

———

The bedroom was sprinkled with black rose petals.

Fang slithered off and chose to spend his evening elsewhere. It was the first time he'd truly granted us privacy.

Low-burning candles were scattered on the dressers and mantels, taking up every open surface available. I'd barely had a moment to take in the romantic gesture when he pressed up behind me and pulled one of my straps off my shoulder.

He kissed the exposed skin, his lips gentle to the surface, moving closer to my neck. His arm hooked around my stomach and pinned me firmly against him, made me feel his hardness right against my spine.

The other strap fell. More kisses.

My dress drooped forward, but it was still too tight to leave my body.

His hand loosened the zipper, and that was when it crumpled to the floor. My bra was snapped free, and then that exposed skin was kissed too. His hungry kisses grew to pants, and he began to grind his arousal hard into me, nearly bruising my skin with the pressure. His free hands grabbed my black thong and pushed it over my ass, leaving me buck naked while he was fully clothed. "Lie on the bed." He said it into my ear, the order given with both authority and gentleness.

I moved to the bed and sat at the edge, every part of me on display.

With his eyes glued to mine, he undressed himself, unbuttoning his uniform then yanking the shirt over his head, showing the rock-hard body that had pressed me into the mattress countless times.

He put on one hell of a show, and it made me swallow.

His arms were so thick, like tree trunks, and the rivers under his skin were the roots. Despite his lack of life, his skin wasn't white as snow like mine was. His skin had a golden color, like he'd spent most of his time out in the sun before he was turned. He undid his belt and then his trousers, dropping layer by layer, kicking off his boots.

Then he stood before me—glorious.

I couldn't believe *that* was my husband.

He walked to me, his thick cock at full salute, and then he cupped my neck as he brought it close.

My lips automatically parted, and I dipped my head to kiss his oozing tip. A gentle kiss turned into more, and then my tongue trailed across his length, feeling that heat in my mouth.

His hand fisted my hair as he tilted his head back, enjoying my mouth on his cock.

Watching him enjoy it made me work harder to make him enjoy it more, but the fun was interrupted when he pulled his dick out of my mouth. He grabbed my hips and tugged me hard, bringing me to the edge of the bed where he could bend me how he wanted me. Then that big dick pushed inside me, his head squeezing past my tightness, and then he sank in. Sank until there was nowhere else to go.

He paused to look at me, paused to bore into my eyes with his. They were brown like the earth, and never again would they shine green like they had after he'd fed on my blood. But they were beautiful in their intensity, especially when he looked at me like that.

At the edge of the mattress, on a bed of rose petals, he made love to me, enveloped me in the love that burned throughout his whole body. He erased the scars you couldn't see, mended a broken heart that no longer beat. He made me forget how it felt to be rejected and replaced. It was hard to believe anyone had ever hurt me...not when a man loved me like this.

16

KINGSNAKE

It was hard to believe that I'd been married before.

Every sensation felt brand-new, from watching her walk down the aisle to slitting her finger for blood and tasting it on my tongue. She felt like my one and only, the only woman I'd ever really loved.

The night of our wedding was spent in erotic bliss. I made love to her over and over, like it was the first time I'd ever had her. I'd let her sleep for hours in between, only to stir her with my hot kisses and anxious hands. Words weren't spoken. The only thing we exchanged were touches and long stares.

When morning arrived, it felt as if only a few minutes had passed. The exhaustion finally hit, and we both slept for hours on end. I was the one who woke up first, finding her cuddled into my body as if a winter storm raged outside.

My fingers stroked her hair as I stared at her.

It took fifteen hundred years...but it finally happened. I found my lover, my equal, my wife.

She opened her eyes soon afterward, immediately squinting because sunlight peeked through the breaks in the curtains. "What time is it?"

"Probably noon."

She ran her fingers through her hair, the covers slipping away and displaying her sexy tits. "Last night was fun." She looked at me with a sleepy gaze and a playful smile on her lips.

"It was." I moved toward her, rolling her to her back and sliding between the soft flesh of her thighs. "I think our morning will be even better."

———

The day passed in the blink of an eye, even though we didn't leave the bedroom. Toward the evening, we shared a shower before we got back into bed, resuming the fuck-a-thon. In my darkest times, I used to spend days at the tavern, fucking all the women who asked for it, lost in the mindlessness of sex.

But now I had that with a single woman.

The evening passed and the next morning arrived, and not a single person came to our door in that time. Viper ruled over Grayson in my stead, and Fang kept himself occupied and didn't disturb me with his presence or his mind.

It was time to return to ordinary life, even though the honeymoon phase seemed to be endless. But I had my responsibilities, and now she did too. "The coronation will be this evening, in front of all the citizens of Grayson. You'll pledge your life and loyalty to the Kingsnake Vampires."

"What do I need to do to prepare?"

"Look hot."

She gave a slight smile before she drank her coffee, even though it had to be midday. "Are there lines I need to remember?"

"No. Viper will grant you the title and hand you the crown."

"I have to wear a crown?" she asked in surprise. "You don't wear one."

"My sword is my crown."

"Then can I have a sword instead?"

"I think you'd look sexy with a crown." Golden and adorned with diamonds, it would look beautiful upon her already beautiful head.

She gave a slight smile again. "I'm not really the crown-wearing kind of gal."

"Alright. A sword it is."

She smiled in victory.

"I have work that requires my attention." I rose to my feet and pushed in the chair, leaving her alone with her coffee and meager breakfast. The food didn't satisfy the hunger, but it satisfied our taste buds. A trip down memory lane, it was a reminder of our time being human, the things we once enjoyed.

"What requires your attention?"

I didn't want to spoil the lightness in our hearts by telling her the truth, so I kept it to myself. "I need to speak with my father. I haven't spoken to him since before the wedding. He's probably eager to return to Crescent Falls, in case Aurelias has returned."

"Should I join you?"

"No," I said. "I need to speak to him in private." I was married to a woman who could read my emotions so well, who was privy to the things I tried to hide. I could close my mind, but that was harder when she knew my mind as well as I did.

She stared at me, seeming suspicious, but let it go. "I'll see you later, then."

I gave her a kiss goodbye then left, walking down the halls of the palace in search of my brothers or my father.

Fang appeared around the corner, his long body trailing far behind him. ***In the ssstudy.***

"Thanks."

Your father is anxiousss.

"I'm sure he is."

As I passed, Fang wrapped around one leg and moved up my torso until his upper body was secured around my shoulders. Like a parrot, he was perched on one shoulder as I carried him to my destination.

I entered the study and found my brothers, drinking in front of the fire. "It's midday."

Cobra held up his glass and took a drink. "While you've had the greatest two days of your life, we've had the worst."

"Why is that?" I sat in the armchair.

"Father." Viper was sunken into the corner of the couch, boots on the table. "He's very insistent that we speak."

"What did you tell him?" In my bliss, I'd forgotten about my father's breath on the back of my neck.

"That we agreed to have this conversation only when we're all together," Cobra said. "And now that we are, it's unavoidable. We need a plan, because once we tell him the truth, he's going to be livid."

"What kind of plan?" Viper asked.

"A united front," Cobra said. "That we've chosen to grant the Ethereal peace. We know how he's going to react, and we need to sheathe his anger. We all agree that the Ethereal who remain are innocent in all this."

"This would be easier if Aurelias were here." The favorite son.

Cobra shook his head. "Aurelias shares his likeness as well as his ideologies. He'd want the Ethereal dead even more than Father. It's probably in our favor that he hasn't returned yet."

He's asssking for you.

"Shit." I'd been out of my bedchambers for ten minutes, and he already knew.

What do I sssay?

"What is it?" Viper asked.

"He's asking for me."

Cobra finished off the remainder of his glass. "It's happening."

What do I sssay?

"Let's do it now," Viper said. "Get it over with."

Tell him to come here. I released a breath and dropped into the armchair. My fingers slid across my temple as the stress captivated me, chasing away all the pleasures of the last forty-eight hours.

He approachesss.

The door opened a moment later, and my father entered, a behemoth even without armor and plates. Muscular and tall like the rest of us, he had a presence that could be felt even with a blindfold on. The first person he looked at was me. "You finally show your face." He moved into the armchair directly across from me.

"I just got married, Father."

"I understand that." His palms went to each armrest. "But a king still has his obligations."

"Viper ruled in my stead—"

"He's no king. You are." Our relationship had soured as quickly as it had improved. He didn't care about my marriage, just his insatiable blood lust.

Both of my brothers remained quiet, like my father would forget they were there if they were quiet enough.

He stared at me.

I stared back.

"It's time to discuss our plans for the Ethereal," Father said. "Unless you have another insignificant matter that's more important."

My closed knuckles propped under my chin. "I have no other matters, Father."

"Good." His hands came together in front of him, regarding me like my brothers weren't in the room. "You've been in their lands, which means you know the way to infiltrate their forest. We'll enter their lands, kill them all, and claim their territory for our own."

"Why?" Cobra blurted. "Why would we want their lands?"

Father took a moment before he broke eye contact with me to look at my brothers. "It's an ideal place for our kind, to live in a mild climate without sun exposure. It's also closer to the kingdoms, the kingdoms that we'll soon rule."

A quiet shudder moved through the room. A shiver that tickled our spines.

"Tell me what you discovered in their lands." When he spoke, it was with a forceful tone, tired of asking the same question he'd asked before.

Cobra shifted his gaze to me.

Viper stared down at the coffee table.

I gave a long pause before I answered. "When we arrived in their lands, we were greeted by Queen Clara, the new monarch of their realm. She granted us kindness and hospitality."

My father didn't blink once.

"They're a peaceful race, living off the earth, not even eating the animals in their forest—"

"I don't care about their dietary preferences, Kingsnake." He straightened in the chair. "You wouldn't have been there for several weeks without reason, and the fact that you refuse to be forthcoming tells me you have heavy news to relate. A king doesn't procrastinate. He meets his challenges head on rather than avoiding them."

I inhaled a slow breath, charred by my father's roast. "The only reason we won that war was because Clara gave us the victory. She told us exactly where they would be and when they would be there."

"And why did she do that?" Father asked, eyes still on me.

Cobra didn't speak.

"In her letter, she said that we were right about all of our assumptions of her kind."

I couldn't read emotions the way Larisa could, but I could feel his anger now, feel it like burning coals in a fireplace.

"Disgusted by her father's actions, as well as a few select members in his inner circle, she helped us because it was the right thing to do. She ended the war between our races and finally established peace. She's a hero."

My father was so angered by what I'd previously confirmed, he ignored everything else I said.

"When we arrived in their lands, the first thing she asked us to do was sign a peace treaty. After what she did for us, I felt she'd earned that. So, Cobra and I both signed—"

"*You did what?*" The room must have grown quiet, because he sounded louder without raising his voice.

"We had to," Cobra said. "It was the only way she would share her people's secrets with us."

"Then she is no hero," Father said. "She's just as manipulative as her father was."

Cobra straightened. "She only wanted to protect her people—"

"I'm assuming she's another woman you've bedded." Father turned to regard him. "Because you're awfully defensive of someone who deserves no defense."

Cobra held his gaze.

"Do you want to know what she told us?" I said, getting the attention off Cobra.

My father dragged his eyes away from my brother to me.

"Before I tell you what she confided in us, there are some things you should know." I dreaded speaking every word, getting closer to the finality that would ignite his fuse. "Clara, along with everyone else in Evanguard, were unaware of these practices. They believed the lies her father told them all, and the lies his father told everyone before his time. They're victims in this."

My father's stare was so hard it was like stone. My words didn't mean a damn thing to him.

"And they've destroyed the very thing that granted them immortality. That's what we did while we were there. We worked with Clara to destroy the obelisk that granted them immortal life. Now they're no different from the humans in the kingdoms. Their glow will fade, and they'll age until time takes them."

His face started to tighten, angry that I still refused to give him the whole story.

"Because of this, the three of us have decided to live peacefully with the Ethereal, to move on from our past and forge a new coexistence. I understand your anger—"

"Oh, you don't understand my anger, Kingsnake," he spat. "But you're about to understand it perfectly once you grow some balls and tell me the truth. The truth that I already know because I can see it written across your damn face." Spittle flew out of his mouth because his lips were moving faster than his mind.

My eyes dropped.

"Say it."

My look was on him once again, not by choice.

"Look me in the fucking face and say it."

I squeezed one of my knuckles so hard it nearly snapped.

"Tell me what they did to your mother."

I did my best to hold his gaze, but I couldn't. The guilt swept me under the waves. The beautiful days I'd spent with Larisa in bed were wiped away, replaced by this sheer agony.

My father had never looked so angry, not even after my mother was killed. "She lost her soul—because those motherfuckers ate it. And you're going to sit there and ask for peace? You're going to pardon their crimes against humanity when your own mother never made it to the afterlife? I've been angry with my sons at one time or another, but I've never been ashamed until now. I'm ashamed of my son. Disgusted by his fucking face. Wish he'd never been born."

My eyes instinctively shut when his insult hit me like a palm to the face.

"If you're ashamed of him, then you're ashamed of us all." It was Cobra's voice, eerily calm despite the tension.

I opened my eyes and watched him take the heat next.

"Because we all agreed to it," Cobra said. "We agreed to it, knowing the truth. It's horrible and we're angry, but every Ethereal who knew about the practice has been killed. We killed every single one of them when we were in their forest. How can we wage war against a people who had absolutely no idea how they maintained their immortality? They were fed a lie by King Elrohir because that was the only way to get them to comply. Once they knew the truth, they destroyed the obelisk entirely on their own. We didn't have to coerce them, because they're as disgusted as we are."

"It won't bring her back, Father," Viper said. "Her soul has been gone a long time. Killing the Ethereal won't change that."

I was so grateful I wasn't fighting this battle alone. I wouldn't know what to do without my brothers. I didn't possess the strength to challenge my father on my own. His words cut me so deeply, like his sword pierced right through my armor and into both of my lungs.

"We've been at war with the Ethereal since the beginning," Cobra said. "Imagine a life free from battle. Imagine one of peace. The Ethereal can remain in their forest, we can remain in our lands, and everything can be as it should."

My father said nothing, looking at no one, his hands slightly moving together as he massaged one set of knuckles. When he found his voice, it was far quieter than it'd been before, but still full of rage. "Our plan was to defeat the Ethereal then rule the kingdoms—"

"That was *your* plan," I said. "The kingdoms have never declared war on us—"

"Because the Ethereal did the dirty work," he snapped. "But once they're eradicated, the kingdoms will grow scared and move for us next. Once they know we've killed their gods, they'll want to kill us."

"Then the simple answer is to not kill the humans," Viper said. "Problem solved."

"They'll still attack us once they realize the Ethereal are too weak to do it themselves." We all talked over one another, everyone trying to get their arguments across.

Voices rose like heat to the ceiling. "I will rule this entire continent and strip the royal families of their titles. It's the only way."

Cobra withdrew, cocking his head slightly as he regarded our father with shrewd eyes. "This isn't about Mother. This is about greed. This is about your obsession for ruling everything and everyone."

Father stared at him. "Whether the Ethereal had taken your mother's soul or not, my plans would be the same. But knowing that they have leaves me with no other choice. The Ethereal who still live have benefited from the souls of innocents. Whether they knew about it or not, they deserve death. I will give it to them."

I had to stop this. "Father—"

He rose to his feet. "Kingsnake Vampires and Cobra Vampires may have declared peace with the Ethereal, but the Originals have not. Stay out of my way—and I'll do what you should have done the moment you entered their lands."

17

LARISA

The seamstress gave me a gown more textured than my wedding dress. This had serpents sewn into the material, the dress only having one strap, which looked like a body of a serpent. There was a prominent slit up one leg, revealing my heeled boots underneath. On top was an open coat, the outside black and the inside lined with red. It was sexy but also powerful, a uniform that matched Kingsnake's but with its own feminine traits.

I waited for Kingsnake to return, but it'd been hours since we'd spoken. The servants told me it was time for the ceremony to begin, that all of Grayson was gathered at the bottom of the stairs of the palace, waiting for me to make my entrance.

I was nervous to assume this power, a power I hadn't earned, only obtained by marriage. It felt wrong to take it, and I wondered if I could just be his wife and not his queen, but I knew what he would say to that.

I reached my mind out to Fang. **The ceremony is about to begin. Where is he?**

Silence was my only answer.

I swallowed, waiting for his voice, terrified by what that rejection meant. **Fang, you're scaring me.**

We need sssome time.

What's going on?

Silence again.

———

The servants guided me to the top of the stairs at the palace. Down one hundred stairs was the first landing, where Viper should be standing to crown me with my blade. But he wasn't there—and all of Grayson stood and waited. Torches burned. The vampires were quiet. All my confidence was shaken by the absence of my husband and brothers.

Husband...it was the first time I'd said it. I wish it were a happy occasion.

Kingsnake finally appeared, jogging through the double doors in his king's uniform, his sword on his hip. Cobra and

Viper appeared as well, hastily dressed for the ceremony that should have started fifteen minutes ago.

Kingsnake came to me, visibly flustered.

"What happened?" I felt Fang slide up my leg and circle my body, taking his place across my shoulders, part of my uniform.

Kingsnake extended his arm for me to take. "We'll discuss it later."

"Is everything okay?"

"Yes."

"Where's your father?"

He winced, like my arrow had struck a bull's-eye. "Later."

I finally took his arm, and that was when the sound of drums began. They matched our footsteps, beating with every step we took on the next stair, my gown and coat trailing behind me.

With his left arm tucked behind his back, he guided me to the bottom, his eyes ahead, his face stoic and regal.

Viper stood, holding the blade across his open palms, his cloak blowing slightly in the evening breeze.

The moment we reached the last step in front of Viper, the drums stopped.

But if I'd had a heart, it would still be drumming hard.

Viper raised his voice so everyone at his back could hear. "Larisa, this crown is bestowed upon you, not only by marriage to Kingsnake, King of Vampires and Lord of Darkness, but your bravery in our last two battles. We would have lost the first fight if you hadn't warned us of the Ethereals' arrival. I present to you your crown, a blade forged with the red diamonds of the Kingsnake Vampires." He held it up for me to take.

I lifted the blade with both hands and examined the pommel, gold with diamonds and rubies, a piece of jewelry that would claim the lives of my foes.

"All hail, Larisa, Queen of Vampires and Lady of Darkness."

———

The ceremony was followed by a grand celebration. It was the first time I saw the vampires participate in festivities. We seemed to be at war so often that there wasn't time to do anything like relaxing and letting loose.

Since they didn't eat food like humans, there weren't tables covered with roasted pigs, smashed potatoes, and other delicacies. Instead, there was booze—and lots of it. A band played music, and some people danced.

But as I glanced at them all, I saw a difference in their composure. Their skin was paler, the color of gray clouds, and they looked...thinner.

Like they were starving.

I'd been so wrapped up in the Ethereal that I'd forgotten about my own people and their plight. The humans continued to be racked by the sickness that refused to abate —and I had the cure hidden away in my bedchambers. Both races were suffering because of my selfishness. I'd spent two days in bed with my husband and didn't think about anyone else, and now that felt unacceptable.

"Is there something wrong?" Kingsnake returned and handed me a glass of wine.

"Everyone looks...thin." The music was loud, and no one was around to overhear my words.

"We've had many battles."

"The prisoners..."

"We've lost more. It's the natural way of things."

The prisoners were humans, humans from my own village, and that made the situation more sickening. "We need to deliver the cure to the humans at once. Their suffering should be alleviated—as well as that of our own people."

A smile entered his lips.

"What?"

"You said our people."

"Well, they are."

"I know." The smile continued. "Just like hearing you say it. First thing tomorrow, we'll leave."

"I'd feel guilty carrying this sword if I didn't."

He took a drink as he circled his arm around my waist. "Now you're thinking like a queen." His lips drew close to my ear. "And I think that's really sexy." He turned his face and caught my lips, giving me a kiss as he tugged me close. "Wife."

It was the first time he'd called me that, and the shivers immediately started. "Husband."

He rubbed his nose against mine, something he'd never done before.

"Kingsnake." Cobra got his attention, speaking to a group of vampires at one of the tables.

"I'll be back."

"You better." It was hard to release my hold on him, not because I was afraid to be alone, but because I would never have enough of that man.

He walked away and joined Cobra, who clapped him on the back like all was well.

I saw the way Kingsnake interacted with his people, always kingly but also approachable. That hadn't seemed to be the case when I'd first arrived here, when people scattered to the opposite side of the street to avoid him. But after the two battles, he appeared to have become a man of the people.

I should do the same.

With my glass in hand, I moved through the various throngs of vampires, the torches catching the light of the merrymakers who seemed to celebrate me...even when I hadn't done enough to be celebrated, in my opinion.

"Your Highness."

I turned at the name, a name that didn't fit me at all.

It was Kingsnake's father, a man I'd only known as King Serpentine. If he had a first name, he never shared it with me. I stilled as his features were exposed in the torchlight. A glass was in his hand, but instead of drinking wine like everyone else, he had something stronger. "I'm sorry I startled you."

His unexpected presence didn't catch me off guard. It was his mood. Infinite and depthless, a pain that stretched in every direction, as if he were mortally wounded underneath his clothing. "You didn't."

A glimmer of a smile came on to his face, similar to his son's. "You aren't the only one who can feel, Your Highness."

"Larisa is fine."

"That's no way to address a queen."

"I hope you don't expect me to address you as such...now that you're my father-in-law."

He was tall like his sons, had the same dark hair and sharp jawline. He was decades older than me, but he was still youthful and strong. "Serpentine is fine."

"You must have had different names...before." They couldn't have been obsessed with snakes when they were human. That must have come later, when they turned and adopted new identities.

"Whatever my name was before, I have no memory of it." He brought his glass to his lips and took a drink. "Kingsnake tells me they've decided to grant a peaceful truce with the Ethereal. His brothers as well. I can only assume you feel the same."

I'd expected him to be angry, but that sadness lingered, as if he felt betrayed. "I understand how hard this must be for you. It would be unrealistic to expect you to agree to this without reservation."

"And yet, that's exactly what my sons expected."

"When Ellasara brought me face-to-face with death, Kingsnake turned me to keep me alive. I was upset with him at first, but once we traveled to Evanguard, I realized that not only my life would have been forfeited without his interference, but my soul as well. He saved me, and I'm so sorry that your wife wasn't saved as well."

His reaction was chiseled in stone, but the pain in his chest seemed to deepen. "My sons have been far less sympathetic."

"I know that's not true. They care. Deeply."

He looked away for a moment. "But they'll never care the way I do. The only one who could remotely understand is Kingsnake, now that he's wed to a woman he so clearly loves. What if it had been different?" He looked at me again. "What if he hadn't turned you—and your fate was the same?"

I held his gaze, knowing exactly what would have happened.

"We both know the answer." He took a drink. "Kingsnake would burn every one of them alive. And yet, he denies what he would have done himself. This is his mother we're talking about, but apparently, his memory is weak because he's forgotten every worldly sacrifice she made for him and his brothers."

My eyes dropped, feeling the sting of guilt.

"Larisa."

I looked at him once again.

"I need you to change his mind."

My new father-in-law had just asked me for a favor, a favor that would bring us closer together and gain his approval, but the knot in my stomach told me I couldn't do it. As much as it pained me to know what had happened to his wife, we had to move on. "I lost my father when I was little. And then I lost my mother a few years ago when she got sick. Both of their souls...are gone. I'll never see them again. Even if I still had my soul, they already lost theirs."

"Then do it for them, Larisa."

"But it won't bring them back." I watched the light leave his eyes as I said it. "It won't change anything. We'll massacre innocent people who despise the practice as much as we do. It would be an irrational genocide."

He hadn't blinked since I'd denied him, and the depth of his sadness suddenly reached new limits. A fire started to burn, the spark that was unleashed once the flames hit the wood. "I understand your reasoning."

I'd expected a much different reaction, based on the fire that simmered beneath his skin. Perhaps he wasn't as barbaric as Kingsnake claimed him to be. He had control over his emotions a lot more firmly than his own son most of the time.

"I admire your commitment to my son. Now that your soul is no longer at risk, you choose to stay with him in this eternal darkness. It's a testament to your love, to forsake a life with children for one with a single man. Raising four sons was the most difficult endeavor of my life, but it was also the best endeavor."

My heart dropped onto the stone ground and splattered everywhere. I felt panic, as if I were trapped in a burning building with no way out. The smoke made it impossible to breathe. I did my best to keep a straight face and control the emotions that had broken loose, but it was a losing battle. "You speak as if this is reversible..."

"Because it is."

The fire continued to surround me. My lungs struggled to breathe. My flesh melted off my bones. "And he knew this?"

"He's always known. When we spoke in Crescent Falls, I told him that I discovered how to execute it. It's a complicated process, but one very few embark upon because no one would ever want to be mortal again." He took a drink as he stared at me, and his expression tightened. "He didn't share this with you?"

I couldn't bring myself to speak. It was too difficult. All I did was shake my head.

"Well, I assume it's because he knew what your answer would be."

I couldn't look at him anymore. Couldn't focus on my reality at all. The rage was so deep that no amount of rain would dampen my flames. "Would you excuse me?" Before he even had a chance to grant my request, I was gone. I set my glass on the edge of a stone wall and took the stairs back to the palace, lifting my ridiculous gown that suddenly felt heavier than a boulder.

The servants all looked at me as I entered, giving quick bows of their heads with salutations. "Your Highness."

I ignored them, entered the bedchambers where Kingsnake and I had made love passionately for days, and grabbed a bag and stuffed it with whatever I could find. I took the vials of venom we'd gathered from our voyage across the sea then headed to the stables.

The stable master was on duty, but he cast a quizzical look at my arrival.

"Fetch me a horse."

He stilled at the order, glancing back at the festivities where Kingsnake remained. "Your Highness—"

"I gave you my order. Now follow it."

He finally saddled a horse and packed my belongings on the sides. "Your Highness, I don't think you should—"

I shoved him against the edge of one of the stalls and grabbed the rope hanging there. I bound his wrists and tied him in place. Out of fear of disobedience, he allowed me. I could tell by the look on his face he would run to Kingsnake the moment I was gone, and I couldn't have him hot on my tail. "It's nothing personal."

I mounted the horse and dug in my heels to take off at a run.

But then I realized...I had nowhere to go.

Grayson had become my home.

My everything.

And now...I had nothing.

18

KINGSNAKE

When I finished my conversation, I searched for my queen.

I assumed she was with Viper, but when I found him, he was tangled up with his favorite prey in a dark alleyway. Cobra remained where I left him, talking with my soldiers because he refused to feed if Clara wasn't his prey. Some of the goblets were full of animal blood, a poor substitute but a curb for the hunger.

I started to walk around, looking in the groups of people to see if she was mingling with the men and women we'd fought beside in the last two battles. But I didn't find her. I didn't spot her thick coat and beautiful hair. *Fang?*

Yesssss?

Have you seen Larisa?

No.

A jolt of fear rushed through me, but I quickly quieted it, knowing there was nothing to fear. Larisa was no longer human, so my own men hadn't turned against me to feed on her flesh. The Ethereal no longer wanted her dead, so she was no longer a target. Nothing was a threat to her.

But that didn't make me feel better.

Perhapsss ssshe retired for the evening.

I moved to the stairs and quickly ascended to the palace doors. I walked inside and headed to our bedchambers, hoping to see her in bed, preferably naked and passed out after all the wine.

But the bed was empty. *She's not here.*

Ssshe must be sssomewhere, Kingsnake. Calm down.

I spotted her coat tossed over the armchair. *She was here.* I moved to the bathroom and pushed the door open so hard it smacked into the wall and left a dent. It was empty.

I went into the closet and flicked on the light.

Her armor was missing.

Why the fuck was her armor missing?

The horror seeped into my veins as I stared, my breathing suddenly deep and ragged, my panic inconsolable. I tried to solve a puzzle without a single piece. Nothing made sense. *She left.*

What do you mean?

She fucking left. That's what I mean. I moved to the stash of venom that we had collected together—and it was missing. *Speak to her. She may still be close.* I dropped my clothes and put on my own armor. Tonight, I was supposed to celebrate my new queen, but I prepared for a war I was terrified to lose.

I will try.

———

I ran down the stairs, and everyone below turned to regard me as my armor reflected the torches. It must have reflected in my eyes too, furious flames about to incinerate anyone who got in my path.

I marched to the stables, my eyes focused ahead, locked in tunnel vision.

"What's happening?" Cobra came to my side when he realized something was amiss.

"Larisa left."

"What do you mean?"

"She took her shit and left," I snapped. "That's what I mean."

A solid three seconds passed, like Cobra was just as confused as I was minutes ago. "Why?"

"I have no fucking idea."

"What if someone took her?"

"They didn't."

"How do you know?"

"Because she took the venom. She left on her own terms."

"Have Fang speak to her—"

"I already tried. She's either too far away, or she's blocking him out."

Cobra walked with me down the path toward the stables. "Did you say something to her—"

"No."

"What was your last interaction?"

"I gave her a glass of wine, kissed her, and then joined you for a conversation."

"And everything seemed fine?"

"Yes." I was exhausted by all the questions when I knew they wouldn't get me anywhere. I finally made it to the stables, but there was no stable master to help me. I marched into the barn to fetch my own horse.

"Your Highness." The stable master sat on the ground, his wrists bound around a metal pole.

My eyes nearly popped out of my head.

Cobra pulled out his knife and cut him free. "Shit, this is bad."

"What happened?" I yanked him to his feet then shoved him against the wall. "What happened to my wife?"

Cobra put his hand on my shoulder and held me back so I wouldn't rip his head clean from his shoulders.

"She—she demanded a horse—"

"And you just gave it to her?"

"She—she's the queen..." He fell back against the wall of the stables, cowering in fear. "She tied me up before she left because she knew I would alert you to her departure."

I wanted to lunge at this motherfucker.

Cobra tugged me back. "Kingsnake, he didn't do anything wrong."

I shoved him off and saddled my own horse. "What the fuck is she doing?"

"Did she say anything?" Cobra asked the pointless question.

The stable master shook his head.

"I need to retrieve my armor and weapons," Cobra said. "I'll grab Viper—"

"He needs to rule Grayson in my stead." It was the quickest I'd ever saddled a horse, which was a remarkable feat since I hadn't done it myself in a very long time. "And I don't have time to wait for you."

"Kingsnake, you shouldn't go alone—"

"I don't care." I grabbed the horse by the reins and pulled him from the stable. Fang snaked up my leg and secured himself around my shoulders.

"Just let me grab my sword, at least."

I mounted the horse and took off.

"Kingsnake!"

19

LARISA

I approached Raventower, the village aglow with the torches that lined its exterior wall. The path turned muddy like it'd rained over the last few days. I approached the main gate, setting sight on the place I'd called home my entire life.

No one manned the gate.

"Hello?"

No response.

"Is anyone there?"

The torches flickered, but nothing happened. "That's not good..." Was I too late? Was everyone already dead from the sickness I could have stopped weeks ago? I dismounted the horse and climbed up the wall, pulling myself up to the ramparts on the other side.

There was no one there.

I looked into the city, seeing the torchlights down the alleyways and around the castle. Even with my enhanced night vision, I couldn't make out the details of the village. Couldn't figure out if it was even inhabited anymore.

I climbed down and opened the gate then retrieved my horse. I walked him through the gate and into the town. The stables had food in the troughs, so I secured my horse and filled his bucket with water before I continued forward.

My boots tapped against the cobblestones as I made my way down the main road. It was so quiet, every step audible. A strong breeze swept through and nearly snuffed out every torch. It made my hair dance in the breeze.

Then it died.

Instead of heading to the castle as quickly as I could, I took my time, looking into the dark houses and seeing no signs of life. The place felt abandoned. Everyone seemed to be dead or had moved on to somewhere else.

As I approached the castle, I saw signs of life. Guards were posted around the stone keep. The wall that surrounded the castle had men posted on the ramparts. The entire town seemed to be concentrated in this one area.

I couldn't figure out why.

Everyone was so fixated on the other side of the wall that they didn't notice me approaching the castle doors. Even the guards entrusted with the protection of the castle looked that way, so they didn't notice me when I pulled on the locked door.

I knocked—and that was what finally drew the attention of the guards.

They rushed me, immediately charging me with their swords.

"Vampire!"

Four of them came at me at once.

I unsheathed my sword and stepped back, deflecting the first hit and then dodging the next. A fight against a human was far easier than one against the Ethereal or the orcs, so avoiding their blades was simple work. "I came here to speak with King Elias. I have a cure for the sickness."

That made every single guard stop. They all stepped back and dropped their swords, looking at one another like one of their own would be able to confirm the truth of my words.

"I need to speak to him."

One of the guards moved to the door and knocked, hitting his fist in different ways to create a specific tune. That seemed to be the password, because someone immediately opened the door.

The guard locked his gaze on me, his reaction the same as the other guards.

"I need to speak to King Elias," I said. "Immediately."

———

I was escorted to his study.

The very study where he'd fucked me over his desk. The one where he'd told me he would marry someone else. The one where he'd suggested an affair, so he could have his cake and eat it too.

I was a much different person as I stepped into that room again—and not just because I was a vampire.

He stood behind his desk and watched me walk in, his eyes empty at first then heavy. A deep breath expanded his chest and he opened his mouth to speak, but then he shut it, as if the words left him.

I knew I didn't look the same. Not only was my skin paler, my eyes lighter, but my body had tightened from my change in lifestyle. Now I had muscles in my arms and legs. Now I wore armor and a cloak instead of old trousers.

He didn't look the same either. He was thin, far too thin for a king.

I approached his desk, feeling like the superior one for once. "What's happened here? No one's in the town. Why are all the guards at this border?"

His mind wasn't as quick as it used to be either, probably because he was exhausted...and starving. All he could muster was a single word. "Werewolves."

"What?"

His hands rested on the surface for balance. "The human population continues to plummet in light of the sickness. As they dwindle, so does the werewolves' food source..."

"Why the fuck does everything eat us?" I snapped. It was the vampires, the Ethereal, and now werewolves. Was that our only purpose? To feed all the monsters?

"They threatened to attack Raventower without donations. I didn't have a choice."

This nightmare just got worse.

"I begged the kingdoms for help, but they have their own problems to deal with."

"What problems?"

"The werewolves are doing the same to them."

After defeating the Ethereal, I'd assumed the worst was over.

"The Ethereal haven't answered our call either."

"And they won't."

Whatever hope he had left in his eyes died.

"We have nothing left to give. The Werewolf King will be here tomorrow—and we'll have no other choice but to fight."

The Ethereal poisoned the humans, and without this cure that Kingsnake and I had risked our lives for, the kingdoms would have turned into a werewolf paradise. Serpentine's anger seemed even more reasonable now. Maybe the Ethereals' crimes really were unforgivable. They could have destroyed the world. "I've brought a cure for the sickness. But I'm not sure how much help that will be now."

"I don't know either," he said honestly. "There are so few of us left."

"Your wife?"

His eyes dropped and he shook his head. "She got sick..."

"I'm so sorry."

"One of her maidens gave it to her. I couldn't even comfort her once the sickness settled in...never saw her again. But that's what most people have already had to go through. And then it was my turn."

"I'm sorry." I didn't know what else to say. The news was so horrible.

His eyes eventually lifted to mine again. "When we lose this battle...and we will...the werewolves will take us captive in their den. Then they'll eat us, one by one. I'm going to tell my men they have the right to claim their own lives, if that's what they wish. An option I may take for myself."

"No."

His eyes hardened.

"We're going to fight."

"You don't understand, Larisa. Werewolves are—"

"I've fought werewolves and orcs," I said. "And now I'm a vampire."

His eyes flinched again, and then a cloud of guilt rose inside him. "I'm sorry...that I let them take you."

It had hurt more than words could explain, but I'd moved on from his betrayal. I'd fallen in love with a man who would never—

My thoughts ceased, hitting something I wasn't prepared to face. My dead heart tightened into a fist like it was still alive, and all the faith I had in love evaporated altogether. Kingsnake had betrayed me three times now. First, he'd promised to let me go and took that back. He'd turned me when he knew it wasn't my wish. And now...this was one far worse than the others. I could forgive the past transgressions because they were inconsequential, but this...this was unforgivable. My husband should be the man I trusted most in this world—and he lied to me.

I returned to the conversation with Elias. "I forgive you."

"How can you forgive me, after what they've done to you?"

I'd fully embraced my immortality until a few hours ago. Now I was lost all over again. "It's not so bad."

"You're much kinder to me than I deserve, Larisa." He inhaled a painful breath. "I betrayed the one person who actually gave a shit about me. I grew to love my wife, but she never loved me. I was just an opportunity. I'm the worst king Raventower has ever seen in its history. Everyone is dead...because I couldn't lead. I stayed locked up in my castle like a coward."

"Elias, this situation is unprecedented. It can't be fixed by a single person."

"You just said you found a cure—so it can."

I pulled the pack off my shoulders and set it down, being careful with the glass vials. "Let's deal with the werewolves. Then we can disperse the cure and move to the other kingdoms to do the same."

"Larisa, a single vampire isn't going to change this outcome. If you brought an army of Kingsnake Vampires, perhaps that would make a difference—"

"They are coming."

His eyes narrowed.

Kingsnake would deduce my whereabouts quickly. The second he realized the venom was missing, he would come for me. I didn't know if he would bring an army, but his brothers would be close behind.

"When will they be here?"

"I'm—I'm not sure. We just need to hold the werewolves off until then."

———

It was the darkest part of the night, an hour before the light started to brighten the sky from midnight black to dark blue. I stood on the ramparts behind the fence and stared into the darkness, seeing their outlines come into view from the torches that we'd erected in the fields.

The one in the lead was dressed in all black, his boots shiny in the torchlight. There were a few men behind him, dressed similarly, some of them wearing hoods as if to block out the nonexistent sunlight.

It was an odd sight, seeing ordinary men approach the gate without weapons or armor, but wearing the smug grin of victory.

I stood on the rampart and looked down below, and then someone joined me.

Dressed in armor that was a few sizes too big was King Elias, his skin sallow like he hadn't seen the sun in years. His men turned to regard him as well, as if it was the first time they'd seen their king in the flesh.

The werewolf locked eyes on him. "Your Highness, so glad you could join us."

Elias stood with his hands secured behind his back, doing his best to appear as a strong king rather than a weak man.

"You know why I'm here." He gestured to the gate directly in front of him. "Let's get going."

"We have nothing left to give," King Elias said. "I'm sure you've surmised that by now."

The werewolf stepped forward. "And I'm sure you've surmised what we'll do if you don't comply. You think these rickety gates will keep my kind out? We'll rip this city apart and feast on every one of you."

"You can try," I said. "But your death with be delivered by my blade."

The werewolf shifted his gaze to me.

As did King Elias and everyone else.

The werewolf narrowed his eyes before a smile set in. "You're a pretty thing, aren't you?" He cocked his head slightly. "But not too pretty to eat."

"There will be no donation today," I said. "We invite you to battle if that's your wish."

"This isn't a poker game, Pretty. Your bluff will cost you a lot more than a hand."

"Then it's a good thing I'm not bluffing."

King Elias spoke under his breath. "Tread carefully."

The werewolf stepped forward. "If you're so brave, why don't you come down here and have this conversation face-to-face?"

"Don't do it," Elias whispered.

"Don't worry, I won't bite," the werewolf said.

"Then I won't either."

His smile dropped.

I turned on my heel and moved down the stairs, King Elias behind me.

"Larisa, I understand you're a nightwalker now, but it's still three-on-one."

"He won't fuck with me when he knows who I am." I walked to the gate. "Open the doors."

"No." Once he gave his order, the men obeyed. "You're going to get yourself killed—"

"The only way to deal with an enemy is to stand your ground. You've let them take from your people long enough. They're bullies, and we know there's only one way to deal with bullies. It breaks my heart to see my home become a ghost town, and I'm not going to sit here and watch them take however little is left." I looked at the guard. "So open the damn gate."

The guard looked at Elias.

Elias gave a nod.

The doors opened, revealing the three werewolves.

"Wow," the lead werewolf said. "Pretty's got spunk."

I walked forward.

Elias joined me.

"What are you doing?" I halted.

"I'm not letting you do this alone—"

"I don't need your help. You're so weak you can barely stand." I faced forward and continued. "I'll handle this myself." I moved ahead onto the open grass, and he didn't follow me.

I made the long walk to the three werewolves, and the one in the lead looked utterly delighted by my company.

He looked me up and down appreciatively. "Maybe you should be king of this place."

"I can't," I said. "Because I'm already Queen of Vampires and Lady of Darkness. I'm sure you know my husband, Kingsnake, King of Grayson, the most ferocious vampire there ever was." A part of me felt guilty for invoking his name when I didn't know what we were anymore. I didn't want to be his queen anymore, let alone his wife, not when he refused to be honest with me, not when he'd hidden something so important to me.

The werewolf didn't cower in fear as I'd hoped. "Kingsnake has done pretty well for himself." He continued to objectify my body with that stare, piercing my armor like he could see my tits in the flesh. "But he's not here. Because if he were, he wouldn't let you anywhere near me. So, I have a proposition for you, Pretty. Come back with me—and I'll spare this godforsaken village you care so much about."

"No."

"Come on. I'll make you forget about that leech—"

"*I said no.* Now leave these lands and never return...or receive our wrath."

"Wrath?" he asked with a laugh. "You and that spineless pussy who let you come out here alone?"

"I don't need his help."

He gave a chuckle as he looked me over. "I may be a were-wolf, but I'm also a gentleman when it comes to a pretty girl. I've humored you up until this point, but I've grown tired of the game. Give me what I want, or you'll receive *my* wrath."

I stepped forward, getting right in his face. "I. Said. No."

His eyes locked on mine, unblinking.

I stared back, holding my ground against this dog.

"What a shame." In an instant, he'd turned, changing from the ordinary human he'd been before into a beast that roared so loudly it made the gate shake.

"Fire!" King Elias yelled to the archers.

The hilt of the sword was in my hand, and I dodged the first swipe of his enormous paw. The last time I'd battled a werewolf, I'd been an ordinary human, so my movements had been slow and sloppy. I was amazed by the way I was now able to dodge his attack. With the speed of the wind, I sidestepped one of his claws and swiped my blade across his torso.

"*Roooaaaarrr!*" With a loud cry, he growled into the night, blood dripping down his fur. He bared his teeth at me, shaking with fury that couldn't be suppressed. Arrows continued to rain down, and then the other two men turned as well.

I was outnumbered.

The first one charged at me.

I sidestepped his attack, but he spun around and smacked his closed paw into my head.

I was knocked backward, my sword falling from my hand.

He was on me instantly, about to slam both of his big arms right into my body to break my sternum and everything connected to it.

I rolled out of the way and grabbed my sword in the process. Before he could get me, I slashed my knife across his heel.

He screamed in fury then stumbled, like I'd gotten his Achilles tendon.

"I told you to leave!"

Spit dripped from his gaping mouth, my murder visible in his eyes. With a limp, he came at me again.

I got to my feet and dodged the attack of another.

The arrows came, but they weren't enough to deflect them.

I was in deep shit now.

One swiped at me, and I ducked just in time, my head nearly knocked from my shoulders.

"Larisa!" King Elias yelled. "Behind you!"

I turned to see the first werewolf on me again, victory in his grasp. With three pissed-off werewolves against one vampire, I didn't have a chance. I'd assumed my royal status would make them scurry like rats into a sewer, but it was a horrible bet. My husband's name wasn't enough to protect me.

Something struck me from another direction, and I was shoved to the ground. I hit the earth, my sword dropping, my world spinning.

"*Hiiisssssssss.*"

I turned at the sound, recognizing that noise anywhere. "Fang?"

Kingsnake made a flurry of blows with his sword, his black cloak dancing as he moved. He sliced the werewolf across the eye then dug deep into his shoulder. His blade flashed with light as it spun, chopping the monster into pieces until he crumpled to the ground.

Fang had the other by the throat, cutting off his air supply so Cobra could impale him in the heart.

Kingsnake was already on the last one, stabbing him in the back because he'd tried to run away.

It all happened in just a few seconds, the battle over immediately once they arrived.

I grabbed my sword and pushed to my feet, feeling a phantom heartbeat in my chest from all the terror.

Kingsnake turned to me, and instead of being relieved that I was unharmed, he looked like he wanted to hurt me far more than that werewolf had. "What the fuck, Larisa?" His body shook as the hilt remained in his hand.

Cobra stood behind his brother, watching the conversation with a guarded gaze.

I stared at my husband.

He stared at me.

He came forward. "How could you do this to me? Do you have any idea what the fuck you just put me through—"

"Wow, that's rich."

He pushed the boundary and became angrier. "*Excuse me?*"

"I left Grayson, which is perfectly within my rights to do because I'm not a prisoner. But that's comparable to what you did?"

"What the fuck did I do—"

"You lied to me."

"And what did I lie about?" When I yelled, he yelled. We screamed at each other on the battlefield, surrounded by dead werewolves and Cobra and Fang.

"That I can be human again."

Within the snap of a finger, the rage inside him died. A pail of water had doused his flames, and now there was just weak smoke.

"You were never going to tell me, were you?"

His emotions were impossible to interpret. There was too much to unravel. But I could definitely see panic—panic that he'd been caught.

"What the fuck is wrong with you?" I shoved him hard in the chest, and he let his body stumble back, defenseless. "I'm the one who has to make the ulti-mate sacrifice to be together, but you wouldn't do the same for me. That's what it comes down to. You could give me children if you wanted to—but you don't."

He breathed, saying nothing.

I wanted him to keep yelling because this horrible truth was too much. I wanted him to say it wasn't true and scream at me for even thinking he was capable of such a betrayal...but he didn't.

"I can't believe you let me marry you."

His eyes stayed locked on mine, but he didn't say a word. His emotions were such a tornado that nothing could be deciphered.

"You have nothing to say?"

"I have a lot to say." Now his voice was quiet, defeated. "It's a lot more complicated than you think—"

"I wouldn't know because you never told me."

"Then let me explain this to you now—"

"This is not how this conversation is supposed to go. You're supposed to scream at me for believing something so horrible about your character. You're supposed to yell at me for leaving Grayson and putting myself in danger. You're supposed to be pissed off at me because I betrayed you by believing this nonsense. But it's true...it's fucking true." The hot tears started in the backs of my eyes, but I refused to let them fall. "Why do the men I love always betray me?"

He closed his eyes, and that was when I felt it.

Heartbreak.

"We're done here." I walked off back toward the gate where King Elias remained. With a solemn expression, he stared at me as I came close. I expected the sound of Kingsnake's boots behind me, expected his arm to grab me by the elbow and yank me back, but it never happened.

He let me go.

20

KINGSNAKE

"You told her." I looked at Fang by the fireplace, where he sat on the rug in front of the flames. King Elias had granted us accommodation without hesitation. In our last interaction, he'd looked at me with fear, but now he looked at me with nothing at all.

Cobra sat in the armchair, one ankle crossed on the opposite knee, his fingers resting across his lips.

I did not.

"Then how does she know?" I snapped. "You're the only one who knew."

"Instead of being pissed off at Fang, maybe you should be pissed off at yourself," Cobra said. "Because you should have told her the truth."

I looked at my brother, murder in my eyes. "I don't need your shit right now—"

"It's fucked up, Kingsnake. How could you not tell her?"

I would never betray you.

Now I carried on two conversations at once. "You're the only one who knew, Fang." I looked at my brother. "And fuck off, Cobra. She finally came to terms with her new life, and I wasn't going to fuck with her head—"

"Don't act like that's the reason," Cobra said. "You can't bullshit me."

"I'm your goddamn brother," I snapped. "Your loyalty is to me."

I wasn't the only one who knew.

"Just because we're related doesn't mean you're entitled to anything," Cobra said. "She's my sister, isn't she? You were afraid if she knew the truth, she would leave you for a human life. Or worse, she would ask you to join her."

"And you really can't understand why I wouldn't want that?" I yelled.

"Of course I do!" he yelled back. "But she deserved the option."

"You want me to be human?" I asked incredulously. "Come on, Cobra."

"No," he said. "But I know Larisa would have chosen you. And that would have made your relationship a million times better. But you fucked that up because you didn't trust her. You had no faith whatsoever."

I turned away, the rage pumping in my veins like I still had a beating heart.

It was your father.

I slowly looked at Fang again, the terror too much. "My father wouldn't betray me..."

Yesss, he would—becaussse it wasn't me.

The room went quiet except for the crackling fire. Pain was stacked across my shoulders, and the burden was too heavy a load. I was wounded on all sides, in battle without my armor, stabbed in the back by my allies rather than my foes. "Why would he do that?"

Maybe he didn't know it was a secret—

"He knew."

"Probably because he's pissed off that we didn't give him what he wanted," Cobra said. "Payback. If he can't have what he wants, then you can't either."

"That's low...even for him." My father and I had buried the hatchet, but he was quick to betray me if I didn't give him what he wanted. It was like a knife to the heart rather than the back.

"All he's ever wanted was to defeat the Ethereal," Cobra said. "He can't think clearly."

My father's betrayal faded into the background because I couldn't do anything about it right now. "I can't lose her." The room went quiet at my words. Neither one of them spoke. Neither one of them gave me words of encouragement.

"You should be talking to her instead of us," Cobra said. "Go."

21

LARISA

I sat in Elias's study, him in the armchair across from me, a fire in the hearth even though it was midday. Most of his curtains were drawn closed and forgotten, like there was no reason to keep them open in daylight when there was no point in even being alive.

"The journey from Grayson is relatively brief," I said. "If they leave a few hours before sunset, they should be here by midnight. In the meantime, we'll be able to stall when the werewolves see us."

"They were unable to return with news because your husband killed them. I suspect they'll assume what transpired and march on our gates with everything they have—while we have nothing."

"But they have no chance against the Kingsnake Vampires."

"But if they don't see an army, they won't believe you," he said. "A couple of vampires may not be enough to convince them."

"They may send scouts before an army," I said. "We may have time."

"I hope you're right." He sank into the other armchair, no longer the handsome man I remembered. The stress had dried his skin, made his hair thin, made his eyes dull. His arms weren't muscular in his emaciated state. "You aren't obligated to stay." He looked at me across the rug. "There's no reason you should die for us. We didn't stand by you when you needed us. You shouldn't stand by us."

"I'm not going to abandon Raventower."

"There's so few of us left. It's not worth it."

"It's always worth it, Elias."

We fell into silence, comfortable silence, something I didn't think would be possible after everything we'd been through. My eyes drifted to the fire, thinking about the man I refused to speak to.

"I'm sorry...about you and your husband."

"Yeah...thanks."

"May I ask what happened?"

I took a deep breath before I shared the story. "He was never going to tell me. Never going to give me a choice. And that's just unacceptable."

Instead of jumping in and ripping Kingsnake apart, he just absorbed the information. "What will you do?"

"I don't know."

"He loves you deeply."

"You don't know him."

"He lied to you because he didn't want to lose you. That's love—even if it's not expressed well."

My eyes stayed on the fire.

"I see that you love him too."

"How so?"

"You've referred to him as your husband when you didn't have to. He's still the man in your heart, even in your anger."

I ignored his assessment.

A knock sounded on the door before the guard poked his head inside. "Kingsnake, King of Vampires and Lord of Darkness, wishes to speak with Larisa. I've informed him she's in your company."

I could feel Kingsnake's rage from across the castle. It started as a simple spark then turned into an inferno. "Send him away." I didn't want to speak to him. It'd been a few hours since our last conversation, and that wasn't enough time for me to calm down.

He shut the door and disappeared.

King Elias remained quiet.

"You can't go in there!"

The door flew open like Kingsnake had kicked it in. He entered the study with flames in his eyes, immediately staring at King Elias and the distance between us, which was the length of the entire room. The anger dampened—but only slightly. "Get out."

King Elias immediately rose to his feet.

I rolled my eyes at the scene he'd just caused. "I don't want to speak to you—"

"I'm sorry to hear that." He rounded on Elias. "*I said, get out.*"

King Elias hurried, leaving his own study and shutting the door behind himself.

Kingsnake grabbed the vacated armchair and pulled it across the rug until it was right in front of me. He dropped into the chair and faced me. "We aren't leaving this room until this is resolved."

"You don't get to dictate the terms of my anger. I'm pissed off, and I'll be pissed off as long as I want. Reconciliation doesn't happen on your timetable."

"But it will happen." It wasn't a question, but it sounded like one, his hope coming through.

I looked away. "Like you've said before...never assume victory before the battle even begins."

His stare remained resolute, but the emotions inside him were like the tide under the full moon. They suddenly became bigger and stronger as they crashed against the shore. "Why are you alone with him in his study?"

"Wow...what a great apology."

"I just don't understand—"

"Because he's the King of Raventower, my home."

"Your *former* home. Grayson is your home now."

"Now my former home as well."

A spark of anger rushed through him.

"And we have an oncoming assault from the werewolves. Trying to figure out logistics."

"And that's all?" he asked in disbelief.

I looked at him head on, my legs crossed with my elbow on my knee. "Kingsnake, no matter how angry I may be with you, there's no way I would ever—"

"I'm not worried about you. I'm worried about him."

"Even if he did try something, the fact that it would upset you means you are worried about me."

His eyes shifted away. "I'm afraid I fucked everything up... and drove you into the arms of your former lover."

"You did fuck everything up, Kingsnake."

He averted his eyes again.

"But you're the man I love...in spite of everything." It was hard just to say that because he'd hurt me so damn much.

His eyes came back to me. "When we played that game with Cobra, you said you hooked up with some random guy at a bar when Elias—"

"You're really going to throw that in my face right now?"

"I'm not throwing it in your face. I'm just explaining my insecurity. And hooking up with Elias is the perfect way to get back at me..."

I looked away, the insult like a slap in the face. "You're the one who betrayed me, but I'm the one who needs to make you feel secure in our relationship?"

He looked away again.

"I feel nothing for that man—except pity. We're married, Kingsnake. I take that seriously. A lot more seriously than you do—since you chose to marry me without giving me my options."

There was a pain so deep in his chest it radiated heat like the sun. He kept his eyes averted, too ashamed to meet my gaze. "We were happy, and I didn't want to mess with it. We finally got past all the bullshit and the hiccups. You'd finally accepted your new reality, and it felt cruel to thrust this information on you."

"I can't believe you were never going to tell me..."

He stared at his hands as they came together between his knees. "Based on your reaction, I know what your answer will be, so I don't feel bad for lying to you. Not at all. Because I don't want to lose you—and now, I will."

"Kingsnake."

His eyes stayed down.

"Look at me."

He gave a subtle shake of his head. "I can't."

"Why do you assume that's my answer?"

"Why else would you be so upset?" He continued to stare at the floor.

"I'm upset because you put your needs before mine—the last thing you should do in a marriage. I'm upset that you've pushed me to make all the sacrifices for this relationship but wouldn't do the same for me."

Now he looked up, his eyes on mine. "That's not true."

"What's not true?"

"I would make the sacrifice—but fuck, I don't want to." He straightened in the chair then sank into the cushion, the pain in his eyes matching the pain in his heart. "I don't want to live a single lifetime with you, watching you get sick and die or watching myself drop dead from a heart attack. Sixty years. Seventy, if we're lucky. Weak and vulnerable to those beings that are stronger than us. It's not the right decision."

"It's still a decision we should have made together—as equals—but you chose to make it on your own. How can I be your queen if you don't share the power? How can you trust me to rule in your stead if you don't trust my opinions?"

He had nothing to say to that.

"Kingsnake...I don't trust you."

He clenched his eyes shut.

"This isn't the first time you've lied to me."

"You can't hold that against me. I couldn't let you go—"

"Because you decided that was best. You didn't give me a choice—"

"And that choice is how we ended up here, husband and wife, madly in love, forever. I'm not sorry." He raised his head and looked at me head on. "I'm not. I'm not sorry for anything I've ever done to make you mine and keep it that way."

My eyes dropped in disappointment.

"You're right...we should have made that decision together. But I was afraid of what you would say. I was afraid of losing you, and you don't fucking understand how much I couldn't deal with that. You have no fucking idea how much I love you."

"I do," I said quietly. "Because it's the way I love you."

It was the first time he took a breath, his emotions smoothing over like a river. "Then forgive me...and let's move on."

"I'm—I'm not ready to do that."

His heart tanked again, the depression spreading through his body like a disease.

His despair broke my heart when I was the one who just had my heart broken.

"I promise I will never keep anything from you ever again. You have my word—"

"You've given me your word before—"

"Our relationship is totally different now."

"I said I need time."

"Larisa—"

"I will forgive you. We will move past it. But right now... I'm just not ready." I gave him the reassurance that he needed, that this relationship was ironclad, that we would be married for as long as we both lived. But I still needed some time to come to terms with the betrayal. "So please give me space. And don't assume anytime I speak to Elias that I'm going to fuck him."

He held my gaze, calm and ferocity both at play at the same time. He seemed to require all his strength to agree. "Alright."

"If you want me to forgive you, then you need to promise me something."

"Anything."

"Promise me that you'll accept whatever I decide." I already knew what my decision was, the only one that would make us both happy. But I needed to know that he would truly make the sacrifice if that was what I wanted, that he would give up something just as important to him as it was to me, that this wasn't a one-sided relationship.

Fear returned, flushing through him like heat. "I would give up everything to be with you. My title. My immortality. My family. Everything. Because you're the single most important thing in the world to me. If that's what you decide, I'll accept it without question. As long as we're together, as long as we can resolve this, the details don't matter."

22

KINGSNAKE

I slept in the four-poster bed alone.

Well, not truly alone, because Fang was there. He stayed on his side of the bed, and I stayed on mine. He was like a dog at the foot, coiled up in a ball, giving off quiet snores when he was in his deepest sleep.

It was still daytime. I could see the light coming through the closed curtains. I found it hard to sleep when my wife was elsewhere. Our honeymoon phase should be in full swing right now, but instead, it felt like we were on the verge of divorce.

I stopped trying to sleep and sat up in bed.

One of Fang's yellow eyes opened.

"You can go to Larisa. You don't have to stay."

I want to stay.

"It's okay, Fang. I know you prefer her company."

Right now, I prefer yoursss.

I rested the back of my head against the headboard and stared at the dead fire.

It'll be alright, Kingsssnake.

"I can't believe he did that to me...my own father."

Sssecrets never die. She would have dissscovered it eventually. And you ssshould have told her.

"Yes, I'm realizing that."

The light lessened, turning a faint blue and bringing the bedchamber into darkness. It was hard to be there, in the very castle where that spineless prick had bedded my wife then left her for someone else. I'd been with lots of other women, but the idea of her being with anyone else...made me sick. Did they fuck in an empty bedroom? The one I lay in that very moment?

A knock sounded on the door. "They're approaching the gate." It was Cobra.

I flung the covers off and got out of bed.

Cobra let himself inside. "Did you sleep at all? You look like shit."

I put on my uniform and my armor, ignoring what he said.

Cobra glanced at the empty bed before he looked at me again. "She'll come around—"

"How many?"

"Twelve," he said. "They must have come to investigate."

"Good. That gives us time for Viper to arrive."

Cobra continued to watch me. "So, what did she say?"

"She's pissed off at me," I snapped. "What do you think she said?"

"But it's not over...right?"

I secured my sword to my hip and grabbed the dagger that I'd left on the nightstand. "No."

He breathed a sigh of relief. "Just sex her up real good, and she'll forget the whole thing—"

"Does it look like she's sleeping with me?"

Now Cobra dropped the topic. "Let's go..."

Fang circled my shoulders, and then we walked out, taking the long hallway toward the front of the castle. We descended the staircase then made it outside, where the ramparts were positioned around the castle. The place was so disheveled and depressing that I wasn't sure what we were fighting for at this point.

We approached the wall, and I spotted Larisa standing next to Elias, her back to me as she looked ahead.

Just seeing them standing next to each other, even if there were several feet in between them, pissed me the fuck off.

She felt my rage because she turned to look at me as if she knew exactly where I was. She locked eyes on me.

I locked eyes on her.

My anger was replaced by a desperate longing. I could try to suppress my emotions around her, but I'd rather she understood just how much I loved her to speed up her forgiveness.

We walked up to her, and it was strange to approach her without sliding my hand into her hair and kissing her. I just had to stand there, look at her like she was a fucking stranger.

Cobra glanced back and forth between us. "How close are they?"

Larisa pulled her gaze off mine and looked at my brother. "Should arrive any moment. Cobra, let me introduce you to King Elias, King of Raventower."

King Elias shook my brother's hand.

I would never touch that fucker.

Larisa looked at me again, as if she felt that sudden burst of rage.

I changed the subject before I said something I shouldn't. "What's the plan?"

"Threats," Larisa said. "What do you know about the werewolves?"

"Not much," I said. "They've always kept to themselves, which is appreciated. They've never participated in political matters of the world. I suspect the sickness has changed all that. At their core, they're human, so this is an excellent time to strive for power."

"How many of them are there?" King Elias asked.

"I just said I didn't know much about them," I snapped.

He stilled at my hostility.

Larisa kept her eyes on me. "We're on the same team, Kingsnake."

"No, we aren't," I snapped. "The only reason I'm here is for you. I don't give a fuck what happens to this prick."

King Elias should cower away, but he remained. "Have I done something to offend you—"

"You fucked my wife."

Larisa closed her eyes, cringing at my outburst. "Kingsnake..."

"And you hurt her." My eyes were reserved for the asshole who was so thin he looked like a little boy. "Yes, you offend me. Your goddamn face offends me. I'm saving your ass when it should be six feet under—"

"*Stop it.*" Larisa grabbed my arm to pull me back to my center. "Werewolves approach the gate, and this is all you care about?"

I turned my gaze on her. "Yes, you're all I care about. No surprise there."

"I care about this village. I care about the people who have suffered while the cure remained at the bottom of my pack. I should have come sooner, and the guilt is suffocating. So, if you care about me, then you'll care about Raventower too. It's the place where I grew up, it's the place where the Golden Serpent bit me in the fields...and brought me to you."

I felt my rage dim slightly.

"So please help me." She pleaded with her eyes, and that was like a hook in my heart. "I need my king..."

"You know you always have my sword, sweetheart." I stared into the eyes of the woman I loved with my whole heart.

And she stared back.

One of the guards shouted from the ramparts. "They're here."

The moment was shattered, and we looked over the edge, seeing the ordinary men approach the gate with the slow gait of arrogance. The previous werewolves had been burned in a fire, and now that was just soot, but the stench of flesh and fur was still in the air. Their leader spotted the campsite and stared, and it seemed to take only a few seconds before he understood what had transpired.

His eyes shifted back to us. "So you've chosen death."

King Elias opened his mouth to speak, but I knew he would only show weakness, so I spoke before he had the opportunity. "As have you—if you don't abandon this crusade."

The werewolf looked at me next, just a glimmer of light still in the sky. "An alliance between men and vampires... This world really is going to shit."

"Leave this village and never return, or suffer the sharpness of my blade."

"You aren't the only ones who need to feed, Kingsnake."

"This isn't about feeding," I said. "This is about power—and don't pretend otherwise."

He showed a smile. "We made a deal with Raventower. They give us humans—or we kill them all. And we keep our word."

"Then keep your word. And I'll keep mine."

The werewolf took a quick look around. "You have no army. A king without an army is just a man. And a single man is no threat to us."

"Just because you can't see an army doesn't mean it's not there. Return with your army and see for yourself."

"I will." That smile remained. "See you soon."

———

"How much time do we have?" Larisa asked.

"A few hours, at most," Cobra said. "I think their den is close."

"I ran into one when I fled from Raventower," Larisa said. "I wasn't very far away."

The first moment we met. I'd felt no attraction or affection —but then I fell madly in love with her.

"When will Viper arrive?" Larisa regarded me next.

"Any moment," I said. "He may arrive at the same time."

"Without the Kingsnake Vampires, we have no chance," King Elias said, looking into the darkness with emptiness in his eyes. "Between the sickness and the werewolves, we're all exhausted. Perhaps we should just surrender or flee."

"We're doing neither of those things." Coward.

"You shouldn't risk your lives for us—"

"But we are," I snapped. "Because my wife has a stronger spine than you'll ever have."

Larisa flashed me her angry stare.

I didn't feel bad for what I said. I didn't say it as a jealous husband, but as a fellow ruler who gave everything I had to my people.

King Elias stared at me. "You have no idea what we've suffered. You have no idea the loss and the anguish we've endured. And when we barely had anything, you marched here and took what few people we had left...and then the werewolves... It never ends. To be perpetually weak and exploited, it's hopeless."

For just a moment, I actually pitied him.

"With the Kingsnake Vampire army, we'll defeat them," Larisa said. "And without them, we'll be able to hold them until the army arrives. Let's prepare for battle." She spoke like a queen, gave orders effortlessly, acted like she'd done this before.

King Elias nodded. "We'll do our best."

———————

A couple hours later, the werewolf army approached.

Viper hadn't arrived yet.

He should have been here by now, so I worried for his well-being as well as my own.

The scout rode his horse through the gate before the doors shut behind him. "A hundred strong."

"That's it?" Cobra asked before he looked at me. "They really did call your bluff, Kingsnake."

"They probably assumed I would call for aid now, and it would take too long for the army to join us." Stupid on their part.

"A hundred is nothing," Cobra said. "We had to deal with ten thousand orcs last time."

"The odds were five-to-one," I said. "But this is a hundred-to-three."

"Four." Larisa appeared, wearing that don't-tell-me-what-to-do expression.

"I don't like those odds," I said to my brother. "We'll need to hold them off until Viper arrives. That trench with fire will only work until the oil is consumed. After that, they'll be climbing up the walls like the dogs that they are."

Cobra gave a nod. "You're right. The two of us will have to take out the ones who do make it over the wall."

"*Three,*" Larisa snapped.

Cobra shifted his gaze back and forth between us before he spoke. "I know you guys are having problems right now, so I'm going to give Kingsnake a break and state the obvious. Larisa, you're decent with the sword, but these are were-wolves. They're orcs with claws, okay?"

"And you forget I'm an Original," she said. "I'm stronger than both of you."

"But not experienced," I said. "Don't take that as an insult."

"Those three werewolves would have killed you if we hadn't gotten here in time," Cobra said. "Kingsnake and I can train you when we have time, but you just aren't as skilled for battle as we are. It's nothing personal."

"Then what would you have me do?" she snapped. "Go eat a snack?"

"Just don't put yourself in harm's way," I said. "Because then I'm going to have to save you. What do you want me to focus on? Winning, or protecting you?"

I knew she was offended by all of this, hurt that she wasn't truly one of us because her skills paled in comparison to ours. But she took it in stride and gave a slight nod. "Fine. But if they bust through that gate, I'll have no other choice but to fight."

"Viper will be here before that happens," I said, knowing nothing would stop my brother from reaching us when we called for aid.

"They're here." King Elias was in his full uniform and armor, his helmet protecting his head.

I looked over the edge and saw all the torches they carried. Werewolves could see in the dark, so it was an attempt to instill fear in all of us. It didn't work on us, but it probably scared the humans shitless. "Light your arrows and prepare to fire." I stepped on King Elias's toes and ran the show, but he seemed too weak and incompetent to do it himself. "Light the trenches."

We'd had little time to construct the trenches around the wall, so they weren't very deep, but it was something. One of the archers lit the arrow and fired it into the trenches, and quickly, the spark turned into flames that sprinted down the trench to the opposite end. The flames leaped up high, and the heat was so strong I could feel it from where I stood.

Larisa came to my side, Fang wrapped around her shoulders.

"I can't believe I'm fighting beside humans."

"A part of us will always be human." She turned her head to regard me, reminding me of a conversation we had in Evanguard. "Right?"

I stared into those brilliant eyes and saw a fire stronger than the one that warmed my skin through my armor. I bathed in her confidence, soaked in her intensity. If an army of werewolves weren't marching on the gate, I'd cup her face and kiss her. "Right."

They stopped behind the barrier of fire, a line of werewolves with open jaws, staring right at me as if I was the one they needed to destroy. The flames were as tall as they were, but that would only last for a couple minutes. The flames would recede with every passing minute, becoming weaker as the oil was spent.

"Fire."

The archers shot their arrows through the flames and struck a few. The light from the blaze must have been too bright for the werewolves to see what was coming, because we hit a few of them and made them collapse right on top of the fire. The fire burned hotter as it consumed the extra fuel.

"*Hoooowwwwwlllll.*"

"*Hoowwwll.*"

They howled into the night, their battle cry.

"Now we pissed them off," Cobra said from beside me.

"Fine by me." I walked down the rampart in the opposite direction and peered into the darkness, hoping to see an army of vampires on horses, to hear the sound of a thousand hooves.

But nothing was there.

———

Our fires took out a decent number of the werewolves, but the flames burned too low, and the first one crossed the threshold. Then the next and then next. Soon, they were all running for the gate.

"Shit." I hadn't thought they would make it this far.

Cobra pulled out his bow and started to fire.

"Fire!" I shouted. "Fire as quickly as you can."

Arrows rained down on the attackers, some aflame and some not, missing their mark and sometimes hitting them in the flesh. But now that they were close, they were invigorated to keep going, to scale the wall and rip off our heads.

Dozens of them made it to the wall and started to climb.

Protect her.

Yeesssss.

I moved to Larisa, positioning myself in front of her so I could kill any werewolf that came close to her.

They made it over the edge and swiped down the guards with their massive claws. Blood-curdling screams pierced the night. Entails dropped onto the ramparts. I kicked back the first one who came over the edge then sliced my blade through the neck of another. Cobra did the same, pushing back as many of them as he could before we lost more archers.

Larisa moved past me and went for one herself, slicing him across the chest then the face before she kicked him back. Another one came up to her side, and Fang was quick to jump and rip his eye out of his face. The werewolf collapsed as Fang gave him another gash on the neck.

Covering my ass and looking out for my wife at the same time was no picnic.

More of them started to pour over the edge.

"Where the fuck is he?" Cobra took down one and then another, but two more appeared from nowhere.

I wanted to ask Larisa to run, but she would never abandon me or her duty.

More of our guards died. King Elias wasn't in sight.

Everything went to shit.

I killed the ones who came for me, already exhausted because Cobra and I were doing all the work so the archers could keep firing. Larisa helped, but she only took out the ones who slipped past us.

Then they stopped climbing over the wall.

"*Hooowwwwlllll!*"

"*Hooowll!*"

"What's happening?" Cobra yelled.

I looked over the edge and...relief.

Viper charged with the army of Kingsnake Vampires behind him. They rushed and chased down the were-wolves on horseback. Other soldiers jumped off their horses and took down the beasts on foot. It was a slaughter, the werewolves outnumbered and with no escape.

Cobra wiped the sweat from his forehead. "Finally..."

Viper wiped the blood from his sword on the fur of his most recent enemy when we approached.

"Took you long enough," Cobra said as we walked up. "What did take you so long?"

Viper only gave him a hard stare.

I clapped him on the shoulder. "Thank you for coming."

"I kept these ones alive in case you wanted to question them," he said. "I'll attend to our wounded and prepare the army for departure." He walked off.

Cobra watched him go. "Why's he in such a hurry?"

A line of three werewolves were on the ground, all bound and in human form. They were the ones who'd run first, which meant they were the most cowardly and, therefore, more likely to talk.

I kicked the first one. "So, here's how this is going to go. You're all going to be killed whether you talk or not. But the one who does talk will get a quick death, my blade straight through their neck in one hit. The ones who don't talk...will be covered in oil then set on fire. Your choice—"

"What do you want to know?" the first one asked, purposely avoiding the stare of the comrades he'd just screwed over.

I nodded to Cobra. "Take care of these two."

"No!" One of them resisted and tried to fight off Cobra.

Larisa kicked him in the head, and that shut him up.

Cobra flashed her a grin before he grabbed him away. "I'll come back for the other one."

The one who remained didn't look pale as a ghost. He looked green as vomit.

I focused on mine. "Are the werewolves doing this to other villages?"

"Yes," he answered immediately. "The Werewolf King is taking the kingdoms for his own. He started with the smaller villages, but he has made it to the Capital."

All of this had happened right under our noses, and we had no idea. "Why?"

"Why not?" he answered. "Why be ruled by humans when humans can be ruled by werewolves?"

"When did this happen?"

"A month ago," he answered.

"I didn't realize there were so many of you."

"We have many different factions. That's why we lie low, so you won't know the threat we really are."

Just when I thought we were at the end of this journey, everything became more complicated. We couldn't walk in there and disperse the cure, not when a werewolf sat on the throne. It was in their best interest to keep the humans sick. "You can eat them even if they're infected."

"Yes."

Shit.

I heard the scream of his comrade when he was lit on fire. But the screams were brief because he either blacked out or died immediately. I kept my eyes on the werewolf who had fully cooperated. "How many of you are there?"

"Hard to say...but at least ten thousand."

I released a sigh. I couldn't look the other way, none of us could, because the werewolves would become so strong that they would come for us next. They'd also gained a monopoly on our food source. This was bad.

Cobra grabbed the other one and dragged him to the stake next.

I had no other questions. "What can you tell me about the Werewolf King?"

After a long pause, he answered. "He's ruthless. Even more ruthless than you are."

The only way we would drive the werewolves out of the kingdoms was if we all banded together. Vampires. Ethereal. Even orcs. "I have no other questions."

———

I walked up to Viper. "We have a problem. The werewolves have invaded the kingdoms. Ten thousand strong. This all happened while we were focused on finding the cure and dealing with the Ethereal—"

"We don't have time for this, Kingsnake. Grab your shit, and let's move out."

"Did you not hear what I said—"

"Our scouts informed me that the Originals have left Crescent Falls and are riding hard in the direction of Evanguard. Unable to communicate with you, I wasn't sure what to do, if I should ride straight to the Ethereal or come to your aid. You know what I picked. The battle was quick, so we may still have time to beat Father before he gets there."

I blinked several times—that was how long it took me to digest what he'd said. "He's going to kill them all."

"Yes."

Another thought popped into my head immediately. "That's why he told Larisa..."

"Told Larisa what?"

"About being mortal. He knew she would be upset...and I would be so distracted that I wouldn't notice his exit."

Viper gave a nod in agreement. "You're probably right."

He'd sabotaged my marriage to get what he wanted. Risked his son losing his wife so he could kill innocent people. My father was a ruthless man, but I hadn't realized he was devoid of all emotion. "We'll head out immediately."

———

I found Larisa bandaging one of the guards.

King Elias was beside them, flat on his back with a gauze wrapped around his shoulder where he'd received a nasty cut from their claws. He looked pale, as if an infection was setting in.

"Larisa."

"Yes?" She continued her work securing the gauze.

"We have to leave."

"Now?" She got to her feet, a line of men still needing her attention.

"Yes. I'm sorry."

"Then I'll stay behind—"

"What exactly did my father say to you?"

She stilled at my abrupt question.

Cobra walked up at that moment, his eyes shifting back and forth between us.

"He asked me to convince you to pursue the Ethereal," she said. "It was a lengthy conversation."

"And you said no."

She nodded. "I told him their execution wouldn't bring back the people we'd lost."

So, he'd tried a different approach, then resorted to the unthinkable last. "Viper just informed me that my father and the Originals are riding hard for Evanguard."

Cobra's eyes snapped wide open.

"I suspect he told you about my secret because he knew it would rip us apart. I would be so forlorn by our estrangement that I wouldn't notice his movements." The betrayal was like acid on my tongue. Vengeance for my mother was more important than his current relationship with his son.

"He rides on Evanguard as we speak?" Cobra asked.

"Yes." I turned to him. "Grab your supplies and your horse. We need to leave immediately."

Cobra took off at a run. He would probably head out before the rest of us, determined to get there as quickly as possible.

I didn't try to stop him. Nothing would stop me if it were Larisa. "I can leave you here with a few men, if you'd like." I didn't know what would happen once I arrived in Evanguard. I hoped bloodshed would be spared in place of reason, but my father had stabbed me in the back, so why would he listen to me? It might turn into a war. Maybe it was better if she stayed. "I can leave Fang here with you."

I assumed she would take the offer immediately, to enjoy her space from me, but she didn't. "I want to help here at Raventower. King Elias informed me that a lot of citizens have fled to live in the wilderness because they felt unsafe in the city. The wounded need care, and I used to be a healer. But...I can't leave you."

Her words made my heart open like a flower.

"I'm not sure how much help you would be if you came. The only people who can reason with him are my brothers and me. And if I can't, then it'll turn into a battle...and I'd rather you not be there if that's what happens."

Her eyes dropped to her chest as she took a breath, thinking about her options.

I stared at her lips, the way they pressed tightly together when she was deep in thought. The armor was so snug on her alluring body. It always gave me chills when I saw her in it, a woman so strong and soft at the same time.

Her eyes lifted to mine again, probably feeling the rush of arousal that flushed through me. "Then I'll stay. There's a lot of work to do here."

I was both disappointed and relieved at the same time. "I'll leave Fang with you. That way, we can keep in touch."

"I know your father has done terrible things, but he would never hurt you or your brothers."

"I'd like to believe that as well, but I'm not sure anymore." I wasn't sure of anything anymore—except this. There was distance between us, but the thread that kept us together remained unbreakable. A million things could have ripped us apart already, but we always held on.

"I'll heal those that I can. Gather up the missing villagers. Bring them back to full health. We'll need all the help we can get to take back the kingdoms from the werewolves."

I nodded. "I'll come back for you. But I won't leave you unless you make me a promise."

"Alright."

"If the werewolves return, I want you to take a horse and run."

Her stare was empty.

"I don't think they will. But I need to know that you'll run if they do. We would have lost that last battle without our army, so there's no way you would be able to handle another assault with nothing but weak and injured soldiers. And it's not worth dying for."

She finally gave a nod. "I promise."

"Then I'll leave you." I turned away without saying good-bye, prepared to grab my horse and ride away without looking back.

Her hand grabbed me by the arm.

A flush of joy moved through my chest, relaxed all the muscles in my shoulders.

She tugged me back to her as she rose on her tiptoes, cupping my face so she could kiss me.

The second I felt her mouth on mine, my arm hooked around the small of her back, and I tugged her into me, squeezing her hard armor against mine, not feeling her flesh but her curves.

It was the best kiss we'd ever had, an ache between our lips, a desperation that showed the depth of our love in the midst of turmoil. My aches and pains faded away, some from the battle we'd just fought and some from the battle of our heartbreak. My hand dug into her hair, and I continued the kiss like no one else was there, like it was just the two of us locked in our newlywed bliss.

She pulled away, her forehead against mine. "I love you."

"I fucking love you."

23

CLARA

Cobra had been gone for weeks.

I thought of him every day he was gone, longing to see his face, to see that smile as he made some inappropriate comment. His absence was supposed to help ease my decision, but it only swayed me even more.

How could I have fallen for a man so deeply, so quickly?

Did that make it less real?

Or more?

My brethren spent their time making their own decisions about their mortality. Some had become so comfortable with immortality that becoming a nightwalker was their only choice. Others chose to live out the rest of their lives as humans. And others...chose to opt out altogether. Too horrified by the reason they were alive, they chose to take their own lives and pass on the way they should have thousands of years ago.

The Ethereal way of life was over now.

We would divide into two groups, half of us joining the Kingsnake Vampires in their coastal town, while the other humans would remain in this forest or find a new life in the kingdoms. It would never be the same. It already wasn't the same.

Now that I no longer had a study, I sat at a table near two mighty trunks. Since the Ethereal were about to be disbanded forever, it didn't seem necessary to have a throne or an office... or anything at all. We'd already become a disorganized people.

Down the path, one of the guards ran, coming straight for me.

My chest tightened, and I rose to my feet, knowing a guard wouldn't run toward me unless it was important. "What is it?" I asked before he fully stopped.

"The Originals march on Evanguard." He spoke through his labored breaths, exhausted from the run and the heavy armor that weighed him down. It was white like an iridescent pearl, but heavy like a stone.

Fear dropped into my stomach like a boulder. "You must be mistaken."

"They bear the black armor."

The Originals were far more difficult than the Kingsnake and Cobra vampires. Their strength was more substantial. Their movements were quicker too.

"We signed a truce," he said. "And they go back on their word this quickly?"

"The truce was with the Kingsnake and Cobra vampires... not the Originals." They hadn't violated any of the terms, but they must have told their father, King Serpentine, the truth of the obelisk and our crimes...and he wanted revenge.

The guard waited for orders.

I was in too much shock to speak.

"Will the Kingsnake and Cobra vampires come to our aid?"

"Yes—if they're aware." I could send a missive now, but by the time they received it and left their kingdoms, the Originals would have already attacked. "They must not know what's going on."

He continued to wait for orders. "Send a missive to Kingsnake and ask for aid. Even if he receives it too late, at least he'll have been alerted to what's happening. In the meantime, prepare every Ethereal for war. The Originals may be stronger than us, but we still have the numbers to challenge them."

He took off at a dead run to fulfill my orders.

I fetched my sword and armor, terrified of what would come next.

———

I chose to meet the Originals for battle rather than remain hidden in our forest. If King Serpentine couldn't attack us directly, he would inflict his wrath on the forest, and we would all rather die than let the trees and creatures suffer because of our misdeeds. So there we stood, lined up for battle, some on horseback and others on foot.

They had already crossed the desert and the arid lands and approached across the open valleys. They started off as black dots in the distance, but then their shapes became more distinct, their darkness a direct contrast to the greenery they stomped on. The closer they came, the harder my heart worked.

My pulse was in my ears.

I knew Cobra would never abandon me. I knew Kingsnake wouldn't take back his word. They hadn't deserted us. They were just unaware of our plight. And by the time they realized it, we would probably be wiped from this earth. We had the numbers to meet them in battle, but we didn't have the strength nor the ferocity any longer.

King Serpentine was pissed, and he wouldn't stop until my head was on the ground.

"Queen Clara!" I turned to my commander, who was positioned at the edge of our forces.

Then I spotted it—a lone rider on horseback. They came from the north, rather than the west. They were astride a brown stallion, and it rode hard, like death chased him from the rear. I turned my horse to get a better look, no longer interested in the army that charged right at me.

As he drew closer, I spotted the dark brown hair...and the brown eyes.

"Cobra."

I dismounted my horse and prepared to receive him.

He didn't slow his horse until he was just feet away from me. He pulled hard on the reins and made his horse take a few steps backward before he jumped down from the steed. He nearly fumbled when he hit the ground, like he was exhausted, like he'd ridden night and day to reach me. "Kingsnake and Viper are right behind me with the army. We didn't know of my father's departure until long after he left." He was nearly out of breath even though the horse had done all the running. "I'm so sorry I didn't stop it—"

"You're here." I moved into his arms and hugged him. "That's all that matters."

He hugged me back, gripping me fiercely.

We indulged in the hug longer than we should, clinging to each other for seconds.

I was the one who pulled away first.

"We had to tell him," he said. "He already suspected everything."

I nodded. "I understand. You shouldn't have to lie about our transgressions. We take responsibility for the crimes we committed—even if we were unaware of them at the time. We are happy to make reparations—if your father is willing to listen."

"You destroyed the obelisk," he said. "Those are your reparations."

I turned to look at him in the distance, seeing how much ground their horses had already covered. "With both our armies, we should prevail. But I'd rather not slay your father—as would you. I know what it's like to have your father killed in battle—even if he did deserve it. I don't want that for you."

His eyes softened, turning into clouds heavy with rain.

"Perhaps we can speak to him."

"I know he's unreasonable right now, but I don't think he'd ever hurt me or my brothers."

I nodded. "I agree. Otherwise, he'd be a lunatic."

Cobra climbed back onto his horse. "Let's ride together."

I moved back onto my white mare, and we left the line of Ethereals and moved into the grasslands between us. We brought the horses to a stop and waited for his father to meet us. As we stood there, the beating hooves grew louder, and the earth trembled.

Cobra and I didn't speak to each other, just stared at the oncoming vampires.

My heart raced in unease, seeing these powerful night-walkers coming to destroy my brethren and my home.

Cobra must have heard my racing heart because he said, "I won't let anything happen to you, baby." He said it without looking at me, his eyes focused ahead.

His father came into view, wearing shiny black armor and a helmet that obstructed most of his face other than his eyes. His armor was similar to that which the others wore, but his plates had more intricate designs. On his chest was a Golden Serpent.

All he did to slow his army was raise one hand.

They all stopped. Every single one of them.

He moved ahead, bringing his horse to a slow walk. He took his time, eyes locked on Cobra's. It was like I wasn't even there, which was fine by me. He finally stopped the horse, and his gaze bored into his son's face.

Cobra stared right back.

Neither man spoke. The horses flicked their tails and shifted their weight. It was quiet, too quiet.

King Serpentine broke the silence. "Get out of my way, Cobra."

"No."

"You think you're enough to stop me?"

"Since I'm your son, I hope so."

The staring contest resumed.

"That was fucked up, what you did," Cobra said. "Screwing Kingsnake over like that."

"I taught him a lesson. Never keep secrets from your wife —because she always finds out. He should have been the man I raised him to be and spoke the truth without hesitation. If she left, then she wasn't right for him anyway."

"That's bullshit, and you know it," he said. "You just wanted him to be distracted."

He stared for a while. "A king is never distracted from his people. That was his error—not mine."

I had no idea what they spoke of. Perhaps I would ask later...if there was a later.

"You've come to Evanguard to murder innocent people," Cobra said. "They had no association with what transpired here."

"They're still alive, aren't they?" King Serpentine shifted his stare to me. "I know Clara has lived a very long eighteen hundred years. She's older than you. Even older than me." His look was full of disgust, like I was maggots in rotting flesh. "Your mother's soul may be the very reason her flesh is so soft." He turned back to Cobra. "Did you think of that? That this woman is only here because your mother is dead."

Cobra continued to grip the reins of his horse. Upright and stiff, he stared, but he had nothing to say.

"We've destroyed the source of our immortality to atone for what our government has decided on our behalf. We're mortals now, and once the souls no longer fuel our bodies, we'll grow weak and become human. Then we'll age...and we'll die. That's the most I can give you in repentance."

His eyes shifted back to me. "And that's not enough."

"It has to be enough," Cobra said. "Because there's nothing else that can be done."

"These monsters have attacked us for a millennium—"

"King Elrohir has been slain, as well as the generals who followed him. Anyone associated with that line has since been put to death. You need to let it go, Father. If Kingsnake, Viper, and I can pardon their sins—so can you. We fought in all of those wars as well. We've lost vampires we cared for as much as you have. If you want to destroy the Ethereal, then you'll have to destroy me too, because I will fight with them against you."

King Serpentine had nothing to say to that.

I heard the sound of many horses and knew that Kingsnake had arrived with his army. They took up ranks with their former enemies and stood with us against our assailant. It loosened the stitch in my chest because I wouldn't lose any more of my people today.

A pair of horses approached us from behind. Kingsnake appeared beside me on Cobra's right while Viper moved to the opposite side.

Now I felt like I didn't belong in this conversation at all.

King Serpentine stared at his sons, looking at each one individually.

I imagined they all stared back at him with the same kind of stare.

Cobra spoke again. "You'll have to kill all three of us first if you want Evanguard that bad."

King Serpentine ignored his words and stared at me. His face showed no emotion, just the way his sons' did, but I knew there was lava running from the backs of his eyes. He held me accountable for every sin—even though I was the one who'd stopped the travesties.

"I'm truly sorry for what my kind has done," I said. "There's nothing more I can give you than the promise of eternal peace and the destruction of the obelisk. Cobra is right. Killing us won't change anything."

"Doesn't mean you deserve to live," King Serpentine said. "I've been called a monster countless times, but I've never taken someone's afterlife, only their blood. If I were you, I would take a dagger to my own heart and end it."

"*Father*," Cobra said.

"For the last time," I said, keeping my voice steady. "I did not commit these crimes. Nor did the people who stand behind me. At the first chance, I righted our sins and destroyed the obelisk. If someone else were in the same position, I'm not sure they would have done the same. You may not like me, and that's okay, but you must admit that I didn't give in to temptation when someone else would have."

King Serpentine looked at Cobra again, as if he knew something I didn't catch. "Now this makes sense. You're fucking her."

Cobra said nothing.

I remembered what he'd told me about the Originals, that they could feel minds. King Serpentine must have felt whatever was in his son's head at that moment.

"No, I'm not fucking her." Cobra chose to deny it. "*I love her.*"

I kept my eyes straight ahead, but a lightning strike surged through my body. My world shook at the declaration, the way he confessed it, not only to his father, but his two brothers as well, something he hadn't even shared with me.

"I will protect her with my life," Cobra continued. "And I will protect her people like they are my own. I wish to part as allies rather than fight as enemies on this field, but I will unsheathe my blade and draw blood against you if you leave me no other choice."

"So you choose her over me," King Serpentine quipped. "Over your own family."

"No," Cobra said. "I choose right over wrong."

A stare-down ensued.

Kingsnake spoke next. "While you've been obsessing over the Ethereal, the werewolves have taken the kingdoms. The Werewolf King sits upon the throne, turning the humans into his subjects."

King Serpentine shifted his gaze to his other son.

"They can eat the infected without consequence," Kingsnake said. "So there's nothing stopping them from growing stronger, while everyone else grows weaker. If we don't cure the humans, we'll run out of food. This is what takes precedence, not this ridiculous vendetta. We need allies if we're to defeat the werewolves. We just conquered a small army of a hundred of them—and they're strong. Stronger than orcs. We need every soldier available if we're to eradicate these monsters from the throne. The Ethereal will fight beside us, not against us, and I need you to do the same."

The air seemed to change all around us, the hostility drifting away on the moving breeze. The werewolf occupation of the kingdoms was disturbing news, but it was probably the only thing compelling enough to get the attention off the Ethereal.

He stared at his sons, but his mind seemed to be elsewhere. He maintained control of the horse absent-mindedly, his thoughts focused on a land far from where we stood.

"The Ethereal will help you restore the kingdoms to what they were," I said. "In exchange, we want peace with the Originals."

"You aren't entitled to requests," King Serpentine said coldly. "Your participation is the least you could do—and you'll do it." He looked at Cobra again. "When we defeat the werewolves, I want sovereignty over the kingdoms."

"You're already a king, Father," Cobra said.

"If you want me to pardon the Ethereal and grant them everlasting peace, that's my price."

"So the only thing that will replace the void of Mother's death is power?" Kingsnake asked incredulously. "That's an equal trade to you?"

King Serpentine gave his son a cold stare. "Nothing will ever be comparable, Kingsnake. But that is my price. We liberate the humans from the werewolf rule and then—"

"You subject them," Cobra said. "That's not a liberation."

"The humans will live their normal lives as they did before," King Serpentine said. "But when I need something, they deliver. I'm much more preferable to the barbaric dog who must have cast a rain cloud over the kingdoms."

"Why can't we live the way we did before?" Kingsnake said. "Without the Ethereal, we'll be at peace—"

"Because the humans can rise up at any time and march on our borders," King Serpentine said. "They're weaker than us, but they also outnumber us. This is my price. Take it, or fight the werewolves on your own."

The Originals were the strongest vampires. A fight would be much more difficult without them, especially when we needed every soldier we could find.

The brothers didn't speak aloud, but they exchanged expressions like they had a conversation in silence. A few nods were exchanged before Kingsnake spoke. "Fine."

"Then our armies will meet in Grayson before we march forward," King Serpentine said. "I'll call the Diamondbacks to our aid from the mountains. I'll see you there." He tugged on the reins and aimed his horse back to his army. "Head out!"

They directed their horses in the opposite direction and took off at a run, their dark colors becoming less distinct as they rode away over the valleys. The sound of a thousand hooves slowly became quieter the farther they traveled.

I took my first full breath since this had begun, relieved that my people wouldn't have to fight on a battlefield today. We'd already suffered so much grief. We didn't need more, especially when we no longer felt like Ethereal at all.

"I'm sorry my father is such an asshole," Cobra said to me.

"It's fine," I said. "I know how that goes."

"Where's Larisa?" Cobra asked next.

"Raventower," Kingsnake answered. "She wanted to stay behind and tend to the injured and find the other residents who have fled into the wilderness. Fang is with her."

"I'm sorry," Cobra said.

"It's okay," Kingsnake said. "We'll be fine."

"Let's rest here for the day," Viper said. "Then we'll return to Grayson at sunset. Kingsnake, you can grab Larisa and meet us there. Queen Clara, your army can join us, and we'll move together."

"Clara is fine."

We directed our horses back to the line, and my people were already relaxed and off their horses, relieved that the attack had been averted. Everyone disbanded and returned to the forest, leading their horses behind them.

I got to the ground, and someone took my horse. I'd barely had my feet on the ground when Cobra was on me, his arm circling my waist as his lips scooped mine into a kiss.

He squeezed me to him, his hands moving into my hair to push it from my face. "I missed you."

Words left me because that kiss was so profound. No one had ever kissed me that way, not even Cobra. My hand went to his wrist, and I looked into those earthy eyes. "I love you too."

———

We went straight to bed. Clothes and armor were dropped on the floor. Our swords were placed on the dining table, side by side. The second our bodies were reunited, everything felt right again. It was as if no time had passed, but our bodies absorbed each other like it'd been a lifetime of separation.

He didn't ask permission before he sank his teeth into my neck, but he didn't need to. That scorching pleasure burst through me, from my fingers to my toes, and I felt high in the clouds.

Hours passed that way, neither one of us speaking, the sun moving across the sky and changing the shadows in the room. While his brothers slept and recovered from their journey, Cobra recovered from his withdrawal.

We finally finished, drops of blood on my pillow, our bodies tangled together under the sheets. His arm was hooked around my waist with my leg hiked over his hip, my wet sex right against his skin.

Fatigue was in his eyes, but he continued to stare at me.

"I'll be here when you wake up." My fingers lightly touched his lips, feeling the thick stubble that had grown over the last few days.

"I want you to always be there when I wake up." The question was in his eyes, but he didn't ask it with his lips. He gave me the option to deflect if I wasn't ready to face it.

But my answer was easy to give. "I'll marry you."

His focused expression immediately relaxed, and slowly that handsome smile came into his face, a lightness in his eyes that rivaled the sun on a cloudless day. No one had ever looked at me like that, like I was intrinsic to their happiness.

"And...I'll turn."

24

LARISA

I went into the deserted town and found the old apothecary shop, which had been abandoned in light of the werewolf invasion. The stock room was full of medicine and herbs, critical for sickness and flesh wounds, but useless against the sickness that had claimed the lives of so many.

I gathered everything and returned to the castle to administer the medications to everyone who showed signs of infection, including King Elias. Several men had died in the attack, but most of them were only wounded. I worked to heal them all, and I instantly had flashbacks to my time in Raventower, when I'd become the city healer because I was the only one who couldn't get sick.

My whole life had been this castle. Changing the sheets on the beds and dusting every surface to keep it immaculate.

And bedding the prince when everyone was dead asleep. I wasn't that person anymore, and it was hard to believe I ever had been.

The healthy soldiers had been sent out to find the villagers who had fled and bring them back to the castle now that it was safe. I hoped their endeavor would be successful, because Raventower felt lifeless without them.

How is he? I spoke to Fang with my mind rather than out loud, so no one would know I could speak to snakes. Might terrify them.

They stopped the attack. Convinced their father to join them in the fight againsst the were-wolvesss.

Oh, that's a relief.

Cobra and Viper will return to Grayson with their armies, as well as the Ethereal, to prepare for battle.

And Kingsnake?

He'sss on hisss way here now.

Good.

He'sss asssked about you many timesss.

I'm sure he has.

I moved into King Elias's room. He was in bed, pale and gray, sweat on his forehead. He was in and out of consciousness, coming to whenever the pain medication wore off. When I approached his bed, he gave a quick jolt.

"It's me," I said gently. "I found that medicine I was looking for..."

He pushed the sheets off himself, revealing the gauze wrapped around his shoulder and chest.

The wound was much better. We were able to beat the infection before it set in. Instead of looking greenish with pus, it was only swollen with inflammation. The skin had started to turn back to its normal color. "It's looking good."

"Then why does it hurt so much?"

I poured the serum into a spoon and fed it to him. "This will take away the pain and knock you out for a long time. I would do your business now, and when you wake up, you should feel a lot better."

"Thanks." His eyes were on the ceiling, never on me.

"We're going to move against the werewolves after we regroup. Remove them from the kingdoms so the humans will have their lives back. I've administered the cure to everyone here, including you, so you don't need to worry about getting sick from the plague any longer."

"If I survive this..."

"You will, Elias. It might take a few more days." I secured the gauze again and adjusted the pressure.

"It seems like you and your husband are having problems."

That heaviness returned to my heart. "It happens. We'll work it out."

"Do you...like being a vampire?"

"It was a hard adjustment at first, but I've come to embrace it."

"So...you've fed?"

"I have."

Now his eyes shifted to me.

"Don't worry, I'm not interested in feeding on you, Elias. You don't exactly look appetizing."

He released a breath.

"Kingsnake is on his way to pick me up. We'll return to Grayson before we attack."

"And what should we do?"

"I don't think anyone here is in any position to fight, unfortunately. The soldiers are searching for the villagers in the wilderness. Hopefully they find them. You'll need someone to attend to you while I'm gone."

"Don't worry about me. You've done enough, Larisa. Raventower was mine to defend...and I failed."

"Raventower will always be my home, so it was mine to defend as well." My hand lightly touched his shoulder, giving him affection before I departed.

"I want you to know...I regretted my decision the moment I made it."

I stared into his eyes before I slowly pulled my hand away.

"Yes, I was attracted to her, but that quickly wore off. Soon, I saw a woman who used me as an opportunity to elevate herself, as well as her family. When I'd speak, her eyes would glaze over like she only partially listened. If I was in a bad mood, she didn't even notice—because she never paid attention. If she were alive now, I don't think she would tend to me the way you have. I was tempted by the crown...but that crown meant nothing in the end." His eyes shifted away, as if in embarrassment. "I should have given it up for you. I should have walked away from it all. I'm not sure why I'm telling you this..."

An epiphany struck me, one that left me quiet for a moment. "You want closure...because we both know this is the last time we'll ever see each other."

———

The soldiers found other villagers and brought them back to Raventower. More started to arrive, somehow hearing the news that the werewolves had been driven out. Instead of empty streets and homes, the town started to fill with people who had lived there for generations.

Larisssa.

"Yes?" I stood in front of the castle, looking at the activity in the village. The torches were lit, and the sun started to set farther over the horizon. Soon, it would be completely dark. That meant Kingsnake was on his way and would be here soon.

I wisssh to ssspeak my mind. Fang was on the ground beside me, his head perched up to stare at the town.

"I'm listening." I turned to regard him, using a damp cloth to clean underneath my fingernails and scrub my skin until every ounce of grime was gone. My hands hadn't been dirty like this in a long time, heavy from attending to the sick and dying.

I tried to convince him to tell you—but he was ssscared. Ssscared you would leave him and he would have no other choice but to follow. He would have to leave behind hisss brothersss and hisss father...and me.

I continued to stare.

I told him you would ssstay. To have faith in your commitment.

"It sounds like you're ratting him out..."

His lie wasn't maliciousss. He just wanted to protect what you have.

I continued to stare at him.

I can't feel his sssorrow the way you can, but I can see it. I can sssee it—and it hurtsss.

————

Kingsnake approached the gate.

I left the castle and went to the wall. The guards had just opened the gate, and Kingsnake's black stallion entered Raventower, carrying his mighty rider upon his back.

I knew the moment he noticed me because a tidal wave of emotion swelled in his chest at the sight of me. He jumped off the horse and approached me, tall and powerful in his armor, his dark eyes gripping me like anxious hands. His intensity deepened the closer he came, his affection wrapping around me and smothering me. He stopped directly in front of me but didn't touch me, his greeting the emotions he knew I could feel.

"You would do it for me?" I said quietly.

It took a moment for him to understand my train of thought, like he hadn't expected those to be my first words. He shifted his eyes away for a second, drawing a deep breath like this conversation was perverse. "Yes."

"You would have children with me? Live one life with me?"

Another breath. "Is that what you've decided?"

"Yes."

Disappointment rushed through him, not just in his eyes, but in his heart. "Then I have no other choice...because I'd rather live one lifetime with you than a thousand lifetimes without you."

Elias had refused to give up his power to be with me. But Kingsnake didn't. That was when I knew I'd found the right man. "As much as I want children...I don't want to lose you. This time together has blown by like the blink of an eye. I know a single lifetime would pass the same way."

The disappointment was replaced by a glorious sunrise in his chest. His eyes lightened subtly as he looked at me. "Forgive me."

I didn't feel an ounce of bitterness. An ounce of resentment. I appreciated him more than I ever had. "I wish you could feel what I feel every time you step into a room." His heart had exploded the moment he'd seen me, and I wished he knew that my heart had done the exact same thing. "Of course I forgive you."

25

COBRA

"I need to travel to the Mountain to fetch my army. It's an arduous journey, so you should stay here." I didn't want to part from her so soon, leave her in Grayson without my companionship, but she needed to rest before the battle. Her blood was more invigorating than any sleep I could ever get. "Viper will be at your disposal."

She looked like she wanted to challenge my decision but probably realized it was the most logical.

"I would marry you now, but I want Kingsnake to be there."

"You want to marry now?" she asked. "Maybe it should wait until after the great war—"

"I may not survive the great war. This moment is all we have. I'd rather not squander it. And I'd rather marry you as a human...then turn you afterward."

"You're going to turn me before the battle?"

"It's the greatest protection you could have. It's been weeks since the obelisk was destroyed. Your glow is duller than it used to be. Your strength already wanes." She would be much stronger as a nightwalker, especially against foes several feet taller than her. "Unless you've changed your mind—"

"No." Her heart rate was slow like water that dripped from a broken faucet. "But you can't die, Cobra. Cursed to live an eternity without you...I couldn't bear it."

"I'll do my best, baby." I kissed her, held her in front of the double doors to the palace, felt so much peace it was as if the world had stopped. For the first time in my life, I had something to live for, something better than booze and nameless women.

But it was also terrifying, because now I had something to lose. "I love you."

She looked at me with those brilliant green eyes, her hair flowing in the wind, and said the words back to me with such conviction. "I love you too."

———

I took the secret tunnel back to the Mountain. It was the ideal path to take because sun exposure wasn't a concern, but it was narrow, so only so many horses could fit side by side. Traveling under the open sky was easier, less claustrophobic.

When I arrived at the Mountain, I spoke to my general. "It's a very long story, but prepare our army for war. The werewolves have taken the kingdoms, and it's time we take them back. We ride to Grayson."

He showed his surprise but didn't bother me with questions. "Yes, Your Highness."

"And release all the humans. They're free to come and go as they please."

He'd been in the process of turning away, but now he did a double take. "What did you say?"

"Release the prey."

"That's our food source—"

"There will always be volunteers."

"For you. But not for the rest of us—"

"Follow my orders, or I'll find someone who will." Once this battle was won and our lives resumed, I would bring my new bride to her home—and she would be repulsed by the practice. Even if she were a vampire herself, seeing us cage an entire town within our walls would seem barbaric to her. She might leave me—and I couldn't bear that. "We'll figure out a way. We always do."

26

CLARA

I tried on the white gown the seamstress presented, two slender straps over my shoulders with a deep cut down the front. There was a high slit up one leg, similar to the dress I'd worn once I'd become queen. When I looked in the mirror, I wondered how I would look once I became one of them. Pale. Lifeless. Cold.

A knock sounded on the door.

"Come in."

Larisa stepped inside. She was in a black dress and boots, no longer in her uniform like she'd been in Grayson for a while. "Wow. That looks stunning on you."

"Thank you." I forced a smile as our eyes met in the mirror. "When did you and Kingsnake arrive?"

"Early this morning. He's still asleep." She came farther into the room, looking at me from the front without the use of the mirror. "You look beautiful. I know Cobra will have a lot to say when he sees you."

"Yes, that man is quite the talker."

Larisa released a quiet chuckle. "I didn't realize you were getting married."

"Cobra wanted to have the ceremony before the battle. Wanted to marry me before...you know."

"I'm sorry, I don't know."

"Before he turns me into one of you." I looked at my reflection in the mirror again.

Larisa stared at me for a while before she took a seat in the armchair. "I detect sadness in your voice."

"It's not sadness. It's... I'm not sure what it is."

"Fear."

I looked at her head on.

"I felt the same way. I wasn't sure if I wanted to be turned, but then Kingsnake didn't have a choice."

"And you've come around since?"

"I have," she said with a nod. "Even if I could change it, I wouldn't. I hope that gives you some reassurance."

"It does. Thank you."

We fell into silence.

I looked into the mirror for a while. "I almost married a man who didn't love me. Now I'm marrying a man I've known for a very short time. It feels right...but I wonder if I'm being hopeful and foolish."

She watched me, absorbing my words and giving them time to digest before she gave a response. "Time is not the best metric for love. Kingsnake and I have been together for a relatively short time, but I know it'll last forever. Cobra has worn his heart on his sleeve with me before. And trust me when I say his love for you is real."

My heart tightened into a fist—and I knew I should treasure that feeling because it would be gone soon. He wouldn't be able to hear my heartbeat anymore...because I would be dead.

"You're taking a risk. I understand it. But if it makes you feel better, it can be reversed."

Every single muscle in my body tightened at that revelation. "What do you mean?"

"I don't know how it works. I just know it's possible. It's probably difficult and complicated, but it can be done. So if you ever decide this was a mistake, there's a way out."

"And you've never considered it yourself?"

She stared for a while before she answered. "I did—briefly. I've always wanted to have children, and that's not possible as a nightwalker. But I would rather have Kingsnake forever than live a short life with him."

"So, he agreed to become mortal too?"

"He did. But it's not the right decision for us."

I looked into the mirror again.

"I think Cobra would do the same for you if you asked."

My hands flattened against my stomach and smoothed out the dress even though there wasn't a single wrinkle. "I don't want to ask."

"It sounds like I made you feel better."

"It's just a big change. A very big change. Feeding on blood...no more sunlight...night vision. It's a different way of life."

She nodded in agreement. "But once you have something to live for, eternity seems like the minimum to aspire to."

27

KINGSNAKE

I stood outside the gate, seeing the Ethereal who had made camp in tents on the field. A short while ago, we'd had a battle on that very field, Ethereal on one side, us on the other, and King Elrohir of Ethereal fell.

Now we were allies.

Cobra's army was visible in the distance, and as they drew closer, their horses slowed. There wasn't enough room for their army inside Grayson, so they would have to spend the day in tents as well.

Cobra handed his horse to the stable master and walked up to me, tireless as if the journey there and back was nothing when he was high on happiness. His hand clapped me on the shoulder. "Brother."

I returned the gesture. "Can we trust your men to behave themselves?" With the Ethereal camped right next door, it could be a bloodbath.

"Everyone fed before we left. Their last meal before we freed our prisoners."

"You released your horde of prey?" I asked, an eyebrow cocked.

"I have."

I continued my quizzical stare.

"I doubt Clara would approve of such barbarism after we asked them to destroy the obelisk."

"Those two things aren't comparable, but I understand what you're saying."

"How is she?"

"Larisa said her dress is stunning."

"It's not the dress—but the woman underneath it." He grinned. "And after tonight, she's all mine."

"After you wed, Viper will be the only one left."

"And it'll stay that way," Cobra said. "That guy is too stiff for a woman—and not in a good way."

I chuckled.

He chuckled too. "You and Larisa are good?"

"We worked it out."

"You sexed her up like I suggested?" He winked.

"I always sex her up."

"Then maybe you got better at it." He clapped me on the shoulder again, and then we walked up to the palace. "Father here yet?"

"No."

"I suspect he'll be here tomorrow. Not looking forward to that."

"Nor am I." It would be strange to come face-to-face, to fight beside him as an ally after he'd stabbed me in the back. I wasn't sure how a conversation would even transpire or if I would accept it if he did apologize.

―――

When I returned to the bedchambers, Larisa sat on the couch with Fang, the two of them playing a round of cards.

"Why do you play if you always lose?"

Larisa put down her card and looked at me. "Ouch."

"Sorry."

"I'm trying to get better." She looked at Fang across from her. "But apparently, Fang is a mastermind." She set down the rest of her cards then walked to me, wearing a black dress that looked good on her sexy body. Her eyes lit up when she stepped closer me, like she hadn't seen me in days rather than hours, and she kissed me like I was her one and only.

I gripped her close and squeezed her ass hard.

She smiled against my lips before she pulled away. "Has Cobra returned?"

"Just arrived."

"So we'll have the wedding tonight?"

"Yes."

"Should we wait for your father?"

"I don't think that's important to any of us anymore."

Her eyes dimmed. "When do you think he'll be here?"

"Tomorrow. After his army rests, we'll leave at dusk."

"About that..." Her arms crossed over her chest. "I know this conversation is coming, so I've chosen to get ahead of it. I'm coming with you. I'm not going to sit on my ass and wait for you to return."

"Larisa, you've seen those werewolves firsthand—"

"Yes, I couldn't hold my own when it was three versus one, but I can handle one on my own. You don't have to put me on the front line with the rest of you, but I can help in some way. Give me something, Kingsnake. The queen of Grayson shouldn't remain in her palace while her people risk their lives."

"Take your pride out of it for a moment, sweetheart. You are not skilled in the blade like my brothers and I. And if you die and I live...I die too."

Instead of rising in anger, her eyes softened.

"You aren't just risking yourself, but *us*. And it's not worth it."

"I understand that, but I can't stay behind. There must be something I can do. What about all the humans who need to be evacuated while this battle is commencing? I could do that."

I inhaled a deep breath, still displeased with that.

"You can have a set of guards with me—and Fang."

"If I could have my way, you would stay right here, sit on your ass, and wait for me."

She stared.

"But I know how egregious that is for you."

She gave a subtle nod.

"I won't be able to protect you, sweetheart. I need you to understand that. I'll be far away, in a different part of the city, as will Cobra and Viper. You can scream my name, and I won't hear it. Fang can call for me, but I would never be able to get to you in time."

"I'll be careful. I'll just get people to safety outside the wall. And if danger comes...I'll run."

"Promise me."

"Yes."

"Promise me you'll abandon your men and the people and save yourself?"

"Yes."

I still didn't like it, but it was the only compromise we would find. "Then I accept."

My mighty fangsss and bone-crushing ssstrengh will keep her sssafe, Kingsssnake.

I know you will.

Her hands planted against my chest then slid down, moving to my trousers so she could slide her fingers up my bare chest. "Looks like we have time to kill before the wedding..."

I was hot and sweaty from working all day, organizing the Ethereal in the fields and then working in my study when the sun was highest in the sky, devising a plan for invasion. "I haven't showered."

"Fine by me." Her fingers pushed my shirt upward, moving it up my chest and then over my head. "You're just going to get dirty anyway."

———

We stood in the shower together, hot water running down both of our bodies, the rivers moving between her tits and down her flat stomach. Her wet hair clung to her skin like glue, and drops fell from the edge of her nose.

She was the most beautiful woman I'd ever seen. I don't know how I hadn't realized it the first time I'd laid eyes on her. Instead of embracing her beauty, I'd focused on her disobedience.

"Can I ask you something?"

"Yes."

"Did you always know the darkness could be reversed...or was that the first time you realized?"

I'd thought this conversation had died and been buried, but it still piqued her interest. There was no anger or accusation in her eyes, so I accepted it as simple curiosity. "I've always suspected it was possible, but we never knew how."

"How did you know it was possible?"

"Rumors...stories. I'd never seen it with my own eyes, but I had to believe it existed."

"And your father figured out how to facilitate it?"

"Yes."

"And how do you facilitate it?"

I stared, feeling a wall rise in my heart.

"Not because I intend to ever pursue it," she said quickly. "I'm just curious to know how it's possible to return the soul to the body after they've been separated for a length of time. It must be magic."

"My father didn't explain the details to me. Said he captured a witch in his lands, and she offered the magic in exchange for her freedom. I'm not sure how it works either, and until I see it actually happen, I probably never will."

"When Clara and I spoke, she was a little nervous about the whole thing. I told her it could be reversed."

"You think she'll go through with it?"

"Yes," she said. "The sacrifice isn't her hesitation. I think a part of her will always be afraid that Cobra will betray her like her last lover. And she just needs to know there's a way out if that happens."

"My brother says a lot of shit, but he's loyal. He would much rather get screwed over than screw someone else over, especially when it comes to a woman he loves. We both know his love is genuine, even if it has been a short while."

"I know."

"After they're married and they've had more time together, all those insecurities will fade." I'd watched Larisa's insecurities fade further and further as our relationship continued, despite my transgressions. After our last fight, her trust in me seemed to deepen. Now we were stronger than we ever were. Once the werewolves were defeated and the kingdoms were liberated, an everlasting peace would ensue, and I looked forward to that time with her. Just the two of us in the shade of a tree, watching the ocean crash against the shore, Fang tangled up in the branches above us.

Her eyes locked on mine, and a subtle smile moved on to her lips. "I know they will."

28

CLARA

I stood in my wedding dress, a bouquet of flowers in my hand, the first flowers I'd seen in Grayson. Their city was stone and wood, serpents carved into the foundation and the pillars. Grass, trees, and mountains surrounded the stronghold, but flowers were nowhere to be seen. I knew Cobra must have sent men out to harvest these from the wild, so I would have something that reminded me of Evanguard in my hands.

Kingsnake moved in front of me. "Cobra has a message for you."

"He does? I'm going to see him in a moment."

"He said if he had a heart, it would race as quickly as yours."

I was on the other side of the palace, but he could still hear it, probably because I was the only living being in proximity.

"Not in fear, but excitement," Kingsnake said. "Are you ready?"

I nodded. "A lot has changed in the last few months. When I met Cobra, I was betrothed to a man I didn't love because the man I did love had betrayed me. And now I stand here...about to marry a vampire...and become one myself."

With his chin dropped, he studied my face, thoughts on the surface of his eyes. "I know Larisa confided her struggles to you. You aren't alone in your doubts and fears. If it's any consolation, I know if this were reversed, Cobra would make the sacrifice without looking back. And I know, going forward, he would make any and every sacrifice for you, even death."

I nodded, knowing Cobra was everything I thought he was.

"Larisa also struggled with her loneliness. Not having a single relation in this world and no ability to make one. But my brothers have become her brothers—and the same is true for you."

"Thank you, Kingsnake."

He extended his arm.

I circled my arm through his, and we moved to the path that led to the cliff. Viper was waiting on the way, and he took my other arm. Together, the three of us walked up the path, my heart a songbird in my chest, and then I saw him.

There he stood, handsome in his king's uniform, his eyes so hard on mine they didn't move. Some would argue I marched to my death, to eternal darkness, but as I stared at his handsome face, I knew it was so much more.

His rigid stare stayed on me, in disbelief at my appearance.

Then his smile broke out, and he issued a low whistle as I came close. "*Daaammmnnn.*" He ignored his brothers as he took my hand and brought me close. He positioned me in front of him and took my other hand. "You ready, baby?"

That charming smile and the way it made my stomach burn melted every fear. All my insecurities seemed to disappear the longer he stared at me, as he encased me in the glow of his love, as he made me feel stunning when no man had ever told me I was beautiful. Every sacrifice seemed inconsequential when he was the reward. "Yes... I'm ready."

———

My legs were hooked around his waist as he carried me down the hall, my arms circling his neck and shoulders, kissing him as hard as he kissed me, my dress a curtain that reached the floor.

He made it to the door and got inside, kicking it shut behind him before he carried me to the bed. He treated my dress like an obstacle between us and didn't hesitate to tug and pull on the delicate fabric, whatever he had to do to get it off. The straps were tugged down, and then he ripped through the buttons so he could finally get it off my body.

He yanked his shirt over his head and pushed down his bottoms in a hurry, kicking off his shoes. One of them flew off and knocked the lamp over, but he acted like he didn't even notice. He dropped his boxers and let his anxious dick free before he grabbed my thighs and tugged me to the edge, so my ass hung off the bed. He guided himself inside, sinking into me in one smooth motion, releasing a satisfied moan when he felt my wetness.

I moaned too, like I'd never felt this man before.

His arm circled under my back, and he lifted me toward him, his other hand planting on the bed to support him as he leaned forward. He gave me hard thrusts over and over, his eyes locked on mine to watch me enjoy them.

Fuck, did I enjoy them.

He seemed to take our wedding night as a challenge to give me the best sex I'd ever had because he did all the work to make me feel good, to make me feel sexy, to make me come as quickly as possible.

I was wet the moment I saw that rock-hard chest, so it didn't take long for me to feel exactly what he wanted me to feel, scorching heat between my legs, a high that made me float to the clouds.

He scooted me up the bed and brought our bodies closer together, his arm anchoring behind one knee as he leaned farther over me, bringing our faces close together as he started to thrust, his dick coated in my come.

I cupped the side of his face and turned my head, exposing my throat and the scars from his previous bites. It would be the last time he would taste me on his tongue. He would have to find my replacement after tonight...and I would have to feed for the first time.

His hand fisted deep in my hair, and he sank his fangs into my flesh, breaking the skin and causing a jolt of pain that quickly turned into the most exquisite pleasure. He pulled the blood into his mouth, and while I became weaker, I also became more relaxed.

We continued to move together, lost in the greatest pleasure. He cut himself off and withdrew his fangs, returning them to his mouth before he faced me again, the only indication of his feeding the small drop of blood in the corner of his mouth. He brought his mouth to mine and kissed me, and I tasted my own blood.

"I love you." He said it against my lips as he thrust, his dick just a little bit harder now that my blood had satisfied his craving.

My hand continued to cup his face and dig into his short hair. "I love you too."

———

Hours passed, and we made love on and off. It was still dark outside, so the other vampires were preparing for war while we were lost in a wonderland. We lay together on the pillows, his hard body flush against mine.

He'd drifted off at one point, but now he was wide awake, looking at me like I was the only thing he ever wanted to look at. "Never thought I'd have a wife, but I knew if I did, she'd be sexy. And you are damn sexy."

My lips lifted in a smile as I released a chuckle. "You're sexy." Drop-dead gorgeous and out-of-my-league sexy.

"Of course I am. You're one lucky lady."

Now I laughed.

"But I'm luckier." He kissed my shoulder and squeezed me tighter.

"Are you ever serious?"

"Only with you." His eyes turned hard as he looked at me, blanketing me with that love once again. "You're a lot more than your looks, baby. I fell in love with this." His hand moved to my heart. "And this." He squeezed my biceps. "Everything else is just a bonus."

My hand rubbed his chest, over the area where his heart would be if it still worked. When I'd pictured what my husband looked like, it wasn't Cobra. It was an Ethereal, someone who would father my children and help me lead my people. But now Cobra felt like the only choice, the man who was my destiny.

"Are you ready?"

His question brought me back to reality, the next step of this marriage. I needed time to properly come into my new state, so the next few hours were critical for the transformation.

When I didn't immediately say yes, his eyes shifted back and forth between mine. "You don't have to do anything you don't want to, baby. We'll figure it out."

"No...I'm ready."

"You don't sound ready."

"It's a big moment. I just needed a second."

He continued to regard me, as if he was unsure if he should proceed.

"It's okay. Really."

He stared at me for a moment longer before he opened the drawer to his nightstand and pulled out a glass vial. There was a tiny bit of venom at the bottom, mostly clear with a hint of yellow. "Drink this."

I took the vial and removed the top.

"Once you drink that, there's no going back. If you don't turn, the venom may kill you."

I stared at the liquid inside before I looked at him again. "Alright." I tilted my head back and got the venom down quickly, coughing the instant I was done because it felt like smoke on my tongue.

Cobra brought his wrist to his mouth and bit himself, piercing his flesh with his fangs. Then he brought it to me to drink, the little drops dripping down his skin and then staining the sheets. Instead of bright red like mine, his blood was black. He didn't bring himself forward, giving me the power to lean forward when I was ready.

I grabbed his forearm and pulled it to my mouth. My tongue tasted the earthy drop, and then I sucked, pulling his blood into my mouth. The taste was like oil and acid, a taste I'd never experienced in my life.

He watched me, his eyes darkening as he watched me drink his blood.

When I'd had enough, he pulled his wrist away. "Now sleep. When you wake up, you'll be my wife—and the Queen of the Cobra Vampires."

29

KINGSNAKE

My father arrived with his army.

The Originals camped out in the field with the Diamond-backs. It'd been a long time since all the vampires had been united against a single foe. Before Larisa came into my life, it'd been several hundred years since the Ethereal attacked us. Every battle ended with loss of life, but neither was ever truly the victor, so those attacks became less frequent.

But now we had a new enemy.

I spotted my father enter Grayson, in the same armor and helmet he wore when he marched on the Ethereals' borders. A large figure with serious muscle density, he was the man I'd always aspired to be. Thankfully, I'd inherited compassion and sympathy from my mother. Otherwise, I would be the barbaric man he'd become.

His eyes locked on mine before he reached me, and then the long walk that ensued seemed to last an eternity. Even before we reached each other, I knew this conversation would be tense based on that stare.

He came before me and stopped.

As we stared at each other on the battlefield, nothing was said.

He was the first to speak. "We'll leave a few hours before dusk. If we ride hard, we should arrive at midnight, and if we win this war swiftly, we won't have to fear the sunlight."

It was exactly as I expected, but I was still disappointed. "So, we're just going to pretend you didn't fuck me over? That's how you're going to play this?"

"We're on the verge of war, and this is your concern?"

"We could both die tomorrow. How is this not your concern?"

"Kingsnake—"

"It's fine. Why did I expect an apology when you aren't sorry? Let's just get down to business and work on our strategy." I turned away and approached the stairs, severing the conversation and any chance of reconciliation.

"Kingsnake."

I stopped when I should have kept going.

"Son."

Don't turn around. Don't turn around. Don't fucking do it.

At the top of the palace steps, I saw Larisa emerge in a hurry, her frantic eyes searching for me.

Because she could feel my distress.

Her eyes eventually found mine, and she glanced at my father behind me, understanding the situation perfectly. Her eyes came back to me with sorrow before she turned away and entered the palace again.

Her face gave me the strength to turn back around.

"I prioritized my vengeance over your relationship—"

"*Our* relationship."

"You should have known it was too big a secret to keep—"

"I should have known my father wouldn't take my secrets to the grave. Fang disagreed with my decision vehemently. He's as loyal to Larisa as he is to me. But he would never, ever do that to me. You're my own father, and you exploited my weakness for your gain."

"I knew she wouldn't leave you—"

377

"You don't know her. You don't know our relationship. You have no idea what would have happened."

"I see that she's still your wife, Kingsnake. No harm was done—"

"No harm was done because my wife loves me more than you ever have. If Mother were alive, she would be ashamed of you. I'm sorry that you lost her. My only compassion for your behavior stems from my imagination. Because if I lost Larisa, I would be inconsolable—and not momentarily, but permanently. But I remember Mother's spirit as well as you do, and she would want us to move on and find peace. She would not want this relentless need for bloodshed and vengeance. She wouldn't want you to sacrifice the relationship with your son to kill innocent people, especially when their deaths won't bring her back. You forfeited our relationship to get what you wanted—and now you can't take that back."

He stood in silence, still as a statue, and probably as empty as one.

"I'm not your son anymore. We're allies—and nothing more."

————

The three of us stood in the study, waiting for Cobra to join us.

Viper was quiet, like he didn't want to compromise his loyalty to me by speaking to Father, which was unnecessary.

The door opened, and Larisa entered with Fang around her shoulders and came to stand by my side. Her eyes were down on the large map we possessed, ignoring my father as much as I did.

Fang stared at him across the table. "*Hiiiiissssss.*"

Fang.

My father stared at him, his stare ice-cold.

Sssnake killer. Blood traitor.

"Is your pet going to be a problem, Kingsnake?" my father asked.

Fang straightened on her shoulder, propping himself higher. "*Hiiiiiiisssssssssssss.*"

"He's not a pet," Larisa said. "Don't speak to him like that again."

He ignored my wife and kept his stare on me. "Is it appropriate to have your woman—"

"*My wife,*" I snapped. "And as Queen of Grayson, it's appropriate for her to stand in whatever room she wishes."

Fang hissed again. "*Hiiissssssssss.*"

My father gave me a hard stare before he looked at the map.

The door opened, and Cobra entered, followed by Clara, who looked different from the last time I saw her. Her skin had been fair, but now it looked like snow. Her green eyes were now viridian, so distinct they looked like two forests. She'd traded in her Ethereal armor for that of the Cobra Vampires, wearing gold and black.

We all stared at her.

Cobra released a grin. "Vampire looks good on her, doesn't it?"

No one spoke, the tension still taut with my father in the room.

I moved on. "They may suspect we're coming. Once they realize their army in Raventower has been destroyed, they'll know that the humans have aligned themselves with the vampires or the Ethereal. I think it's reasonable to assume victory would have been impossible otherwise. So we don't truly have the element of surprise."

"But I doubt they would anticipate the Ethereal forging an alliance with the vampires," Viper said. "As we've been at war for thousands of years, that's simply impossible. We will have the element of surprise, because by the time they realize we're marching on their gates, they'll be unable to prepare for the onslaught."

"Assuming the humans don't fight for them," Cobra said. "This should be a quick defeat."

"But if they do fight for them," I said. "That will drastically change things."

"How could the werewolves enforce that?" Cobra asked incredulously. "The second we arrive, they'll turn on them."

"Unless the werewolves have poisoned their minds. Told them that a vampire ruler is worse than a werewolf," I said.

"That's a stretch," Cobra said. "Considering we've pretty much left them alone."

"Why else would we march on their gates?" I asked. "Out of the goodness of our heart?"

"Kingsnake is right," my father said. "Why would we risk our lives for theirs?"

"Because the werewolves will come for us next," Cobra said. "The vampires and the humans just became allies."

"We need to be prepared for anything," Viper said. "We need to assume the humans will fight against us, and if they don't, then our siege just became easier."

"The werewolves are vicious," Clara said. "We've dealt with them occasionally in our history, but they're distinctively displeasing. I've met the Werewolf King, and he's sinister. I can imagine he would threaten the humans with anything to get their compliance. Such as, if they don't fight for the werewolves and they win, each soldier will lose either their wife or their firstborn."

It was barbaric, but believable.

"Then we should assume the worst," Viper said. "We'll need to divide their attention to multiple points." He grabbed the wooden pieces and placed them on the map. "I have enough explosives for these three locations. We blow the wall, and our armies will enter the city through these passages."

"Why these locations?" Cobra asked.

"Because these streets lead straight to the castle." I dragged my finger across the map to show Cobra. "It's a straight shot where we need to go. The Werewolf King will sit upon the throne and wait for the battle to end. We kill him, and the others will flee."

Cobra nodded in understanding. "Good plan."

"Viper and I will lead our men in the first passage. Cobra will lead his men down the second. And King Serpentine will lead the Originals and the Diamondbacks down the last passage." Too angry to address him as my father, I chose to insult him instead, to disregard our shared blood. "Larisa will be in charge of evacuating people from the streets. Clara, would you like to help her?"

"I will lead my people alongside the Cobra Vampires," she answered. "I belong in battle. I've trained my entire life for it."

I looked at Cobra.

He didn't object to it. "Then we have a plan. Prepare to depart in a few hours."

————

I handed our belongings to the stable master then approached Larisa's horse. I checked the saddle to make sure it was secured properly. A few months ago, one of my men had fallen off and broken his neck because the saddle wasn't secured properly. I never forgot that, so now I always checked, and I checked Larisa's first.

Cobra was beside me, securing his blade into the side bag. "Nervous?"

"No. You?"

"No."

"Then why did you ask?" I turned to him.

"To see if you would be honest—which you weren't." He faced me in his full battle armor, his helmet hooked to the saddle behind him.

"We've won every battle before. We'll win this."

"Viper has always said arrogance is what gets you killed."

"I'm trying to make you feel better."

"I'm not really worried about me." He came closer. "I'm worried about my wife...which still sounds weird to say. I've seen her in action, and she's great. Not as good as me, but pretty damn good. But now I worry."

"I know how you feel."

"I would ask her to stay back, but I know she wouldn't. She wouldn't look weak in front of her people either. If she doesn't lead them into battle, who will? They won't follow one of us."

"You fell in love with her because she's strong. You can't ask her to stay behind."

"Yeah, I know. But now I gotta watch her back as well as mine. Never done that before. Only worried about my neck."

I didn't know what to say. Nothing would console him.

"You're lucky Larisa agreed to stay behind the army."

"She's not the fighter that Clara is. She's still a novice. She's stubborn but not unreasonable."

Cobra grabbed his gloves and secured them onto his wrists.

That was when I noticed his hands. "You've chosen not to wear rings."

"Jewelry isn't my thing. Just makes it harder to grab the hilt of my blade."

"What about her?"

"She doesn't wear one either."

It was an interesting choice, but I didn't pass judgment.

"I don't need a ring for women to know I'm married."

"Then how will they know?" I asked.

"Because my hand will be on her ass." He grabbed the pommel of the saddle and pulled himself onto the horse.

Clara came into the stable at that moment, wearing the armor Cobra had provided for her, looking like his queen.

He watched her secure her blade to the horse and climb onto her white mare.

Larisa came next, stunning in her red-and-black armor, my lifelong companion wrapped around her shoulders. Her dark hair moved in the breeze, her cape flowing behind her, the woman who'd captured my gaze and held it.

Her stare met mine when she felt my thoughts, felt my admiration. "Are you alright?"

"You know I'm alright."

"I mean with your father."

"My brothers can continue their relationship with him. But I've chosen not to."

Instead of being relieved, she looked displeased. "Nothing has changed between us—"

"That's not the point."

"I know what he did was wrong, but he's your father—"

"He didn't apologize to me."

Now she was quiet.

"He's not sorry. Not sorry for hurting me. Not sorry for anything. He chose to ignore the issue or make excuses."

She still had nothing to say.

"I don't want to talk about this again."

"Will you let him sit on the throne if we win?"

Death would be the only thing that would stop him at this point, and I wasn't willing to cross that line. "I don't care what he does."

———

Larisa

There were far too many of us to take the same route to the kingdoms. Some of us went under the mountain through the hidden passage and the Dead Woods, but others took the more dangerous road over the mountain. Now that winter had ended, snow wouldn't be in their path, so it was much easier to pass that way.

We made it to the valleys and Raventower, the first kingdom closest to Grayson, and continued forward. There were smaller kingdoms and villages outside the main city, but Magnion was the center of the kingdom, where the High King Orion ruled over the smaller kingdoms. A long time ago, the other kingdoms had moved behind the protection of the new wall in exchange for giving up their sovereignty. There were other kings, but their titles were only to preserve their line and status. In truth, they really didn't mean anything, not when one true king ruled over everyone else.

I was certain King Orion was dead at this point. The Werewolf King would have killed him the second he'd invaded their kingdoms. Probably decapitated him and ate his head just to scare the shit out of everyone.

The wall was visible in the distance, taller than most castles, impenetrable from the outside. My night vision allowed me to see things in the pitch-darkness over great distances. I was certain we could see them, but they couldn't see us at all.

We had to blow up the walls to enter, but I bet the werewolves would simply use their claws to climb over the edge —like fucking cockroaches.

Viper maneuvered his horse to come to Kingsnake's side. "I'll plant the devices and have the men detonate them simultaneously. In that time, we'll need to break into the three groups so we'll all be ready to charge once the way is clear."

"Understood," Kingsnake said.

"We'll travel on foot to avoid detection." Viper dismounted his horse, gathered his men and his supplies, and departed.

Now this truly became real.

Kingsnake met with Cobra and his father. "Let's separate our armies. Once those walls come down, we charge. Those with horses go first to clear out the people in our way."

"Got it." Cobra nodded to him. "Good luck, brother."

Kingsnake said it back. "Good luck, brother."

His father turned his horse away and said nothing.

Kingsnake turned his attention to me. "I need you to move to the rear now, sweetheart."

It was time to say goodbye.

I stayed on my horse and stared at him, unsure what to say.

He was empty, no emotion whatsoever, as if this was a regular day.

I suspected he'd cleared his mind for me, tried to assure me this was nothing to worry about.

But I would worry anyway. "Please be careful."

"You know I will."

I couldn't hug him on the horse. Couldn't kiss him. Only stare. "I love you."

A flush of emotion swept through him, like every other time I said it. "I love you too, sweetheart."

I tugged on the reins of my horse and moved to the back, away from the rows of soldiers, away from my husband, the king who would lead our people to victory...or defeat.

———

I stayed in the rear with the small army Kingsnake had deployed to protect me. Fang was wrapped around my shoulders, his eyes focused ahead as he waited for the explosives to tear holes through the walls.

"Are you scared?"

No.

"You think he'll be okay?"

Kingsssnake has survived many battles.

"But were any of the battles like this?"

Thisss isss the firssst time werewolvesss have been our foes.

"And that doesn't scare you?"

I have faith. As ssshould you.

Suddenly, the world shook as the first explosive catapulted blocks of stone into the sky. It happened so quickly, but everything moved so slowly. The stones seemed to hover in the air before they slowly came back down to the ground. Then the second wall and third wall detonated simultaneously, the sound deafening on the ears. It spooked my horse, and he shifted and turned, stomping his hooves on the earth in distress.

"It's okay, honey." I pulled the reins tight to get him to still.

I saw the armies charging in the darkness, three different lines of soldiers of Ethereal and vampires heading into the city to kill everyone who got in their way. I remained at a safe distance, protected by my own calvary, but the sight was so stressful that I was relieved Kingsnake had asked me to stay behind. "It's happening..."

"Hooowwwwlllll!"

"Hooowll!"

"Hooowwwllll."

Like dogs howling at the full moon, the werewolves' cries pierced the sky.

30

KINGSNAKE

I rode hard down the streets with my men behind me. The moment the first wall was breached, horns sounded in the night to signal our entry. Archers scrambled for their bows and arrows and fired down on us as we entered the city.

I was far past their fire, so I continued to ride hard, heading straight to the castle far in the rear. My father, Cobra, and I would go right to the castle to take out the Werewolf King and end this battle swiftly to lessen the lives that were lost. Viper and Clara would direct our soldiers to meet the fury the werewolves and men would thrust upon us.

They were unprepared for our attack, so it took time for their foot soldiers to enter the city to meet our blades. By that time, I had ridden far up the street, a group of my guards behind me, running past the humans who screamed and retreated into their homes. I hoped Cobra was having the same ease as I was.

The castle was just in sight—and that was when I saw the werewolves appear. Like gargoyles, they swarmed all over the keep, as if they climbed with their clothes on. Enormous creatures with black-olive eyes that shone in the moonlight.

They guarded the entry to the keep—and that told me exactly what I needed to know.

The Werewolf King was right inside.

I hopped off the horse and ran up the stairs, my men behind me. My sword was unsheathed, and I spun it with my wrist, ready to slice into fur and muscle. They released snarls and growls but remained by the door.

More vampires flooded up the stairs with me, and then they were cornered.

A stare-off ensued, brief, because then the fighting began.

Two rushed me at once, and I ducked under the mighty paw that would have struck me against the pillar. I sliced my blade across the ankle of the one on the right, and he staggered sideways, giving me time to slice the other across the neck. "Go for the ankle!" Their legs bent in the opposite way of ours, so slicing the back of their heel made them lose all sense of balance.

Vampires and werewolves dropped to the ground, forming piles of bodies as we continued to fight for entry into the castle that housed the coward who chose to hide behind closed doors.

The others climbed down from the top of the castle, and one jumped on me.

I was knocked to the ground, my sword flung from my grasp, and that ferocious beast dropped onto my chest so I couldn't move. He snarled at me, spit dripping onto my chest plate like drops of rain. Hot breaths washed over me, and not in the affectionate manner of a pet.

I reached for my dagger and stabbed him in the leg over and over, but he screamed and remained on top of me, about to bite my head off.

Then a sword stabbed him through the chest, making him go still, and he toppled onto the ground beside me.

With a quick glance at the blade, the golden hilt and the black malachite told me exactly whose it was. I yanked it out of the flesh of the beast then turned to see Cobra fifteen feet away, a pile of bodies around him. I tossed the blade to him, and he caught it with a single hand. "Thanks."

"You owe me one." He turned away and continued the fight.

Another werewolf jumped down, but this time, I dodged it by rolling out of the way. I sliced my blade through his ankle, and instead of making a simple cut, I severed it straight through.

He screamed like a kicked dog, unable to balance on bone. He tipped over, and another vampire stabbed him through the neck.

The immediate danger had passed as the werewolves climbing on the castle had been defeated. When I turned to look at the city, I saw vampires fighting both humans and werewolves in the streets. Archers were on some of the buildings, shooting at one another and into the crowd below.

Cobra jogged to me. "We've got to break down this door and get inside the castle."

"I thought the humans would turn against them."

"Maybe they will once the Werewolf King is dead." Cobra started issuing orders. "Cut down that pillar." It was made of wood, deep mahogany, carved with deer and bears because the humans had always been obsessed with hunting.

The vampires worked to chop it free until it toppled over like a new fallen tree.

"Let's move."

We all picked up the pillar and started to ram it into the door.

The door didn't move, like it was a solid wall.

We did it again and again, but there was no give.

My father appeared, blood stained on his armor from butchering all the werewolves and humans who got in his way. He quickly realized our intention and ordered his men to help. He took a spot at the front and helped us ram into the doors.

Finally, they shifted—a little.

"Again!" my father yelled.

We continued to ram the wooden pillar into the door, our men standing behind us to watch our backs. It took a solid five minutes to make the door give at the hinges, for the material to dent from our force.

Finally, the door caved open, and half of it dropped off the hinge.

"Forward." My father went first with his men, and arrows immediately bounced off his armor because an assault waited for us.

We poured inside, human archers everywhere, raining arrows down on us all. They were merely a sacrifice, because once the vampires rushed in, they were cut down where they stood, another graveyard of bones.

"Let's separate." My father took his men one way.

"Come on." I nodded to Cobra, and we both headed a different way, entering the castle with low-handing chandeliers throughout the rooms, thick rugs in maroon and midnight blue, portraits of the king hunting in the wild, and grand fireplaces that could roast an entire boar.

We moved through the empty rooms until we approached another set of double doors, even bigger than the ones that had prohibited entry into the castle.

"Must be the throne room," Cobra said. "The little bitch is hiding."

I moved around the room, seeing if there was another way inside, but all I found was a solid wall that enclosed any other rooms. High up toward the ceiling were stained-glass windows, but they had to be at least twenty feet in the air, inaccessible. "We'll have to break down this door too."

"Hooowwwwwllllll!"

We both turned at the sound, hearing it from the front.

Cobra looked at me. "Ambush."

"They cornered us." I turned to the men. "Bar the way with anything you can find. Archers, prepare your bows."

The werewolves poured in, coming from behind, at least three dozen, and we didn't have ample room to fight.

Then the doors behind us opened at the same time, and more came from the rear.

"Shit," Cobra said. "This is not good."

I sliced down the ones who came at us from the rear, relying on our men to take out the ones who flooded in from the front of the castle.

Cobra got punched in the face so hard that he rolled to the floor. His sword dropped, and when he reached for it, another werewolf kicked it away and sneered.

I had only a second to react, and with all my strength, I sliced my blade right through the stomach of my foe so his entrails spilled out. I grabbed my dagger and threw it into the eye of the monster about to take my brother's head. I got the other with my sword, making him fall right beside Cobra.

Cobra took the opening and crawled to his sword, turning over just in time to stab the beast about to descend. The knife stuck him through the spine, and he was gone immediately. "Thanks."

"Now we're even—"

A werewolf stronger than all the others grabbed me and threw me across the room, fifteen feet into the air, making my body hit the wall so hard my armor caved in slightly. I fell to the floor, and that knocked the wind out of me.

"King of Vampires." The Werewolf King was nine feet tall, taller than all his brethren, and his fur was midnight black, while all the others were a mix between gray and black. "Lord of Darkness. And soon, Lord of Death."

I pushed to my feet with my sword in hand, refusing to show weakness for the way he'd thrown me around like a fucking rag doll.

Cobra fought off two werewolves at once, trying to get to me but unable to break free.

The Werewolf King sneered at me. "You think I didn't know?" He came closer, his black eyes like oil. "You think Raventower is strong enough to defeat my army alone? No, I knew you were coming, Kingsnake—and you should have assumed I knew."

I spun my sword around my wrist and moved to the side, ready for him to lunge so I could find an opening. The neck and the ankles were their weaknesses, but this would be more challenging because he was bigger...and stronger.

"You want to play." He tightened into his defensive stance, ears folding back, his teeth extended.

"I want to kill."

"Be my guest." He lunged at me, but it happened so fast.

Without knowing how it even happened, I was thrown across the room and against another wall, twelve feet in the air. My back hit the wood, caved in my armor more, and then I landed hard against the tile.

A cold laugh came from his mouth, standing there while werewolves and vampires fought one another, bodies piling on top of one another.

"Kingsnake!" Cobra tried to break free, but a werewolf came from behind, and he was forced to save his own neck since he couldn't save mine.

Fuck, I might die.

The Werewolf King came forward. "No vampire can kill me."

I was on my feet, staring at a foe three feet taller than me, with a muscle mass that was several times greater than mine. He threw me around like I weighed nothing, like my armor was a set of knitted feathers.

"Did you think you would be the exception?" he asked with a laugh. Now he was just toying with me, knowing it wasn't a fair fight, that I had no chance of killing him, so he might as well fuck with me. He came closer, cutting me off from everyone else. "I'll rip your head clean from your shoulders and stick it on a pike so everyone can see, including that prey you've made your wife."

I felt sick, not because of my impending death, but the heartache I would leave behind. But I wouldn't beg for my life. I wouldn't ask Fang to save me, not when he was too far away and powerless against this monster.

I had to fight.

I reached for my dagger and threw it as quickly as I could, aiming for his heart.

He was quicker, angling his arm in the way and taking the blade in the forearm. He twisted his arm back and forth to regard the blade and the dribble of blood that stained his fur. It was inconsequential to him. Utterly.

He looked at me again. "Kinda tickled." He pulled out the dagger and tossed it aside.

Werewolves couldn't speak in their wolf form, but for some reason, this one could, and that made it even more sinister.

He rushed me, and by a miracle, I dodged it and sliced my sword across his side.

But he immediately grabbed me and threw me again, hurling me into the wall across the room.

I collapsed again, and that was when I recognized the injuries under my armor. He would beat me until I couldn't stand, in too much agony to move, and then he would rip my head from my shoulders and eat my corpse.

There was no way out of this.

Fang. I pushed myself to my feet and grabbed my sword. *Tell her I'm sorry...and I love her.*

Nooooo!

I shut off my mind so I wouldn't have to listen to his grief. Wouldn't have to listen to whatever message Larisa would have in return. With my sword gripped in my fingers, I straightened and faced my foe, refusing to give up until I was dead.

"You've got more spine than I realized," he said. "Too bad I'll have to snap it." He swiped at me, and I moved out of the way, digging my sword deep into his side. But it didn't slow him down, and he grabbed me in his paw and slammed me down into the floor before he threw me again.

This time, I hit the floor and didn't move.

My sword was still in his body, and he left it there, like a badge of honor.

He drew close, his feet audible against the tile, even over the sounds of battle.

I pushed myself up, but barely, everything shaking, bones broken. I slipped, and my knees hit the tile.

"I almost feel bad." He sneered at me, his smile toothy.

I forced myself up, to die on my feet rather than weak on the floor. But it took all my strength to stand. Took all my strength not to collapse back and let him finish his torture.

He grabbed me by the chest and forced me off the floor, holding me like I weighed absolutely nothing. Then he reached for my head, his claws digging into my neck and jaw, drawing blood as he prepared to rip me into pieces. "Any last words, King of Vampires and Lord of Darkness?" He mocked me, mocked me on the verge of my death.

"Fuck you."

A growl erupted from his open mouth, and he moved to twist my head.

But then he screamed and dropped me to the floor.

I hit the tile again and looked to see my savior, hoping it wasn't Fang and Larisa.

"Do not touch my son." In his black armor with the Golden Serpent on his chest, my father swung his blade for the knee of the werewolf and then the stomach. He had only an instant, the werewolf so distracted by the unexpected assault that he dropped his guard.

I forced myself up and grabbed my dagger, pushing myself forward to stab him where I could.

The Werewolf King grabbed my father and threw him against the wall just as he had with me.

I stabbed the blade right into his ankle, over and over, tearing apart the tendons and the flesh.

"*Hooooowwwwwwwllllll!*" He screeched like the wounded animal he was and toppled sideways, blood pouring from the wound.

The wound wouldn't kill him, so I jumped on top of him and grabbed my blade still in his stomach. I grabbed it by the hilt just as his eyes widened in terror. He was about to swat me off when I pulled out the blade and stabbed him through the front of his neck, pushing through the spine that attached his head to his body.

He went limp, dead instantly.

Now that it was over, my body couldn't go on, so I slumped to the floor, in pure agony over the broken ribs, the broken leg, the broken arm...everything was broken. The fighting continued on around me, sword on sword, screams of terror as vampires and werewolves lost their lives.

My mind started to fade. My eyes closed.

"Son." I felt a hand against my chest then warm fingers against my cold skin. "Son, stay with me." He gave me a shake.

My eyes opened again, but momentarily.

"I'm sorry for what I did."

I heard the words, but my mind was in too deep of a haze to care.

"I love you, son."

My eyes closed. And they didn't open again.

31

LARISA

Fang didn't try to talk me out of it.

I rode my horse through the streets toward the castle, dodging the fighting that raged on either side. Werewolves attacked Kingsnake Vampires and Cobra Vampires. The white armor of the Ethereal was in a pile from all the dead. It was just shouting and screaming and howling.

We were halfway there when the howls began.

"Hoooowwwwl!"

"Hooowlll!"

"Hooowwwwlll."

Werewolves stood on the rooftops and at the top of the castle, issuing their calls for others to hear. It must have meant something, because the werewolves started to run through the streets toward the main gate. The fighting ceased as they made their exodus. They ran right past me, ignoring me on my horse.

The Werewolf King is dead.

"You understood that?"

I underssstand a sssurrender when I sssee one.

I continued to gallop down the path to the castle, gripping the reins like my life depended on it. "Can you reach him?"

No.

I had hot tears in my eyes, knowing the worst had come to pass. Kingsnake would never say that to me unless it was the end. Wouldn't torture me if there was any hope whatsoever for his survival.

I jumped off the horse when I arrived and ran into the castle. "Kingsnake!" I ran through the empty rooms, past the dead werewolves and vampires, not seeing my husband among any of them. "Kingsnake!"

"In here!" It was Cobra.

I ran, Fang slithering behind me.

I nearly tripped when I came in the door. "Where is he?"

Cobra wore a grave face, pale as winter. Clara was behind him, arms crossed over her chest, purposely not looking at me.

"Where is he?" The tears came and poured down my cheeks, the truth as clear as words on a page.

"He fought the Werewolf King and prevailed, but..."

"Oh no..." My hand cupped my mouth to stifle the tears.

"He was beaten severely—"

"Where fuck were you?" I snapped. "Why didn't you help him?"

He kept his voice steady. "I tried...but I couldn't."

"You didn't try hard enough."

"He's still breathing, Larisa. He might pull through. He might not... I don't know."

"He's...he's still alive."

"Yes."

Fang had already left, slithering across the tile to another area in the room.

I turned from Cobra and followed him, finding Kingsnake on the floor, his face so bloody he was unrecognizable.

His father was there, removing the chest plate that had been so damaged it looked like a herd of horses had trampled it under a thousand hooves.

I collapsed to my knees beside him, seeing his chest rise and fall deeply, like he was in unimaginable pain.

His father said nothing. Didn't look at me. Just grieved.

My hand reached for his, and I grasped it. "I'm here...." Silent tears fell down my cheeks.

His father placed his hand on his shoulder. "Come on, son."

Fang wrapped his body around his head and shoulders, resting his head on one of Kingsnake's arms. He closed his eyes, and two yellow tears streaked from the corners.

We sat there together, all of us praying the man we loved would come back to us.

———

We carried him to an empty bedchamber upstairs, unable to return him to Grayson in his condition. I sat at his bedside with Fang, feeding him blood, keeping an eye on him to make sure he continued to breathe.

I hadn't slept in three days.

I was too afraid if I did, I would wake up...and he would be gone.

His father and brothers came to visit, stood there and stared at his sleeping face. They didn't speak to me. I didn't speak to them.

I already felt like a widow.

Cobra entered the room, no longer in his armor and uniform, but regular street clothes. The battle had been won days ago. The werewolves had returned to their dens. The humans had cleaned up the city that we'd destroyed and liberated. Life went on—but not for me.

Cobra pulled up a chair and sat at his brother's side. This was how all the visits went—spent in silence. He stared at his hands in his lap and didn't even look at his brother. "The Werewolf King was nine feet tall...thicker than twelve oxen put together—"

"I don't want to hear this."

"He fought valiantly. If it were me...I wouldn't have lasted nearly as long."

"Stop."

"He's still here, Larisa." He lifted his chin and looked at me. "If he's made it this long...I think he'll pull through."

"Please don't get my hopes up."

"I think hope is exactly what we need." His eyes shifted to his brother. "His face looks better."

The change was hard for me to see, because I stared at him every day, all day.

"Have you checked his bones?"

"I—I don't want to see."

"You want me to check?"

"Just—just leave him alone." If his body could heal, it would happen naturally. I didn't want to touch anything and cause him pain. I didn't want to do anything to interfere with his healing.

Cobra turned quiet.

"I'm sorry...for what I said before." I'd blamed Cobra for Kingsnake's state, and that wasn't right. "I was just upset—"

"It's okay, Larisa," he said in an empty voice. "I should have tried harder."

"You would have helped if you could."

"I wish it were me instead of him...whether he lives or dies."

My hands gripped each other as the pain rushed through me. I looked down at my fingers, forcing myself to keep it together. "What's happening now?" If I didn't change the subject, I would break down.

"My father has become King of the Kingdoms. In return for their liberation, he will rule them. Their lives will resume as they did before, but sacrifices will need to be made, an eternal gratitude for what we've done here."

"The humans shouldn't be ruled by a vampire..."

"I agree. But I don't care enough to stop him. No one does."

Kingsnake would care...if he could care.

32

KINGSNAKE

The Werewolf King snarled at me. "I'm sorry for what I did." He snarled again. "Son, stay with me." He swiped his claws across my body, ripping my head from my body. I saw it on the floor, staring back at me with a horrified expression.

I jerked upright and stared at a dark wall, breathing hard, my clothes soaked in sweat. It took several seconds for me to understand I was in a bedchamber. Moonlight came through the open window. I had no idea where I was, but I knew I was alive.

Kingsssnake, I'm here. Fang propped himself up on the bed, his yellow eyes like glowing candles in the dark. He didn't slide over my body to come closer to me, out of fear of touching me.

"Larisa...." I searched for her, finding her asleep in the chair at my bedside.

Ssshe hasssn't ssslept in four days.

"I'm alive..."

Yessss.

Fang must have woken her up, because she gave a jolt as she awakened, her eyes snapping open and searching for mine. When our eyes locked together, she gave a gasp so deep it was like she'd been underwater until her lungs begged for air. She left the chair and came to me, her hands cupping my face as the tears streaked down her cheeks.

My eyes watered as I watched her weep for me, witnessed all the pain I caused. "I'm sorry—"

"It's okay. You're here." She brought her face to mine and pressed a kiss to my forehead, being as gentle as possible, like I was fragile as glass. "You're here with me."

———

I sat up on the pillows Larisa had provided for me, conscious but still in serious pain. When I moved my leg, I cringed when I realized it was still broken. So was my shoulder. So were my ribs. If I was better than I'd been five days ago, I couldn't tell the difference.

Viper was the first to see me. He came to my bedside and reached for my shoulder, but at the last second, he thought better of it. He withdrew his hand before he touched me. "How do you feel?"

"Terrible." The worst I'd ever felt, at least physically.

Fang was coiled into a ball at my side, staying with me every moment of every day.

Larisa had fallen asleep in the chair again after she'd notified everyone that I was awake.

Viper glanced at her, her small body curled up into the armchair. "Maybe I should come back later."

"I think she's knocked out cold," I said. "First time she's let herself sleep deeply in five days."

He nodded. "Yeah, she's been a mess." Viper had never been good with words, and he wasn't good with them now. "I've never been so scared."

"I know."

"I didn't know what would happen."

"I'm surprised I'm alive, to be honest." When I'd closed my eyes for the last time, I thought that was the end. "What's happened?"

"Larisa didn't tell you?"

"We didn't say much…" It was all stares and tears. There would have been lovemaking if I were capable of it.

"The werewolves fled the kingdoms after you killed that dog. Father took the crown, saying his subjugation is a fair trade for their liberation. Their way of life won't change as long as they pay him for his sacrifice."

"Why am I not surprised…"

"How did the Werewolf King get that big?"

"No idea." I couldn't believe I'd lasted as long as I did. "Did you chase them down?"

"We let them go. We were more focused on you."

I nodded in understanding.

"It's going to be a while before you can move."

"I know," I said. "But I'm alive…so I can be patient."

———

Larisa showered and changed her clothes. It was the first time she took care of herself because she had been too afraid to leave my side. Now she was in a dress, with her brown hair clean and combed. She fed me vials of blood regularly, donations from the humans we'd liberated.

She brought me pain medicine, stuff that she used to use in Raventower. She mixed it with the blood she fed me to mask the taste, and when it kicked in, I finally relaxed. The constant pain made it harder to sleep, but once she chased that away, I was able to rest.

I finally asked the question that was on my mind. "Why hasn't my father come to visit?"

She sat in the chair at my bedside, not sharing the bed with me because she was afraid she would accidentally press on something she shouldn't and hurt me. "He wasn't sure if you'd want to speak with him. I told him I would let him know if you asked for him."

I stared at her face, feeling both anger and affection for my father.

"He didn't want to upset you while you're trying to heal."

"I want to see him."

"Alright." She left the chair and walked out of the bedchambers.

Fang perched up to meet my gaze. ***You're feeling better if you want to sssee him.***

I suppose.

I'll bite him if you wisssh.

That won't be necessary, Fang.

419

He coiled back into the ball.

A moment later, my father entered. Larisa must have stayed elsewhere because she didn't join us. In his king's uniform, he approached, his look of affection replacing his typical coldness. He walked up to my bedside and placed his hand on the back of my neck, gripping me the way he had when I was a boy, in one of the few places I was unin-jured. "You look a lot better."

"I look better than I feel. My bones are still broken."

"It takes time. There's a lot more trauma than those broken bones that your body has to heal." He released me and sat in the chair Larisa had vacated. One ankle rested on the opposite knee, and his hands came together in front of him, elbows propped on the armrests. He just stared at me.

I stared back. "Thank you...for saving me."

"Don't thank me, son."

"Were you injured?"

"A scratch in comparison to you."

"I saw him throw you against the wall."

He gave a subtle shrug. "I'm not back to where I was, but I will be. Whatever the consequences may have been, they were worth it. Your life is more valuable than mine will ever be."

I didn't know he felt that way. He never shared affection with me, either physically or verbally. "I'm glad you're well."

His stare absorbed mine for a while. "You mean that?"

I nodded.

"You forgive me?"

"I do."

He took a breath, the air coming in quick but releasing slow. "Thank you."

"Viper tells me you've taken the kingdoms for yourself."

"I have."

"You think that's wise?"

"Doesn't matter if it's wise. That's the deal we made."

"If you rule the kingdoms, then this entire continent is vampire territory."

"As it should be." He relaxed in the chair, his hands gripping the edges of the armrests now that we talked about business.

"We have our kingdoms, Father. Can we leave the humans in peace?"

"The Ethereal are the ones who took away that peace when they poisoned them. I can protect the humans from the werewolves. I can only take what we need. I can prevent an attack on the vampires. Keeping your friends close—and your enemies closer."

Nothing I said would change his mind, so I chose to let it go.

"Viper and Cobra have begun distributing the venom. You should see the line."

"Do we have enough?"

"Not sure. Even if we don't, most of the humans will be immune now, and that's all that matters. The others will die off, but the stronger ones will survive. Eventually, this disease will disappear. All will be right with the world—once you're well."

———

I was stuck in bed for weeks.

Weeks.

The longest I'd ever been consumed by an injury. Or in my case, injuries. It would be easy for me to snap in my frustration, but I remembered the moment I'd realized I would die. The moment I'd told my wife I loved her for the final time. The pain I felt at that moment was infinitely worse than what I felt now.

This was nothing.

I sat on the bed and played cards with Fang while Larisa sat in the armchair, reading a book.

Fang put down his last card.

"Wow, you are good at this."

Told ya. He slipped his tongue in and out.

Larisa didn't take her eyes off the words on the page. "He cheats."

Liessss.

I grabbed the cards and returned them to the pile before I shuffled them. My broken bones had realigned themselves and solidified, but the pain told me I needed more time before I could put on my armor and walk out of there.

Another round.

"You've kicked my ass three times in a row."

Ssso?

"I'm not interested in it being four."

Then get better.

I set the cards on the nightstand.

Fang curled his body up and gave me that disappointed stare.

"You're taking bed rest better than I thought you would." Larisa closed the book and set it on the nightstand.

"Bed rest is better than being dead."

Her eyes softened. "It is."

"When I thought I was going to die...I felt like shit for leaving you behind. I'll take bed rest over that any day."

———

My armor was too broken to be repaired, so it was replaced with a brand-new set. Black and red, with black serpents over the red pieces and red serpents over the black. It was polished and shiny, containing no scuff marks from previous battles. New armor for a new beginning.

I looked at myself in the mirror once everything was secure, thinner than I used to be, because lying in a bed for three weeks had weakened my muscle tone. But once I was back to my previous routine, it would return.

"How are you?" Larisa spoke from behind me, her body blocked by mine.

There were aches all over my body, all in places where things had been broken, but those might never go away.

"Never better." I turned around to face her, to show her that I was the man she remembered, not the cripple who had been stuck in bed.

Her eyes lightened as she looked at me, her head tilting slightly. She stepped into me and hooked her arms around my neck to kiss me. On her tiptoes, she reached hard for my mouth.

My arms scooped into her body and lifted her, bringing her perfectly level with my mouth so she could kiss me exactly as she wanted.

She stopped treating me like a fragile piece of glass that would shatter into infinite pieces at the slightest touch. She embraced me as a healed man, a man as strong as I'd been before I was beaten to within an inch of my life. That was a great feeling.

We were supposed to depart the kingdoms and return home, but now that I had her in my arms and her mouth on mine, I steered right back to the bed and dropped her onto the sheets.

Fang immediately let himself out and shut the door with his tail.

She was in her uniform to travel, so I slid off her boots and dragged her pants over her ass until they were at her ankles. I undid my pants enough for my cock to come free, the plates of armor too much for me to push down my trousers any farther. But it was enough to pull her into me and slide inside, finally reacquainted with the woman I loved.

She gasped for me the way she always did, her hands reaching for my hips as she bent her knees toward her waist.

My hands gripped her waist, my thumbs touching in the middle of her stomach, and I thrust hard, finally enjoying one of the best reasons to be alive. I looked down at her as I took her, as I claimed her as mine again.

She rocked with me, panting and writhing, her nails digging into my flesh as she held on. "Kingsnake..."

33

LARISA

We returned to Grayson, the cloudy coastal stronghold that always had a cool breeze. Now that I was a vampire, I appreciated the climate more than I ever had before. It allowed me to enjoy the day as well as the night, while protecting my skin from the sun's harmful rays.

Now that most of the humans were immune to the sickness, food for the vampires was no longer scarce. Even after the war, there were still enthusiasts, and even more appeared now that the Werewolf King had been defeated. Most of them were interested in Kingsnake, but he passed on them all and gave them to the others.

For the first time, life was simple...peaceful.

I almost didn't know what to do with myself.

Kingsnake and I continued our honeymoon, the one that had been interrupted by his father's sabotage, and it wasn't until a week after our return that we left our bedchambers and checked on the well-being of Grayson.

Kingsnake was back to how he'd been before, just with a new addition of scars from his near-death experience. We entered his study, where he worked at the desk, and I sat in the armchair near the fire. A book was in my hands, and Fang was curled up on the rug in front of the fire, like a dog that liked to lie in the sun.

"Kingsnake?" I shut the book.

Kingsnake picked up on my tone and didn't answer me from the desk. He joined me in the sitting area, taking a seat on the couch and reaching for the decanter of scotch there. He filled his glass without offering me anything and took a drink. "Yes, sweetheart?"

"You think it's smart to let your father rule the kingdoms?"

He stared at the fire. "I knew this would come up eventually."

"It worries me."

"Even if I disagreed with it, which I do, there's nothing I can do."

"You could ask."

"I made my disapproval very clear. As did my brothers." He looked at me again. "After the battles we've fought, I don't have it in me to pursue this. I'm sorry to disappoint you, but I'm tired of butting heads with my father."

My eyes shifted to the fire.

"If he were abusing the citizens or doing something nefarious, it would be different. But regardless of who sits on that throne, it's always going to be someone corrupt. It's always going to be someone who puts their needs before everyone else. If anything, perhaps this will narrow the divide between humans and vampires."

My eyes came back to his. "I want peace as much as you do."

"Then let's live in peace. And if it becomes a problem, we'll deal with it then."

A knock sounded on the door.

"It's open," Kingsnake said.

Cobra entered, followed by Clara, both of them dressed for their departure. "It's time we return to the Mountain. I'm eager to show my queen her new kingdom, as well as her subjects who have decided to join us in darkness."

Kingsnake left his glass behind and joined his brother at the entryway. "And the Ethereal who have decided to remain human?"

"They'll return to the forest," Clara said. "Now that King Serpentine has what he wants, I doubt he'll think of them again. And hopefully, the werewolves will never figure out their location."

I came to Kingsnake's side and faced them, my brother-in-law and sister-in-law. "I'm sad you're leaving."

"Me too." Clara smiled. "But we're a short ride away."

"We'll visit," Cobra said. "But we haven't had a proper honeymoon..."

"I get it," Kingsnake said quickly, not wanting any more details.

Clara and I hugged. "See you soon," I said.

"You too." She squeezed me before she let me go then hugged Kingsnake next.

We all exchanged hugs, saying goodbye after a long time together.

"We can talk about this later," Cobra said. "But it's been on my mind since we left—"

"Aurelias." Kingsnake immediately flushed with discomfort, the weight sitting on his chest.

Cobra gave a nod. "Yeah."

"He's been on my mind too," Kingsnake said. "I thought he would be back by now."

"I agree," I said. "Maybe he couldn't get a ship or something."

"Then we should go get him," Clara said. "If he's a brother of yours, he's a brother of mine."

"He's a good guy," I said. "Just rough around the edges..."

"Then we're in agreement," Kingsnake said. "We'll set sail and search for Aurelias."

Cobra nodded. "Come to the Mountain in a week. We'll ride to Crescent Falls and sail together. Viper can handle our kingdoms while we're away."

Kingsnake nodded. "Sounds like a plan."

Cobra and Clara walked out and left us alone in the study.

"You think he's okay?" I asked, loving Aurelias the way I loved Viper and Cobra.

"I think he is," Kingsnake said. "That's what I believe anyway..."

———

Kingsnake and Larisa have found their happily ever after, but Aurelias has begun his own journey at the bottom of the cliffs. His tale is next, and we'll see his love story with none other than Huntley and Ivory's daughter...it's gonna be gooooood.

<u>Order The Forsaken Vampire now!</u>

Printed in Great Britain
by Amazon